Doctor How

Doctc

Mark Speed

Published by Terra Supra Limited
Registered in England and Wales no. 8109753

www.terrasupra.co.uk
Nothing is black and white

For the avoidance of doubt, this is a work of parody.

Doctor Who and TARDIS are registered trademarks
of the BBC.[1]

---

[1] No, really – they are.

About the author

Mark Speed finished writing his first novel at the age of fifteen. His comedy writing has appeared in newspapers as diverse as the London *Evening Standard* and *The Sun*, and been broadcast on BBC Radio 4 Extra. He performed his solo comedy, *The End of the World Show*, at the Edinburgh Fringe in 2011 and 2012.

Amongst other postgraduate and professional qualifications, he has a Master's degree in Creative Writing from City University, London. In 1995 a chiropractor told him he'd never run again. Sensibly, he gave up chiropractors, and has since completed several marathons and a couple of Olympic-length triathlons. He occasionally does irresponsible things like scuba and skydiving.

In case you hadn't guessed, he's a 'polarity responder'.

Other works by the same author

Doctor How and the Rings of Uranus (short story)

Apocalypse Later: A guide to the end of the world by Nice Mr Death

Britons in Brief (anthology)

More about the author is available from these sources:
Goodreads: https://www.goodreads.com/MarkSpeed
Amazon Author Central:
http://www.amazon.com/author/markspeed

Author information and more writing:
www.markspeed.co.uk

To Lynne Arnot

Thanks for getting me started, and for saving my life

Author's note

Doctor How asked me to write this series in British English. Original manuscripts in Gaelfreyan and Squill will be available when your civilisation reaches the necessary level.

Similarly, Doctor How uses the Imperial system of measurement, rather than the Metric: the French were wrong on a truly cosmic scale. Other characters are stuck using Metric because they don't know any better.

Prologue

I keep six honest serving-men

(They taught me all I knew);

Their names are What and Why and When

And How and Where and Who.

 Rudyard Kipling

 (extract from *The Elephant's Child*)

Chapter One

"The driver insisted he was rammed by another taxi, Sarge," said the constable. "Said he rolled once from the impact, then the other vehicle rolled the cab onto its roof. He swore the other vehicle came to rest on top of his."

"Tell me, what am I supposed to believe?" asked Sergeant Hughes. "The invisible cab?"

"The evidence does point to another vehicle, Sarge."

"The only thing that could have driven away from an impact like that is a tank, constable."

"Sarge."

"No trace of alcohol in his system. What about drugs?"

"Didn't seem the type, to be honest, Sarge."

Hughes grunted. "Maybe it was aliens?" He looked up. The rain had cleared now, but a layer of thick cloud sat at around a thousand feet, glowing orange-brown from the glare of the distant streetlights of Dagenham. Dawn was still two hours away. "Maybe they're up there, laughing at us?"

The constable knew better than to answer.

"And no vehicles in those fields, and no trail of detritus?"

"Not that any of us has been able to find."

Hughes looked at the wreck of the cab, which lay at a slight angle on its roof. The driver had been lucky – the impact had destroyed the front passenger side completely. The cab was designed to withstand crushing, and it would have taken considerable force to compress the body as much as it had been. Fire and rescue had had to cut the driver's door off to get him out. He walked around to get the best view of the underside. Elements of the underside were crumpled, consistent with something heavy having lain on top of them.

"The fuel tank, constable."

"What about it, Sergeant?"

"That's a very clean cut."

"I assume it happened as a result of the impact, Sarge."

"No, that's a cut. An impact would have twisted it, probably sheered away some retaining bolts; dented it. There's no denting. This was cut."

"Fire and rescue?"

"Why would they cut the line to a fuel tank?" The fire and rescue team was packing the last of their gear. Hughes called their 'guvnor' over. "What do you reckon, Steve?"

"Someone's cut that," said the fire officer. "Pincers. Two blades. One here, and one here. You'd need about five-hundred pounds of pressure to do that, minimum. Here, Roy!"

Another fire officer came over. "Guv?"

"You know anything about this?"

"Nah. Clean job that, though."

Hughes thought for a moment. "You'd need one of those pneumatic pincers for this, wouldn't you?"

"Dirty great things," said Steve. "You've seen 'em often enough. Weigh a ton. Judging from the angle, maybe a ten-foot man could've done it. Cab would've had to have been on its side for us mere mortals to do it. And there's no way we're going to hack into a diesel tank with a casualty trapped inside, is there?"

"Well, thanks for the clarification."

"That's not one of ours anyway," said Roy. "Our pincers' jaws are smooth. Look at the edges of the cut – the blades were serrated." He grabbed the constable's torch and shone it on the clean edges of the cut to show the pattern left by the serrated edges.

"Thanks, lads," said Hughes.

"Until next time, Hughesie," said Steve, and walked back to his truck.

"Yeah, there's always a next time in this game," said Hughes. The emergency lights on the rescue truck went out. It throttled up and roared off into the gloom. He turned to the constable. "And you were first on the scene?"

"Yes, Sarge."

"And the vehicle was on its back the whole time, and there was no ten-foot Jolly Green Giant with a pair of pincers?"

"No, Sarge. I was here four minutes after the incident."

Hughes sighed. "Two bits of metal from the underside of the other vehicle coming together from opposite directions to cause a laceration in this steel alloy. Doesn't sound likely, does it?"

"No, Sarge."

"Besides which, we have no other vehicle, constable." He took a deep breath in order to be able to deliver an even bigger, more theatrical sigh, but stopped. He let his breath out and sniffed the air. "I don't smell forty gallons of diesel, constable. Do you?"

"Sarge?"

"The driver said he was coming back from the depot, having filled up for tomorrow. Where did the diesel go?"

"There was no spillage, Sarge. You can see from the ground that –"

"Nothing. No diesel. I get it."

The wreck was cleared away just as dawn was breaking. A few minutes later the remaining patrol car removed the last of the cones and drove off just as the Essex rush-hour was beginning. The greatest volume of traffic was heading in the opposite direction from the cab, into London.

As he walked back to his own car, Sergeant Hughes glanced into the field adjacent to the dual carriageway and saw a thing of wonder – a mound of fresh earth sitting in the middle of a field of four-inch spring barley, some fifty yards from the site of the impact. The lines of the seed-drill went straight through it, from left to right from his point of view, so it had been made after the crop had been sown. There were no tractor marks anywhere near it, so it could not have been made by a machine. He'd grown up in rural Essex, and he knew a molehill when he saw one. This was *some* mole.

He clambered down the embankment, noticing a crushed sapling and cuts into the grass at approximate right-angles to the direction of travel of whatever had left the site. The top bar of the wooden fence at the bottom of the embankment was freshly broken, and splayed out into the field. The break revealed fresh wood, with no points of weakness; something much heavier than a man had snapped it. He examined the top of the bar, and found abrasions indicating that whatever had come over the fence was not only heavy, but hard.

The cuts he'd seen in the grass continued into the soft earth of the field and stopped at the base of the molehill. Unfortunately, they'd been made before the rain had stopped, and were parallel to the seeding-lines, so they weren't as distinct as they could have been. The furrows had been flattened in some places, and had the tops cuffed off in others. Nevertheless, he took out his tape measure. The mound itself was about ten feet in diameter and five feet high. There was a whiff of diesel.

He couldn't blame his team for having missed this. Not in the dark and the rain. Even if they had seen it, would they have wanted to believe it?

He turned and looked back. Only from this angle was it clear that something around six feet wide had made its way down the embankment into the field, across it and then… and then literally gone to ground. He took a photo which encapsulated the path down the bank and through the barley.

He laid out his measuring tape against a couple of the cuts in the earth and took photos showing their length, and the distance between them. As he did so it began to dawn on him that these were footprints, and he wished that he were not alone. The cuts, or what he assumed were the actual feet of the footprints, were some fifteen inches long and three wide. In aggregate they looked somewhat like the tread marks a tracked vehicle might make, except for the fact that the distance between them was not of an exactly regular pattern.

He looked at his muddy shoes and realised that somewhere beneath them might be something with serrated jaws that could cut through steel alloy. It had multiple feet that were capable of digging into earth.

He trod as lightly and carefully as a soldier in a minefield until he reached the embankment, then scrabbled up, grasping at tufts of grass, up onto the reassuring solidity of the tarmacked road. Once he had his breath back he looked across into the field. From this angle all he could see was the molehill and his own footprints, such were the angles of bent vegetation and the furrows in the field. He scanned the surrounding fields and saw nothing else out of the ordinary. He ran across to the other side of the dual carriageway and had a look there. Nothing.

What troubled him wasn't just that whatever it was didn't seem to have come out from the molehill, but that there seemed to be no clue as to where it had come from.

He got back into his car, and his professional training kicked in. He was conflating evidence: a road traffic accident with a couple of difficult-to-explain features had occurred. In a nearby field he'd seen the tracks of a diesel-powered earth-moving vehicle. Of course, there was the matter of a sober taxi-driver reporting a non-existent second vehicle, and the cutting of the fuel tank.

Twenty years of service or not, he'd be a laughing stock if he reported this. He drummed his fingers on the steering wheel and wondered whether he should call a colleague to verify it. Wasn't there a retired copper who had a website about UFOs? He'd look for something similar, or maybe log it there.

Chapter Two

He wasn't patient by nature, but when dealing with other species protocols had to be observed. He forced a smile, gritted his teeth, and knocked for a third time. "Mrs Plensca?" he said. "It's Doctor How." He fingered the wooden coat hanger, wishing he didn't need it.

The apartment door opened on a chain and two beady black eyes set on a pale face looked at him through the three-inch gap. The eyes blinked; the door closed. There were low, muttered voices in an alien language. The chain rattled and the door opened just enough for him to enter the apartment.

Mr and Mrs Plensca were as naked as the day they were hatched. Their mouths were flattened beaks, with a single nostril hole placed directly in the face behind. In everyday life these features would be disguised by a biomask; a living tissue which would give the wearer a human face. Their appearance would be accepted as well within the normal, and rather wide, range of faces in London. Its variety was one of the many features which made the city so attractive.

Beneath the translucent skin of their bodies he could make out their respiratory systems – blue-green pulsing veins squeezed between skin and organs. He didn't look any lower than chest-height. Whilst nudity in private was the norm for this particular culture, one just never knew about other taboos. The face – or at least the primary sensing area – was always a safe bet.

"You are how?" said Mr Plensca, bowing.

"Very well, thank you," said Dr How, returning the bow. "And I trust you and your lady wife are well? Do excuse me a moment." He placed the coat hanger on the door handle, unlaced his shoes, and put his socks in them. Next came his suit trousers, which he placed on the bar of the hanger, being careful to line up the creases. His jacket went on top, followed by his shirt. He slipped his underpants off and, after a slight hesitation, put them on top of his socks.

"We can help you how? Or this is a social visit during the holy month?"

"Oh. Happy Rindan holy month to you both. It slipped my mind, but then it's once every – what – three-and-a-half Earth years, isn't it?"

"Very good, Doctor. We have been here only two, so it's our first away from home," said Mrs Plensca, looking at her husband with what looked like fondness. "You observe our protocols well, for which we thank you. You would like to eat with us? My husband is an excellent... cook."

"Thank you so much, but I'm quite full." He'd made the mistake a few years ago of eating with the previous consul and her husband. Little wonder she had hesitated over the word 'cook', since the cuisine was entirely raw, and usually slimy in nature. There was an awkward silence. He beamed a smile at the couple and looked at them expectantly. They looked at each other, then back at him.

"We can help you how, Dr How?" said the consul.

"I thought I could help you."

"I assumed this was a social call."

"Ah. I received a message that your invertor was malfunctioning."

"Our invertor is functioning well, Dr How. Voltage and power are both satisfactory. We thank you for your concern."

"How odd." He turned and reached back into his jacket pocket for his smartphone. He tapped in his passcode and showed them the screen. "See? Got the message half an hour ago. I wasn't busy, so I thought I'd drop by."

"It really is most attentive of you, but we have noticed nothing."

"May I take a look?"

"By all means, Doctor." The consul waved her hand in the direction of the kitchen.

As his feet dug into the carpet he wished he'd brought disposable blue wrappers with him. Who knew what microbes or dirt he was picking up? The kitchen floor was tiled, but the sudden coolness against his feet felt awkward in a different way. He opened the fuse box and looked at the invertor. It was just as he'd installed it a decade earlier when the first Rindan consul had arrived. This was basic technology even a human could understand: it just took the domestic electricity supply and converted it to the frequency and voltage required by the occupants of the apartment. He checked the telemetry device attached to it by sending himself a test message to his phone. He pinged it back and it sent him a history. The device had not sent an alert to him. Not today, not ever. Perhaps the problem lay elsewhere?

"There is a problem, Doctor?" asked the consul.

"I wouldn't mind checking your utility cupboard, if I may." The consul nodded her assent, so he put on his underpants and opened the apartment door. The meter box was in the corridor, just outside. His feet felt even more exposed on the hardwearing blue communal carpet. This was a public space – he could only imagine what filth found its way in from outside. He squatted down and opened the door.

He heard the door of the apartment opposite open and a female voice say, "Oh!"

He twisted round and saw a middle-aged woman staring at him, open-mouthed.

"Landlord services," said Dr How. "Heating

malfunction, do excuse me." The door slammed shut. He muttered to himself about social protocols and looked inside the cabinet.

The electricity meter spun steadily, and the wiring was fine. He'd just closed the door when something struck him as odd. He opened it again and checked. The water meter was turning. He stuck his head back into the apartment, where the consul and her husband stood waiting politely. Just off down the hall he heard footsteps, so he nipped back into the living room and closed the door behind him. He took off his underpants and bowed again. The Plenscas bowed.

"Do you mind if I…?"

The consul once again swept her arm.

He checked the kitchen. As he'd thought, none of the appliances were on.

"All is well, Doctor?"

"May I just use your facilities?"

"Facilities?"

"The bathroom."

"Doctor, I –"

Before the consul could reply, he raced through the bedroom. Although the door to the en-suite was closed, he could hear that the shower was on. The consul was right behind him.

"Doctor How, this is most –"

He whipped open the bathroom door. There was no one in the shower cubicle, but it was far from empty. One wall was covered in what looked like polyps – greyish-green tubes about two inches in diameter and five inches long. They drooped contentedly under the warm shower. He estimated there to be two dozen.

"Doctor How, I must protest in the strongest –"

"Mrs Plensca, what do you think you're doing?"

"I'm sorry, Doctor," said Mr Plensca. "These are my

responsibility. I planted them."

"My husband was growing them for the feast at the end of the holy month," said the consul. "They're a traditional food for the final meal."

Doctor How took a couple of deep breaths to calm himself, and wished he hadn't – the smell from the polyps was not a sweet one. "Mrs Plensca, you do not have a breeding licence for these."

"We're not breeding them, Doctor," she said. "We're just growing them."

"These are an unlicensed alien species. What happens if their eggs spread into the sewer system?"

"Really, they are quite harmless, Doctor," said the consul.

"Excuse me," said her husband. He opened the door of the shower cubicle and threw some powdered food at the wall of polyps. "Feeding time," he explained.

Delicate latticed red fans flicked out of the tubes to grab at the particles washing past them. Dr How had to admit that they did look rather beautiful.

"Sexual or asexual reproduction?" he asked. "Adult or infant?"

"Unusually for such a lower-order species, they are sexual," said Mr Plensca. "This is the female infant stage."

"And no males hanging around?"

"No males."

The Doctor looked hard into Mr Plensca's eyes. "No others of this species, apart from what I see here?"

"None."

"Irrespective of your wife's status, you realise that this breach means I now have the authority to search this place from top to bottom? Or, worse still, get a Squag to do it?"

The Plenscas looked at each other, then at the Doctor.

"We will eat them all by the end of next week," said the consul.

The Doctor sighed. "Now is that the end of next Earth week, meaning a week today? Or is it next Rindan week, meaning about the middle of next month?"

"Happily, both are the same. It is end of Rindan holy month," said the consul.

The Doctor smiled and patted her and her husband on their naked shoulders, then wished he hadn't.

"Look, what I really object to is the outflow going straight into the London sewers. It's also wasteful, both of energy and water. I know it looks plentiful on Earth, but you have to remember that this is a primitive society. If you could rig up a closed system it would be much better."

"Thank you for being so accommodative," said the husband. "We must insist you have a polyp."

"Thank you, but they don't agree with me."

"No, it is tradition. You come to Rindan house in holy month, you must have polyp."

"I really must be getting back home. Lots to catch up on. Can't wait for you to prepare one."

"No preparation needed, Doctor. Eat raw. Like… Like *oyster*."

"Oysters are a bit smaller. One gulp. These look… big."

"Yes, you must take one, Doctor. Bad luck if you don't." Mrs Plensca left the bathroom.

"Here. This is nice one," said Mr Plensca. He reached under the spray and touched the foot of a polyp. The whole mass of polyps shrank back against the wall, their orifices shrinking small and tight, like a tapestry of anal sphincters. He peeled the base of one away from the tiles as his wife came back into the room holding a Tupperware box, which she handed to him. He let some of the warm spray fill the box and then put the tight polyp in it. He presented it to Dr How with a bow.

"Thank you," said the Doctor.

"It must be eaten in the next six hours," said Mr Plensca,

21

"Otherwise it will begin to go off."

"I can't imagine how bad that would smell," said Dr How, to puzzled looks from his hosts.

The three of them went back through to the living room and the Doctor hurriedly put his clothes back on. "Well, thank you again for the polyp," he said.

"It was nice to see you, Doctor," said the consul.

"Enjoy the rest of your holy month."

The door closed behind him. He stepped to one side, put the coat hanger and Tupperware box down and took his shoes off. He leaned back against the wall, removed the sock from his left foot, took out a hygienic wipe from his pocket, unwrapped it and rubbed it over the sole of his foot. He put the sock back on and put his left foot back in the shoe. He was wiping the sole of his right foot when the door opposite opened again. The middle-aged woman stared at his bare foot, the coat hanger, and the Tupperware box.

"Germs," he said. "You can't be too careful, can you?"

He made his way out of Du Cane Court and up Balham High Street without further incident, coat hanger and Tupperware box in hand, then turned right at the combined Tube and overland station. On Sundays the service was half-hourly, which was too long to wait for such a short distance, so he walked up past Tooting Bec Common. Murphy's Law being what it was, a couple of minutes later a train rumbled its way up towards Streatham Hill, with a couple of pistol-shot reports as the train went over the points and the electricity sparked from the third rail.

A couple of green parakeets squawked loudly as they flittered between trees. They were another invading species that had been introduced unintentionally – no one knew exactly when, or by whom. Whilst they added an exotic air to the parks and gardens of London and Kent, they played havoc with the indigenous wildlife.

There was still no explaining the invertor, and he wondered if the Plenscas might think it had been a ruse to enter their apartment. *His* apartment, he reminded himself. He was, after all, their landlord. And he did have other caretaker responsibilities – not just to other consuls and out-of-towners in other apartments throughout London. A look to his right was the only reminder he needed as to why this was such a plum posting: lush grass and old oaks. Even the railway embankment was teeming with life.

He took a deep breath. A delicious twenty-percent oxygen, mixed with unreactive gases. A strong but reasonable gravitational field, giving a decent pressure and thus a habitable temperature range for any water-based species – which was most of the known universe. Or, at least the known *Pleasant* universe. He had a predilection for trips to Earth's Carboniferous period, for the thirty-percent oxygen content and the sight of the gargantuan insects it supported – dragonflies three feet long and multi-coloured butterflies with six-foot wingspans being his favourites.

The invertor. He mulled it over. It hadn't sent a message. What, or who, had? A rogue message was highly unlikely. Conclusion? He'd been hacked. By whom? Or was it by *Who*? Unlikely, if not impossible at the moment.

He walked on, up the gentle slope and into the Telford Park Estate. He'd bought one of the solid red-brick Victorian houses off-plan from Telford himself, some thirty years after the railway had arrived in Streatham Hill. Nothing too extravagant – just a semi-detached. It was spread over three floors and a cellar, with three receptions and five bedrooms. He liked the castle-like appearance of the design – the front of the house had a faux turret and the roof sloped into crenellations, rather than guttered eaves. Spacious enough for his needs, but nothing that would attract too much attention in that kind of neighbourhood. Mr Telford had been surprised at the modesty of the Doctor's modest choice, given the substantial sum Telford had just paid him for this, the last enormous parcel of Doctor How's land.

It had been one of his longer-term investments – over eighteen-hundred years – having bought it in AD43 as the Emperor Claudius' troops invaded Britain to reinstate Verica, exiled king of the Atrebates. There was nothing like war to devalue the price of real estate, and the previous owner had been only too happy to be able to take the gold and flee north. Few things do more for the value of land than the enforcement of the rule of law, so although he had to pay a higher tax to the Romans he was happy to do so as the rent he received more than covered his initial investment. He'd not needed to visit much in the Dark Ages that followed – just the odd scare with a few projections. The Black Death had proven tiresome owing to a shortage of competent administrators but the rest, as they say, was history.

The Doctor didn't *need* all that land and the wealth that came with it. However, he'd always felt that it was important to have a genuine sense of attachment to a place. It gave him something to bat for, and he enjoyed seeing the development of cultures over such long periods – the changes in customs and religions, the evolution of language and the inexplicable, nonsensical fashions. And the people – although he was essentially a loner, he did love to meet the great and the good of each period, as well as the ordinary person on the street. For him, the game of fantasy dinner-party guests was played for real. And having the land and wealth of the well-heeled made it so much easier to be accepted, and to entertain. He was fondly remembering a dinner with H. G. Wells when he came within sight of his house.

Old Mrs Roseby was in her front garden, pretending to water her roses. His heart sank.

"Good morning, Mrs Roseby. Lovely day, isn't it?"

"Good morning, Dr How. Rain expected later."

He cast a deliberate look at her tin watering can, drawing her eyes to it.

"You can't be too careful with roses at this time of year. Besides, the weather girl looked foreign. Them foreigners don't know the British weather so well, do they?"

"It's all done by computers, Mrs Roseby. Big computers. She's just a presenter."

"Don't trust them computers either. When I was a girl –"

"When you were a girl, the very first proper computers saved the free world by breaking the Nazis' secret code, Mrs Roseby. Trust me, it'll rain later. And roses really don't need that much water. Deep roots. Now, was there anything else on your mind?"

The old woman put down her can, its clang on the brick path betraying its emptiness. "Your dog frightened the life out of my Albert."

"Albert the cat?"

"Yes. Poor thing nearly had an 'eart attack. Your dog slammed up against the door and barked and snarled like a... Like a…"

"Like a guard dog?"

"Yes! Like a guard dog."

"Well, that's reassuring."

Mrs Roseby was confounded, so he moved further down the path to his front door. She shuffled after him on her side of the wall.

"I've never seen that dog in all these years," she said. "You ought to let it out for exercise. That's why it's so ferocious. It's a miracle it doesn't eat that cat of yours."

"Two salient points to bring to your attention, Mrs Roseby. First, my apparently ferocious dog has not eaten my cat after all these years. Second, would you really want a ferocious dog out on the street?"

"Well, I... I... You never even let him in the garden."

"He's agoraphobic. I'll have a word with... With Bonzo. He'll be quieter in future. I promise. Good day, Mrs Roseby." He put his key in the lock and turned the brass handle. The handle felt just a touch different. He sniffed his hand and concentrated. Fried food and human hand-sweat, plus an undertone of cheap soap. He'd had a visitor. An unwanted one, by the sounds of it. He took a sterile bud from his pocket and rubbed it all over the handle, then popped it in its matching test tube and put it back in his pocket. He'd get the DNA analysis later. He pushed a button and the UV disinfecting lights on the sides and ceiling of the porch came on. He gave himself a five-second twirl in their invisible rays. His white shirt glowed a pleasing blue colour. The door to the house was open, and he closed it after entering.

"Trinity," he called.

A large black cat with the musculature and movement of a panther padded down the stairs and across the polished oak floor. It rubbed against his legs.

"Mrs Roseby tells me you've been quite loud. She's probably listening for an over-excited dog right now."

The cat looked up at him with her green eyes and gave two deep, throaty barks which reverberated around the hall.

"Good girl. Now, is this who came to call?" He presented the palm of his hand. The cat sniffed it and gave a miaow of assent.

"I wonder if that's the same person who hacked us, Trini." The cat tilted her head.

"Yes, I think we've been hacked." The cat hissed and stuck her tail in the air.

"Oh, we'll get him, don't worry about that. Now, I've brought you a little treat from the Plenscas. How do you fancy a bit of raw Rindan polyp?" Trinity gave a loud growl and followed him through to the tiled kitchen, rubbing his legs.

He set down the Tupperware box in Trinity's eating area and she purred as he removed the cover and presented it to her with the foot of the polyp facing her. The polyp pulsed, feeling the surge in available oxygen. Its red fan flicked out into the air. Trinity looked at the Doctor, then sniffed the creature's foot. It shrank to half the size. If a cat could have shrugged, that's what Trinity did. She bit the foot and the creature squeezed itself tighter. In a couple of swift movements she had just the top of the polyp showing in her mouth. It flicked out its red fan beyond Trinity's nose and she caught it in her teeth. She gulped down hard, then opened her mouth to show Dr How the red innards, which had been pulled out from the body. She chewed the innards and the fan.

"Oh, that's the best bit. I see. Clever girl."

He put the Tupperware box in the dishwasher and washed his hands with disinfectant soap.

Trinity licked around her mouth and sat back, purring. He stroked her head and she pushed back against the palm of his hand.

"Oh, my dear Trini," he said, "I have a feeling we're going to be terribly busy very soon." She looked up at him and gave a low, questioning growl. "Oh, I just know."

Chapter Three

If there was a right side to the A23, then Streatham Hill lay on it and Tulse Hill on the other. Whilst the former could boast famous former residents such as James Bond actor Sir Roger Moore, the latter's former residents tended to be more infamous than famous, and to serve their time at Her Majesty's pleasure. If they were lucky, it would at least be nearby in either Brixton or Wandsworth prison, where friends and family could visit more easily.

It had been a hard day at the office for Dr How; it always is for members of any intelligent species who have to answer to a Dolt. He'd left his Spectrel to figure out the identity of his hacker, and when he'd checked in at lunch it had given him a name, a location and a background. One thing the Doctor had learnt was that action should be as swift and decisive as possible. He used his work computer to access his Spectrel, and used it to perform a hack of his own.

The address was only a mile or so from his home, and getting within walking distance merely involved taking a different bus up from Brixton Tube station. Distance was a strange concept in London compared with anywhere else, even for someone as well-travelled as Dr How. The neighbourhood on one side of a road could be radically different from that on the other. In east London he'd seen slum housing next to bankers' apartments, as if the physical world had been Photoshopped by a political satirist.

The A23 headed due south to the coast, and was

nicknamed the Brighton Road after the city at its southern terminus. The A205 – the South Circular – went directly east-west. Streatham Hill lay to the south-west of the crossroads, and Tulse Hill to the north-west. They were polar opposites. If the Luftwaffe had had a plan to destroy Tulse Hill in the Second World War, and to sap the morale of its inhabitants by making their lives a misery, then they had failed utterly in their mission. Unfortunately, the plan had been taken up in the Sixties by enthusiastic young urban planners, and had succeeded on a scale that would have delighted Hitler.

When he'd invested in Du Cane Court in Balham as it was being built in the Depression of the Thirties, the Doctor had known it was a winning prospect. It had overground rail services to Victoria, Clapham Junction and London Bridge. The newly-extended Northern Line connected it with just about anywhere else in London you'd want to go. Designed as easy living for the well-off, Du Cane Court had filled with minor West End stars, who could get home from a show in the West End in twenty minutes. Streatham Hill, then the 'West End of South London' was just four minutes away by overground rail. Although Tulse Hill did have an overground station, it was not much used by residents and therefore not much used at all; there being no reason to visit the area.

He got off the bus and walked up the hill to the squat, brutalist five-storey block of flats. His sense of being watched didn't come from the CCTV cameras perched on custom-built poles and masked within mirrored protective globes. The cameras were probably more of a disincentive, rather than a true deterrent.

His bespoke black suit and white shirt were his everyday wear and his uniform. And, like a uniform, it was a signal to whoever was watching him that he wasn't afraid of being noticed, of being different. His business attire showed that he meant business.

There had been a long and successful campaign against anti-social behaviour by the local council. One part of this was the CCTV; the other increased physical security. The stairwell had been secured with a steel gate against entry by drug-users looking for somewhere dry and private to take a hit.

He walked up to the entryphone and took out a little oblong object the size of a pocket knife, with a surface of brushed metal. He swept it over the keypad and heard the buzzing as a solenoid pulled back the bolt. He pushed open the gate and went through. The eyes were curious now – warier. But he sensed they were turning to another subject of interest. He took the stairs up to the third storey and looked at the door of number thirty-eight. The dark blue paint indicated that it was not privately owned. On this type of estate, the doors of the tenants who'd opted to buy at a discount were generally fancier. He'd not noticed any in this development, and it was little wonder. He rang the bell.

The footsteps were heavy, and the door was answered by a plump Afro-Caribbean woman in her forties. Her clothes were cheap but smart. "It's Kevin again, innit?" she said, before he could utter a word. "I swear I will disown that boy one day."

"Is he in?"

"Nah, he's out with his mates. Well, he's out. Whether they're his mates or not is another matter. He's had his dinner so probably won't be back soon." She paused. "I hope it's not serious. Mind if I see some ID?"

"My card, Mrs Thomson. Here."

Mrs Thomson examined his card. "What does someone from the Technology Transmission Department at Imperial College want with my son? Anyway, I need to see photo ID. Sorry."

"Certainly. My driving licence."

She examined the Doctor's licence but kept his business card. "Good enough. Won't you come in, Dr How?" She put his card on the mantelpiece, next to a wedding picture of what he assumed was Mrs Thomson and her husband – an older white man with black-framed glasses. "Tea?"

"No, thank you. I wasn't planning to stay long."

"Come." She took a seat on a black leather armchair and motioned him to a place on the matching sofa. "I take it you're not about to offer him a position as an associate professor?" She let out a cackle and slapped a substantial thigh, which wobbled.

He smiled. "Unfortunately not, although I don't doubt that your son is smart enough."

"*Reeaaaally*?" she said. "I just wish I could direct that brain of his into something more productive. Like so many young ones, he's not got the focus. Lord knows I've tried to make him knuckle down. ADHD I think it is. I see it a lot up at the hospital. I work in A&E. The younger ones, they just don't have the patience to sit quietly. Can't read a book or a magazine. Always fiddling with their phones."

"As I said, he's certainly smart enough to be able to hack into a pretty secure environment."

"Oh, no. Not that again. I told him it's dangerous. You hack into the American systems now and they extradite you and put you away for decades. I can't afford no fancy lawyer. It's him and his conspiracy theories, you know. UFOs and all that nonsense. I mean, I always tell him that if aliens were so smart, why in the name of God would they bother with us? Eh?" She shook her head.

"I suppose it's at least stopped him from getting into other sorts of trouble. His record says he was cautioned for a few petty offences – shoplifting and the like."

"Ah, you know about that. That was enough for him. He's fairly legit now – computer repairs, phone unlocking, that sort of thing. Works out of his bedroom." She flicked her head in the direction of a hallway.

"Yes, I know exactly the sort of thing. Password resets on stolen PCs and iPads. Unlocking smartphones."

"What can I do, Dr How? It gets him a modicum of respect on the estate. He's like his dear departed father – smart, but not the kind of man who can stand up to other men. Not physically, at least. But he has a good heart, I promise you. Maybe one day he'll set up a proper shop down in Brixton. I always hoped someone would take him as an apprentice at one of those places in the arcade, or Brixton Village."

"It would certainly be a good use of his talents, Mrs Thomson. It's been nice talking with you, but I have to get on."

"Would you like me to get him to write you a letter of apology, Doctor?"

"Heavens, no. Just tell him that if he tries that stunt again he'll find his hard disc reformatted. He has quite a collection of programs on it, so he knows how many days it'll take to download and reinstall them. Tell him I mentioned that. Oh, and tell him I'm not bluffing. I wiped out his high score on Bioshock." It wasn't all that had happened to Kevin's computer. He wasn't sure whether Kevin knew just how much trouble he might be in.

"Serves him right, Doctor. I'll let him know. You take care on the way out. Do you know where you're going?" She rose to let him out.

It was dark outside, and the night was overcast and moonless. The streetlights on the estate were of the mercury-vapour variety used for industrial parks, giving a stark white light with a hint of pink.

"It's not much of a walk home from here."

"Best stick to the main road, though. Bye-bye, Doctor. And thank you for not being too hard on the boy."

He trotted down the concrete stairs, footsteps echoing

around and out of the stairwell. He pressed the green exit button, the gate buzzed, and he was out onto the tarmac.

There was a route round the back of the block, and that was his fastest way to the South Circular, and home. Attention wasn't on him, but he was very interested in seeing who it was on now as he walked stealthily towards the service area at the rear of the flats. He stopped at the corner of the building and listened.

"I told you, I know *nothing*," said one voice.

"Jesus, Kevin. The Feds knew exactly who and what they was lookin' for. They went straight into Joe's and nicked him. His brother says they even quoted the serial number of his laptop at him, and it matched. Boom – straight in the van, no arguments."

"Spyware," said another voice. "Shopped him. You said that machine was clean when you was done with it."

"I swear it *was* clean," said Kevin.

"You got careless. Know what happens when fruit gets handled carelessly, Kevin?" said the first voice.

"It gets bruised," said the other. There was the sound of scuffling, then the noise of a body being bounced off something large and hollow.

"I don't know nothing," said Kevin.

"How comes you got a nice friendly visit from the Feds ten minutes ago, eh? Giving you a reward from Crimestoppers, was they?"

"On my life, I don't know who that was. It can't have been a Fed. You saw him – he wasn't wearing a stab-proof vest, was he?"

"So if he wasn't a Fed, who was he? Went straight through the gate."

Dr How stepped out from behind the corner. "It's easy if you have one of these," he said, and held up the oblong metal object.

Kevin's two interrogators had him pushed up against

one of several giant dumpsters. They loosened their grip. All three stared at the suited man.

"Whoa, it's the Feds," said the larger of the two assailants.

"Good evening, officer," said the other. "We was just having a quiet word with young Mister Thomson here."

"I assume you've finished now, gentlemen?"

"Who's asking?" said a much deeper voice. A chunky youth stepped out of the shadows. "My Dad always told me to ask for ID. No warrant card, no conversation."

"Consider me just another one of Kevin's customers who wants a word," said the Doctor.

"Who are you?" asked the chunky youth. "You're on my turf. You ain't got no visa and you ain't paid no *entry fee*. Know what I'm sayin'?"

"Do excuse me. I thought this was public property. I didn't realise you were King of the Dumpsters."

Chunky's companions knew better than to laugh. Kevin's eyes opened in terror. There was a *snick* as a blade opened in Chunky's right hand. It glinted as the youth pointed it at Dr How's face.

"Just a word of advice, mate," said one of the youths holding Kevin. "Now would be a good time to show some *serious* respect."

"Yeah, and like maybe say your prayers if you don't," said the other. Kevin was pushed back against a dumpster and all three advanced on the Doctor.

"Kevin," called the Doctor, "I want you to look away now."

"No need," said Chunky. "He didn't see nothin'. Did you, Kev?"

"Nothing, I swear," said Kevin.

"Cover your eyes, Kevin," ordered the Doctor. He raised the metal object above his head. Its brushed metal casing reflected the light in a diffuse, unthreatening way. The trio's eyes followed it.

"Wh –" Chunky managed, before a blinding flash lit up the service area.

"Come, Kevin," said the Doctor. He pocketed the object and walked past the youths, who were rubbing their eyes and crying in agony. Chunky stumbled into a dumpster and fell over, letting out a fresh scream as he fell on a broken bottle and cut his shin. The Doctor grabbed Kevin by the lapel of his anorak and pulled him to his feet.

"What have you done to them? We should get an ambulance. My Mum's a –"

"They'll be alright in a few minutes. Your he-man might do well to get a tetanus jab though." Still holding Kevin by the lapel, he marched him off along the narrow path that led to the South Circular.

"Oh, I get it. It's like in *Men in Black*! Cool, man!"

"No, not really. They'll be a bit confused as to what happened, but they'll just associate you with pain from now on. You're coming with me."

"Jesus, I can't believe it. You're like Agent K."

The Doctor swung Kevin round. "Get this into your dense little head, Kevin. *Men in Black* is fiction. What is fact, my friend, is that you are in serious trouble. Maybe more trouble than you could ever imagine."

"With who?"

"No, not with Who. With me. With How. And some other people. I don't know who."

"I don't understand."

"You understood enough to hack into my systems. Then you came knocking at my door. I'll be needing answers, Kevin." They reached the South Circular. The rush-hour had finished, but there was a steady stream of traffic as they turned and headed west.

"Now, you either come with me and give me some answers, or you go back home and face your mother's wrath. And I'll also trash your computer remotely."

"You'd have a job. I'm the *best*."

"Really? Guess who put the spyware on Joe's machine that got him nicked?"

"Well, it wasn't me."

"I know."

"So it was you?"

"No, it wasn't me. I don't know who or what it was, Kevin. And if I don't know who it was then if I were you I'd be very, very scared right now."

They reached the busy junction. Seeing a gap in the speeding traffic, the Doctor grabbed the youth's arm and forced him to run across the dual carriageway to the traffic island. They caught the last seconds of a green light on the other side. They were now heading south along the A23.

"But I don't understand."

"Never play a game you don't understand, Kevin. You broke someone's rules and you paid for it."

"What's the worst that could happen?"

"Oh, *gosh*, Kevin. What do you think the King of the Dumpsters was going to do to you after Joe's court case over the stolen laptop?"

"I could have talked my way out of it."

The Doctor stopped and turned to face the youth. "*Really*, Kevin. You might have found it a whole lot more difficult with *no teeth*."

"Look, it wasn't –"

The Doctor continued his brisk walk. "Just suppose – I don't know how good you are with hypothetical questions, Kevin – but just suppose whoever did that to Joe's laptop – I say 'Joe's' laptop, but of course it's stolen –- just suppose they did that to every single machine you've hacked in the last two months."

"They couldn't. Could they?"

"Oh yes, they could, Kevin. And can you just imagine

how unpopular that would make you in your manor? Yes, I can hear your little brain working like mad now. Part of you's thinking that things might be quite a bit easier with the boys in the slammer. But it's not a full flush, is it? And then they do get to come out in a few months. Not so much fun then. Not so easy to talk your way out if it, is it?"

"Jesus. How do you know all this?"

"Because I did you a bit of a favour, sunshine. I stopped it from happening. I'll show you everything when we get back to my place, which – as you know – is but a short distance away."

"I'm not going in that house with that mad dog of yours. He'll kill me."

"He's a she. Still, we'd better make sure you get off on the right foot with her. Here, let's get her a tin of dog food."

They ducked into a small independent grocer's. The Doctor scanned the tins. "Hmm. Rabbit. I think she'd go for that. I remember her catching something small, cute and furry once. Trouble was, it only looked cute. Pure evil, it was." He declined a plastic bag. "She prefers things raw, and I rather suspect this is cooked. Still, it's the thought that counts, isn't it?"

They crossed the dual carriageway, then headed down the leafy road which led into Telford Park Estate. The noise of the traffic quickly died behind them. A couple of hundred yards later they were at Dr How's front door. "I'm not quite sure whether she's expecting you," he said as he unlocked it. "She can be a bit funny with strangers, so you'd better leave the introductions to me. But I'm sure she'll like you. Eventually."

Kevin crept warily into the porch behind the Doctor, who closed the front door behind him. He clicked the timer switch and the UV light came on. "If you'll just raise your arms, that would be great."

"What's this?" Kevin noticed his white shoelaces

glowing.

"UV light. Kills bacteria. Can't be too careful. You'll find I can be a bit fastidious where hygiene is concerned. Get used to it." He opened the door to the rest of the house and they went in.

"Trini," called the Doctor. "We've got company." There was no response.

Kevin screamed and grabbed the door handle, unable to turn it in his panic.

"What is it?" asked the Doctor. The youth was now in petrified shock, his back to the door. The Doctor pushed him away from the exit, out into the hallway. A huge spider covered in short jet-black fur, its head the size of a bowling ball and a body twice the size, was dangling on the end of a single sliver of silk, its legs spread out three feet on either side for balance. Its eight green eyes were locked into Kevin's, less than two feet from his face. Its mandibles twitched. Kevin let out a small choking noise.

"What's the matter, Kevin? Have you got arachnophobia?"

Kevin choked back a gurgle.

"Oh, Trini. You're not hypnotising him, are you? I'm so sorry, Kevin. It's one of their hunting strategies in the wild for larger kills. She doesn't get much of a chance to practise it these days, but even so, it's a bit rude. After all, she's not intending to kill you. Not that I know, anyway."

"C-c-c-c. S-s-s-st –"

"Can I stop her? Yes, of course. Trinity, would you please let Kevin go?"

The spider rose silently on her silken sliver and, with a flick of her body, stood upside-down on the ceiling, eyes still fixed on Kevin.

"Come on, let him go." Trinity backed off to a point in the ceiling just above where the stairs began. "Oh, very well." He turned to Kevin. "She wants to show off. It's her favourite party trick. Watch this."

The Doctor went up to the third step. Trinity dangled a hind leg. The Doctor jumped up and grabbed it, as if it were a trapeze bar. She held that leg steady whilst she crawled back to her previous position in the middle of the hall ceiling. "Pretty impressive, isn't she? Capable of holding thirty times her own bodyweight."

Trinity dabbed the spinner in her rear on the ceiling and spun out a fresh sliver, returning the Doctor gently to the floor. She flashed back up to the ceiling on the silk, then dropped to the floor without a line, landing silently on her feet in front of Kevin. She backed off a few feet, to the end of the corridor next to the stairs.

"Now, she's said hello to you. It's only good manners that you say hello to her."

"H-h-h-h-h. T-t-t-t-t. Ht."

The Doctor shook Kevin by the shoulders and waved his hands in front of his eyes. "Come on, snap out of it. She's not going to bite you, lad."

"H-h-h-hello, T-Trinity," said Kevin.

"I thought the cat had got your tongue there, Kevin." The Doctor looked down at his guest's jeans. "At least you've not wet yourself."

If a spider could have laughed, it would have looked like Trinity did at that moment – her head nodding and mandibles twitching.

"In the wild, with larger prey, they hypnotise them first, you see. Bit like a snake does. Then the next thing you know, you're dead. Or probably you don't know at all, because you're dead, come to think of it. Whilst she's got you fixed with her two big eyes, the others are busy working out the physiological details – what sort of sensory systems you've got, how good they are, muscles, central nervous system, circulatory system – you know; veins, arteries, that sort of thing. Then she'd probably either paralyse you or just slash an artery. Or, if you're smaller, chop your head clean off. If your head's the important bit, that is. Normally the case, but you just never know, do you? Well, she does. Obviously. Or at least, she does if you make the mistake of giving her a few seconds to work it out. Are you better now?"

"She's not a dog. She's a spider."

"And they say science education is on the decline in this country. Well, not exactly a spider, but near enough. Let's just call her the most efficient predator I've ever met. She's not from round these parts, you know."

The Doctor turned to address Trinity. "Kevin's actually very thoughtful. He insisted we stop and buy you a can of this." He held up the tin of dog food. Trinity's attention switched to the can, and he handed it to Kevin. Her attention stayed on the can.

"Good girl," said Kevin. "I hope you like rabbit?"

Trinity's rear legs straightened with a twitch that made Kevin start.

"I'd take that as a yes, Kevin. Now, how about you just give her the food? She's in feeding mode now, and you don't want to leave her in that state without giving her something. Quickly."

"Do you have a tin-opener?"

"I hardly think *that* will be necessary, Kevin."

The youth turned, open-mouthed, to the Doctor.

"She likes a bit of activity with her feeding. Look, if you're still a little scared why don't you just throw it to her?"

"But –"

"Oh, for heaven's sake. You're not going to hurt her. She likes to play with her food. She's a *predator*, for God's sake. Don't you get it?"

Kevin lobbed the tin underarm in Trinity's direction. It wobbled in its arc, but the spider reached out a front leg and caught it noiselessly in a paw. She set it down in front of her the right way up.

"She's not going to…?"

"No, she doesn't eat metal. A bit of bone, yes, but metal? No. Be sensible."

"What's she doing?"

"Reading the label, of course. What do you expect?"

Trinity grasped the tin with one leg and slid it under her mandibles. There was a pop, and then a tearing noise. She rotated the can in increments, each marked by the sound of metal tearing. The top fell off, hit the floor and rang for a couple of seconds as it settled down. Trinity gulped down the contents with her mandibles. Once the bulk was finished she tore the can at the sides and cleaned out the last morsels of food.

"Wow," said Kevin, as Trinity scuttled off in the direction of the kitchen, carrying the ripped tin and its lid in her mandibles.

"Yes. She does make your native species look a bit – I don't want to be unfair here – a bit *underdeveloped*, doesn't she?"

From the kitchen came the sound of a tin being rinsed and then thrown into a recycling bin.

"Y-yes. Does she attack humans? Is she the dog I heard?"

"Everything attacks humans. Bacteria, viruses, insects, dogs, mice, fish. Anything will attack a human if you annoy it enough. And, unfortunately, humans seem to specialise in being annoying. I put it down to your curiosity. And your blind ignorance too, I suppose. Of course, you mostly don't mean any harm – but you never seem to get the message, do you? I often wonder if, as a species, you're autistic. Or maybe a touch too arrogant for your own good."

"You mean you're –"

"Not human? No."

"What are you, then?"

"I brought you here to answer a few questions of my own. The answers to yours will become abundantly clear over time. But right now, for your sake, you have to answer mine. Those are the rules for now."

An oversized black cat with green eyes padded into the hall from the direction of the kitchen. It purred and rubbed itself against Kevin's legs. He bent down and stroked its head, and it pushed back into his hand.

"Are you, like, not afraid that Trinity's going to eat your cat?"

"Trinity is the cat."

Trinity opened her jaws and gave a large meowl. Kevin whipped his hand away.

"I think she likes you," said the Doctor. "And not as a foodstuff, either. That's a relief. Particularly for you, I suspect."

The Doctor had insisted Kevin wash his hands thoroughly in anti-bacterial soap in the downstairs bathroom, then given him a cup of hot chocolate for the shock he'd suffered.

"I think I recognise some of the artists you have on your wall," said Kevin, as they descended the stairs to the cellar. He'd never met someone this well-to-do; nor had he been in a house like this one – not as an invited guest, at least – and was struggling for conversation. "Those kinds of prints can be very expensive, can't they?"

"*Prints*? Those are originals."

"But I swear I saw a something like an Old Master, and maybe a – what's-his-name? – a van Gogh. Something in that style, anyway."

"Oh, Vincent spent a few years just down the road in Brixton. Surely you knew that? His uncle got him a job at Goupil and Cie, the art dealers, who then transferred him to their place on the Strand. Walked to work every day. He was happy here, for a time. Such a shame when Eugénie rejected him. He'd done the odd sketch, so I told him it would be good therapy – take his mind off things. We kept in touch. I sent him some woollen colour swatches after he moved to Arles, and he sent me that portrait back in return. I was mortified – poor chap was on his uppers by then. I sent him enough rent money for a quarter. Probably blew it on absinthe. You can't meddle too much in the lives of others."

"He sent you a portrait of *you*?"

"Of course. Very much the done thing in those days. Right, if you'll sit here for me, please." The Doctor pulled up a second chair in front of a large oak desk. The only item on it was a laptop.

Kevin sat down and looked around the bare, white room with its flagstone floor. He was glad Trinity hadn't joined them. "What's the phone box for?" There was a traditional red British telephone box in the corner of the room opposite to where they'd come in. It was in pristine condition. The red paint seemed to pulse with the deepness of its red, and the glass panes reflected the white walls so brightly he couldn't see inside.

"Can you just *concentrate* and stop asking questions?"

Kevin swung his chair round to look at the screen of the laptop.

The Doctor adopted a sober tone. "Look, we need to get to the bottom of this. You tried to hack me, but you also tried to hack someone else. They didn't like it one iota, and they were going to make you pay for it. Now, I need to know who it was. Clear?"

"But why should you care?"

"Because they also hacked me. I know who you are, but I don't know who they are. No offence, but I think they are a considerably greater threat to me than you are. Now, think back to what you were doing."

"Well, you know, I was just, like, surfing some stuff on

the dark web, you know."

"Come on, hurry up. How did you come across me and my system?"

"Oh, I could see there was all this activity. An IP address somewhere in Dagenham. Something looked a bit odd."

"What?"

"I've never seen code like it before. People have styles. It just seemed… I dunno. Alien."

"Go on."

"Well the characters wasn't even recognised by my system. You know, the characters wasn't supported by any font I could find."

"Not even something that supported Ancient Greek, Cyrillic script, Arabic, Thai, something like that?"

"Nah, nothing. I parsed it in all these fonts and it was all just nonsense."

"And so you did what?"

"Chopped it into binary and started crunching."

"And?"

"And it still didn't make much sense. Then I realised a big chunk of it could be turned the other way and used as graphics."

"Turned the other way? What do you mean?"

"I sorted it into blocks. There was a repeating bit of code. Did I mention that?"

"No; a critical detail you missed out. Never mind. Go on."

"It was a map."

"Of?"

"I don't know. I only got part of it."

"But you saved it?" Kevin nodded. "We'll look at it later. Now, that was the passive thing you were doing. What was the active thing that made them hit back?"

"They were snooping around an IP address in Streatham Hill, using the Dagenham thing as a proxy. I mean, what's something of that kind of industrial strength interested in something around my 'hood for?" He saw the Doctor wince at the thought of being considered in the same neighbourhood as himself. "Well, we's all south of the River, innit? No one loves us."

The Doctor sighed. "You're right. North Londoners will never get it. Keep going."

"So I hacked them trying to hack you. So it wasn't really that I was hacking you indiscriminately, or anything. I was kinda hacking them hacking you."

"Hack not, lest ye be hacked."

"Sorry?"

"Go on, Kevin. Go on."

"And your system was using the same sort of code, except that I couldn't convert it to graphics or nothing."

"At that stage, neither my system nor theirs would have been using graphics."

"And then I realised that the whole reason I could see any of this in the first place was that they'd been using the Dagenham address as a proxy but using me as a masking IP all along. I was on the inside, if you see what I mean."

"Which is why I couldn't see their IP address."

"And that's it. End of story. Next thing I know, I'm shut down. So what do you reckon?"

There was silence for a few seconds, whilst the Doctor thought. "I have a cousin in Dagenham," he said. "I do hope he's alright. You see, this," he indicated to his laptop, "is an antique."

"No it's not, it's a tasty bit of kit, that."

"Kevin. It's an antique. Well, okay, it's not an antique. Technically an antique has to be at least a hundred years old. But what I mean is that it's really primitive. This is to my sort of computing what flint axes are to a machine gun."

"Nah, you don't know –"

"Take it from me, lad. It's Stone Age. I just use it as a

convenient interface. Now, what could be better than to hide behind a curious young man who's interested in conspiracy theories, and happens to live within walking distance? Let's have a look at your map, shall we?"

"It's on my computer back at home."

"The entire contents of which I have here."

"That's theft!"

"Kevin, another little saying for you: He who lives by the sword, dies by the sword. You were lucky to have intercepted the graphics because the rest of it would have been gobbledegook to you. Or anyone else, for that matter. Here we are." An image resolved itself on the screen.

"Yeah, that's it. It's a map. Not like any map I've seen."

"That's because it's a geological map, Kevin. Let me just fiddle with a few of these files." The Doctor ran a secondary program. "There you are. A 3D map of... of the geology of an area of Essex."

"What's all them coloured layers?"

"Those are rock strata. See, on the top there, is what's called the alluvial layer. That's the soil and clay laid down at the end of the last Ice Age. Underneath that you've got successive layers of older formations, from the blue clay through which the Tube system is built, down to sandstone, shale, and what have you."

"So why's someone looking at that?"

"You want to map it to see if there are valuable minerals down there. Coal, for example, or oil. In this instance, the data seem to have been stolen from a company which was interested in shale deposits."

"Like shale gas."

"Oh, you *do* watch the news. Good man."

"I don't get it. Someone who's interested in shale gas is interested in hacking you."

"A couple of obvious things here, Kevin. First, you might notice a small dotted area of some complexity if I zoom in… like so."

"Yeah, gotcha. Looks like plans for something underground."

"Exactly. We don't know what, though. The second thing is that when you try to hack someone like me you're generally not merely interested in hacking."

"I was."

"Yes, well you're just insatiably curious. If you hack someone like me you're interested in neutralising me."

"What makes you say that?"

"Because whoever did it had already hacked my cousin. They were using his machine."

"You mean your cousin has a computer like a machine-gun too?"

"If we're sticking with that analogy, yes."

"You recognise the code?"

"Yes, it's Gaelfrey."

"Gallifrey? You're Dr Who, innit?"

"No. I'm not Dr Who. I'm Dr How. And it's *not* Gallifrey." The Doctor's tone switched in an instant from patient to irritated. "I don't want to hear that word in this house. Or *any*where around me. Understood?"

"Jesus, Doc. Sorry, man. Like, I didn't realise you was so sensitive."

"Sorry. I overreacted. You weren't to know."

Kevin twisted awkwardly on his seat. "Look, I need you to level with me. You're like… You're like the Doctor, innit? And that." He pointed at the phone box. "That thing over there is like the TARDIS."

Doctor How sighed deeply. "Yes, and no. I am *a* Doctor. There is no *the* Doctor, except in fiction. And except in one person's head in particular." He spat out the last sentence with some bitterness, but regained his composure. "Despite my assertion to the contrary, you think I'm Dr Who, don't you? A real-life Time Lord?"

"Yeah, man. It's like *way* cool."

"No, Kevin, it is not way cool. It is not even – as you mistakenly say in your street patois – *like* way cool. It is an enormous responsibility. A huge burden. Yes, a pleasure at some times, and it does occasionally have its privileges. It serves well my taste for art, for example. But most of the time it is bloody hard work. Do you understand me?"

"Like don't have a cow. I was just asking."

"Forget everything you know – or think you know – about Dr Who and Time Lords. It's a fiction. Do you understand?" Kevin nodded. "It's a fiction taken up unwittingly by the BBC, touted by a megalomaniac back in the Sixties. He's made my job a dozen times more difficult, and nearly trashed the entire universe into the bargain."

"So is that your –"

"No, it's *not* my TARDIS, Kevin! That's a misnomer."

"A…?"

"A *misnomer*." Kevin looked at him blankly. "It means wrong name. It's a misnomer put out by the BBC. TARDIS is actually a very rude word in my native language and nearly one in yours if you changed the 'a' for a 'u'. A certain someone, who will remain nameless, thought it would be terribly amusing. According to the BBC, TARDIS is supposed to mean Time And Relative Dimension In Space." The Doctor was now ranting wildly. "Can you believe the sheer *gall* of these people? Like they actually *know*, like they *understand* how the physics works?" The Doctor glared at Kevin, who shook his head.

"Let me tell you what it's like. It's like a troop of monkeys – and I mean *monkeys*, like baboons; not chimpanzees, not even *apes* – coming up to your very sophisticated saloon car with individual climate-control for each passenger, and a hi-fi system that would fool a bat. As you drive your state-of-the-art car through a safari park this troop of purple-bottomed baboons comes up to your car and calls it "Oog". And then – and then – then, they have the cheek to first of all *capitalise* the entire thing, so it's not Tardis, it's T-A-R-D-I-S, just to spell out the first letters of exactly what these monkeys think the physics is that they can't even begin to comprehend. And after that they march down to another baboon who calls himself a lawyer and they register it as a trademark. So if I wanted to write my own biography, *my autobiography*, and I wanted the boneheaded human reader to understand the concept by way of using the word TARDIS, some baboon with a Technicolor™ bottom specialising in intellectual property law could demand money with menaces through the good courts of baboon society. And all this," spluttered the Doctor. "And all this after I saved your – forgive my crude colloquialism here – after I have saved your sorry collective Technicolor™ asses on more occasions than I care to remember."

Silence hung in the air. The Doctor was breathing deeply.

"And was that thing you used…?"

"No. It's *not* a Sonic Screwdriver. Such a thing does not exist. How in God's name *could* it? How could you *possibly* have something working on sound waves in the vacuum of space?" The Doctor slammed his fist on the desk.

"You has like got issues, hasn't you?"

The Doctor slowly closed his eyes, then reopened them. "Yes," he said quietly, "I have issues. I have issues about this and many other things. First of all, it's *Gaelfrey*. A script-editor misheard it and renamed it Gallifrey, probably because it didn't sound quite right for use on early evening Saturday television. Second, it's not a TARDIS, it's a *Spectrel*. That stands for Space Expanding-Contracting Time Relationship. I only use a capital for the first letter, because I consider it a proper noun, and no longer an acronym. I only call it that because it sounds nice in your language and gives you a set of words you can easily remember. It doesn't actually explain the physics any better than the word TARDIS, but I find that if I don't at least attempt a fancy name that sounds like a vaguely convincing – albeit absurd and nonsensical – explanation, then you humans don't trust it. Third, it is a Tsk Army Ultraknife. I will explain some other time just how idiotic it would be to call something so sophisticated a Sonic Screwdriver. Clear?"

"Yes, clear, boss."

"*Boss*?"

"Just a turn of phrase. Respect, innit?"

"Now, as it happens, fate has thrown us together. I recognised your thumbprint on the back of one of my Turners upstairs."

"What do you mean?"

"I mean your thumbprint is on the back of one of the pieces given to me by the painter J. M. W. Turner."

"How –"

"My system scanned your prints and matched them. Oh, don't worry about the damage. It's history. And I was reconciled to it long ago."

"But I never touched your Turner! How could I have?"

"That's quite literally another story, Kevin. You and I have to get through this one first."

"You mean…?"

"Yes, you're my new assistant and it looks like we're destined to have a series of adventures together. Welcome aboard. Please, call me Doctor. We have work to do."

"Wow, this is so cool, man!"

"I keep telling you that it is *not* cool, Kevin. It is highly dangerous. Oh, and if you think you're going to wander around telling all and sundry about your new position, you're very much mistaken."

"But can I not tell my Mum?"

"I suppose she has a right to know something, yes. But be careful what you tell her."

"Hang on just a second. Have you, like, had assistants before, yeah?"

"A few, yes."

"So, like, where are they now?"

"Dead, mostly."

"*Dead?*"

"You know, old age. For the most part."

Kevin goggled at him. "For the most part?"

"Yes, for the most part." The Doctor patted him on the shoulder. "Stick with me and do as I say and you should be okay. Before I forget, we'll start by giving you a couple of hundred quid for some new clothes. Here." He handed Kevin a wad of notes from his wallet. "For God's sake don't spend a penny of it on what you call *bling*. Clothes only, and I shall want to see itemised receipts. Understand me?"

"Yes, boss. Doctor."

Chapter Four

The filling station had run out of diesel at around seven-thirty at night. A customer had been filling the tank of his SUV when it had run dry after just a few litres. Just seconds earlier, the indicators had flashed a low-level warning. Mr Patel, the station's owner, had thought it was an error, given that the bunkers had just been filled that morning. If a member of his staff had been on duty at the time he'd have thought he'd been duped – conned out of a delivery. But the gauges had indicated that his tanks had been filled with the same amount of diesel and petrol he'd signed for.

This had left only one possibility, and it filled him with dread. Unfortunately, the seriousness of the incident had meant the involvement of the fire brigade because the only rational explanation was that the diesel bunker had suffered a catastrophic failure. If that were the case, his insurer was going to face a hefty bill. It wasn't just the repair of the structural damage – there was the clean-up bill to consider. The surrounding ground would be contaminated, and would probably need digging out. He'd be out of business for months, at least. If it had leaked into the sewers then there was the potential for a massive explosion.

It was now ten o'clock, and he was standing on the other side of the police cordon watching the fire crew flush the drains with industrial detergent to reduce the fire risk. He was thankful that he wasn't in a residential area, and that he didn't have a couple of hundred displaced households pouring their ire on him. All he could do was watch the figures on the forecourt and wait for any news.

A police patrol car pulled up onto the forecourt and a sergeant got out. "Alright, Hughesie?" said Steve. "Makes a change, eh? No one hurt. No motors."

"I was going to ask how long you're going to be," said Sergeant Hughes. "We've got a hell of a big diversion."

"Just about to take a look inside. Got a specialist coming in from Tilbury for a butcher's. Refinery fire officer. Private, so we'll have to charge him out of budget."

"I suppose you don't get many of these."

"Serious business, ruptured fuel bunker. Think back to the Buncefield explosion in 2005. The petrol one seems to be intact, but there's always the danger it'll go. Diesel ain't quite so bad, but petrol – whoof!"

"What caused it?"

"Search me. Happened very fast from what I hear. You'd expect a slow leak – a crack, something like that. This is pretty new, too. Mr Patel over there said it's no more than four years old. So if one bunker's failed suddenly then you have to think in terms of something big like subsidence. But the thing is that the concrete's reinforced, and a good six inches thick. Enough to stand on its own. You could take one of these out and crash a car into it, I should think. We don't get earthquakes here, but they're designed to withstand them."

A couple of firemen wearing breathing apparatus lifted off the inspection hatch.

"Right, here we go," said Steve. He put on his breathing equipment and walked forward twenty feet to join the other two men. He lowered himself onto the concrete beside the inspection hatch. One of his men handed him a heavy duty flashlight. He put it into the tank and leaned his head inside. He let out a muffled yell and dropped the light. There was an echoing bang as it hit the bottom of the tank, and a scuffling noise from inside. Steve jumped to his feet and ripped off his mask.

"Get back!" he yelled. From inside the tank came the unmistakable sound of masonry hitting concrete, then something that sounded like earth being thrown onto the floor of the chamber. All four men froze, listening to the sounds. After a few seconds, there was silence.

"What was that?" asked Sergeant Hughes.

"No idea," said Steve, shaking. "I could swear there was…" He shook himself. "Let's take another look. Roy, you want to have a butcher's too?" He took another torch, and he and Roy crept forward to the inspection hatch. Steve poked his head cautiously over the side of the hatch and flashed the torch around, keeping his hand at ground level. He then put his head into the hole, reached in and shone the light around. He pulled his head back out and indicated to his colleague to do the same. Hughes couldn't hear what they were saying.

They got back to their feet and pulled off their breathing apparatus just as a private car rolled to a halt on the forecourt. The driver got out. He was a portly man in his fifties wearing jeans and a casual shirt, looking all the more haggard for having been called in from home.

"Evening," he said. "Steve Jones? Dave Swann. The two men shook hands. "You're one of Parkie's boys, ain't you? How is the old dog? We were on blue shift together back in Basildon."

"Ah," Steve brightened. "Yeah, Dave Swann. Parkie's doing alright. Close to retirement now, of course."

"Yeah, I got out eight years ago. Sit on me arse in an office now. Risk-assessment and contingency planning mostly. What's the bother here?"

"Need your advice. More your thing, mate. Leaking tanks and that."

"Cleared the drains, I see," said Dave, thumbing back

towards the firemen who were finishing up with the detergent.

"Owner says there's pretty much a whole tankful gone into the surrounding area," said Steve. "Catastrophic failure. Now, I was expecting a fracture and a slow drain."

"Most likely scenario, yes. Not likely it's just sprung a leak." Dave looked around. "Especially not with building regs the way they were when this was built."

"Right, if you wouldn't mind doing the honours, then. Tell me I'm not imagining things."

Dave pulled on a protective suit, and was given breathing apparatus and a flashlight. He accompanied Steve up to the hatch and looked in. There was a muffled exclamation and Steve lay down on the ground next to him. There was an animated discussion, which was unintelligible from where Hughes and Roy were standing.

"Doesn't make sense," said Roy to Hughes.

"How?"

"It's six-inch thick steel-reinforced concrete, right?"

"Yes."

"Well, it looks like something's actually… I dunno how to describe it. Something's punched in to the tank."

"Punched in?"

"Yeah, the reinforced steel has been cut and bent inwards."

"You mean cut?"

"Clean edges."

"Just like if you'd had some of those big pincers? Just like the fuel tank of that taxi the other day?" Roy looked at him. He nodded.

Steve and Dave came back to join the other two men.

"What's the verdict, gents?" asked Hughes. "Can I reopen this side of the carriageway?"

Dave and Steve looked at each other. Steve nudged Dave. "You're the expert mate. And you're getting fees for this."

"There's nothing inherently wrong with the structure," said Dave. "So the remaining tanks are safe in themselves."

"Okay," said Hughes.

"And the diesel has drained away. And I mean really drained away. Effectively. Deep. Very deep. That's why Steve's lads didn't find any contamination in the drains."

"So what happened?" asked Hughes.

"Well," said Steve, "we reckon this is one for the Old Bill. It's been half-inched, hasn't it?"

"What do you mean?"

"Someone's nicked the diesel. They've only driven something in there and nicked it, haven't they?"

"Get off, mate," said Hughes. He stared at Steve, and the fire officer smiled at him.

"Well, me and Dave reckon someone's crashed a drill-bit, or a pig from a pipeline into it."

"A pig?"

Steve looked at his feet. "Yeah, you get these motorised things that can go along old sewage, gas or water pipes. As they inch forwards they break the old pipe and push the fragments into the surrounding earth. They pull in fresh pipe behind them. Plastic stuff that's good for the next hundred years or so."

"I think I know the things you mean," said Hughes. "I saw the water people using one in a road a few years ago. About three feet long and maybe six inches wide?"

"Yeah, that's the job."

Hughes ordered his men to begin taking off the diversion. The filling station would remain shut until someone a couple of ranks above him could talk to one of Steve's superiors in the cold light of day and decide what to do. Dave Swann said his goodbyes – he'd be one of the experts consulted the following morning.

"Here, let's have a talk," said Hughes. "I can drop you

back at the station."

"Sure, mate," said Steve. They walked to Hughes' patrol car and got in.

"What did you see when you first looked down there?"

"This big hole. The concrete had fallen into the tank. The steel reinforcing rods had been cut and bent inwards. I've never seen anything like it. I was stunned."

"Stunned enough to drop your torch?"

Steve looked back at him.

"Look, we've known each other – what – maybe fifteen years. Not exactly Christmas card list, but… you know, we're professionals." Steve nodded. "We've seen some bloody horrible messes out there," he thumbed in the direction of the dual carriageway. "But I've never seen you flinch." Steve nodded again. Sergeant Hughes cleared his throat. "I'm going to guess that the hole was about two metres across. Right?" Steve perked up. "I'm also going to guess that there was quite a bit of soil pushed back into that tank. Am I right?"

"How'd you know? Roy tell you?"

"No." Hughes took his camera out from the back seat and switched it on. "Have a look at these. I took them after everyone else left the other day."

"This is the taxi that crashed into another vehicle, right?"

"Yeah, the vehicle that didn't exist. Let's scroll through to the ones that didn't make it to my report. Here you go. This is what I saw in daylight. See? Big mound of earth. Then I saw these tracks leading down to it. Something heavy, maybe a couple of metres wide. Something pretty heavy, but the imprints aren't as regular as you'd expect from a big tractor tyre or a tracked vehicle."

"And this was right next to the crash scene?"

"The team did look for the mystery vehicle in the immediate vicinity, but there was nothing. Remember, we couldn't find any tyre marks – not even any glass that didn't belong to the cab. No way you could have seen it in the dark."

"Sure, I'm not saying your guys didn't do their job. I'm just wondering why you're showing me this."

"Steve, this happened about four miles from here. Right? Heavy enough to dent a black cab. Two metres across. Something that can apparently cut through reinforced steel. And all it leaves is a molehill. Did I mention the molehill smelled of diesel?"

"So what did you say in your report?"

"I didn't."

Steve said nothing.

"And I was going to ask you what you're going to put in your report."

"As I said, the only conclusion me and Dave could make was that something broke in. Had to be one of those pigs. Or maybe a drill bit from one of those fracking operations. The diesel would have just flowed off into the hole, wouldn't it?"

Hughes was silent for a moment. "There are no two-metre wide pipes around here. And I doubt very much a pig's going to be able to reverse with a dirty great pipe trailing behind it. Plus, I see no construction crews. As for a fracking drill – be serious."

"What other explanation is there?"

"Steve, level with me." Hughes squeezed the fireman's shoulder. "I heard the noise. That wasn't a machine. I want to know what it was."

Steve turned to stare out of the passenger window for a few seconds, then looked Hughes in the eye. "This is between us, right?" Hughes nodded.

The fireman took a deep breath and then sighed. "It was black and shiny. Big thing. I only saw what I think was the back of it. And a couple of legs."

"*Legs*?"

"That's what they looked like."

"Go on. What did the rest of it look like?"

Steve paused before replying. "A cockroach. A beetle sort of thing. You know?"

Both men stared ahead through the windscreen at the passing traffic. It was Hughes who broke the silence. He picked up the camera and scrolled to the photos of the tracks. "A six-foot wide beetle would probably leave footprints like that, wouldn't it?"

"A big beetle that likes diesel. I'll let you file your report first – stealing fuel is a police matter."

"Nah, Steve. A six-foot wide beetle with a stomach full of diesel is a fire hazard."

The laughter of relief left them in fits for a couple of minutes.

"Look," said Steve, taking controlled breaths. "Dave's going to report it as a stray pig or a drill-bit from a fracking company. There'll be a search and it'll turn up nothing. That's none of our concern."

"Until someone gets killed. I was going to send these to a website I've heard about. They deal with reports about the paranormal from police officers. All anonymised. Usually it's UFOs and all that rubbish. It'll be a nice change from the usual content. Send me your pictures and I'll submit them at the same time. I can't just do nothing, can I?"

"You're right. Maybe someone reads that stuff. Maybe they can figure it out."

Chapter Five

"Mrs Thomson, please. If I could just expl –"

"You got no right to be calling him a baboon, Dr How."

The Doctor held his phone slightly further away from his ear. "I didn't call him a baboon, Mrs Thomson. I compared the entire human race to a troop of baboons."

"Well, that's still racist."

"No. If anything, it's species-ist. Racism is what human beings do to each other when they're from different races. I was trying to explain to your son that, compared to – let's say, an advanced extraterrestrial species – human beings are baboons." He wondered just how much Kevin had blurted to his mother.

"You're filling his head with all sorts of nonsense about UFOs and aliens. I was hoping you'd talk some sense into the boy. You're supposed to be a scientist, for God's sake."

"People get ideas into their heads and you can't get them out. I'll have a word with him."

"Alright then. Now, if he's going to be your apprentice then he needs an employment contract. And he's worth more than minimum wage doing what he does with computers."

"But I just gave him two hundred pounds for clothing last night!"

"Two hundred quid doesn't go far these days, Doctor. And if he's going to damage his own clothes then you're just paying for wear and tear."

"Let's start again, Mrs Thomson. My extensive

background checks revealed that Kevin has no history of gainful employment. And may I remind you that two days ago he hacked into my computer? I'd have been perfectly within my rights to report him to the police. However, I believe in restorative justice and I'm giving him a chance."

"You're gonna keep him out of mischief on the estate?"

"Believe me, he's not going to be anywhere near the estate at all. He quite literally won't have the time to get into trouble."

"Well, I suppose I ought to be grateful that a man of your education is willing to give him a chance, Doctor. What sort of hours will he be working at your office?"

"At the moment I'm taking him on in a strictly private capacity, Mrs Thomson – so he won't be coming to the university at all. He'll be helping me with personal projects on an *ad hoc* basis. He'll be able to do some of the work from home, but you might expect some longer periods of absence."

"So he'd get overtime for those?"

"*Overtime*?"

"Yes, or a shift allowance."

"Mrs Thomson, I've always rather thought of the position of my assistant as an honorary one."

"That's exploitation. He won't be able to claim any benefits or training allowance if he's with you. You're wealthy enough, by all accounts, Doctor."

The Doctor fumed, but tried not to let it show in his voice. "Last night you said you were ready to disown him. Now I feel I'm the one being exploited here. Perhaps I should just leave him to rot with his wonderful peer group on the estate?"

"Okay, okay. Some kind of honorarium, then. And out-of-pocket expenses."

"Out-of-pocket expenses I can do. I'll also feed him. He'll have opportunities to make money on his own account after I teach him."

They came to an agreement to pay the benefits Kevin would have been due, plus a bonus based on his performance. Quite what the performance targets could be, the Doctor was at a loss to imagine. If he didn't perform well then he'd be dead – it was as simple as that. How times had changed since he'd employed his last assistant. None of the previous ones had better get wind of this, or he'd have pay demands stretching back millennia.

He heard the unmistakable clumping noise of Dolt coming down the corridor. Technically, Dolt was his supervisor but not his boss.

The Dolts were a parasitic species which had set forth to occupy every civilisation in the Pleasant universe. Once another species reached a certain level of organisation and rule of law, the Dolts would begin to infect the host. They would begin by establishing a powerful colony within the civil service, lending it an air of professionalism and efficiency. Once trust had been established, the infected civil service would send out its tentacles by way of red tape into other non-governmental organisations and private bodies. The enforcement of increasingly petty, pointless and intrusive rules would induce a form of terrified paralysis in the unfortunate host society. In a panicked bid to keep within the ever-tightening noose of apparently benign and well-meaning legislation, every organisation – private and public – would infest itself with Dolts. Efficiency would decline as rulebooks burgeoned and staff spent more time filing pointless reports rather than doing their jobs. The host civilisation's entire gross economic product would therefore go into sustaining the maximum possible number of Dolts. There they would stay, in complete control of the now-placid and incapable society.

Their first invasion of Earth had been a mixed success, taking place in around the year 235AD. The Roman Empire had reached a size and level of sophistication that had triggered their sensors, and they'd moved in. Within a few generations the population of Rome had swollen past a million – most of whom were unemployed and sustained entirely on free wheat hand-outs and grisly entertainment. The presence of a million idle freeloaders was a knife to the throat of a terrified government.

The Praetorian guards had been there to maintain the status quo but operated by nonsensical Dolt rules. They were paid to protect the Emperor but would offer the position of Emperor to the highest bidder, murder him a few months later, then hold another auction to line their pockets. Fifty years later they had their ideal candidate in power: the emperor Diocletian. Eventually taxation rose and productivity fell to the extent that the currency had to be debased. Hyperinflation set in and the whole Roman Empire collapsed. Other, less advanced civilisations without Dolts filled the void. The Dolts were victims of their own success.

A few centuries later the Dolts had regrouped, but the best they could do was to instigate the Crusades; a triumph of stupidity over reason and sanity. A few hundred years after that, Western civilisation had recovered and experienced the Renaissance. For a time, it had looked like the Spanish Empire would triumph, as they conquered new territories in South America. The Dolts had remained scattered throughout the imprint of the Roman Empire, and had made their move. As they exerted their influence on the Spanish, wealth from the new territories was used to subsidise pointless public buildings, rather than invest in a meaningful economy. Like the Roman Empire beforehand, it began to rely on plunder and conquest just to sustain itself. An expensive Armada was formed to invade England, with the signature Doltish idea of having more priests on board the ships than soldiers. A cargo including forty thousand barrels of olive oil and eleven thousand pairs of sandals had ensured that their gunners didn't even have room to use their cannons, which were vastly superior to those used by the English fleet. The Armada had been doomed before it set sail, thanks to the Dolts.

Then came the Enlightenment. In Britain, the Industrial Revolution had begun with a vengeance – there began the biggest migration of humans from country to city yet seen. New technologies were invented and exploited. Science and innovation made rapid progress. The British defeated the dictator Napoleon and their empire stretched to every corner of the globe. The first professional and independent civil service in the world was born. Standards were unified from one end of the British Empire to the other, and enforced by an army of highly trained civil servants.

And then the Dolts had moved in. First to go was Brunel's wide gauge railway. His seven-foot gauge enabled faster, larger, safer, and more efficient railway transport. In 1846 a parliamentary commission influenced by submissions from Dolts ruled that the standard gauge of four feet eight and a half inches made more sense – if only to themselves. It was game over for the British Empire from that point forth. No colonial outpost was safe, and with the independence of India in 1947 the Dolts had nearly a fifth of the world's population in their stranglehold.

Outside of any civil service, a one-party state was ideal for the Dolts. In the absence of either of those, MBA programmes and Economics degrees were the next best bet to infect ordinary humans with Doltish ideas about the way the world should be governed. Since the Second World War, the host societies had been spewing out over-confident graduates from these programmes to stem the inexplicable decline in their economies. It was a feedback loop gone haywire – the worse their economies became, the more graduates with Doltish ideas were demanded. The more Dolt-influenced MBAs and Economists were appointed, the faster the economies were clogged up with Dolts, or humans with Doltish ideas. One had even reached the lofty height of President of the United States, managed to offend two billion people with his inappropriate use of the word 'crusade' and launched an unwinnable and unaffordable war against a noun.

This, at least, was the Doctor's own hypothesis about Dolts. He couldn't prove it, but that's what it looked like to him, based on the evidence he'd seen with his own eyes. One day he'd write an academic paper about it.

Dolts were known for their complete lack of empathy and their inherent lack of imagination. His supervisor, Dolt, was no exception – indeed, he was the archetype for the species, unable as he was even to think up a humanoid surname for himself other than Dolt. The University's confused and over-polite administration staff had at first documented his name as D'Olt – as the President of Imperial College was Sir Keith O'Nions at the time of his appointment, and one didn't make the sort of mistake one made with O'Nions' name more than once. Dolt's loud protest of "I'm a *Dolt*. A plain Dolt; nothing more than a *Dolt*!" had passed into institutional lore.

The Doctor himself had been at the university since before its amalgamation from several different institutions. It was always far easier to inveigle one's way into an organisation at its foundation, and even more so when it was formed from so many varied constituents. He'd nudged Prince Albert towards forming the Royal College of Chemistry by private subscription back in 1845 and been awarded a role in supervising the transfer of technology from research into industry. A knighthood had followed, as well as the role of visiting professor, though he never let himself be called anything other than Doctor. Imperial College had been born from its predecessors in 1907 and it had taken a further 79 years for its human overseers to form its world-class Technology Transfer department, which he happily let do its job – just so long as the technology had passed the transmission guidelines.

There was a knock at the Doctor's door; precise, measured, and exactly the same as every other knock Dolt had made on it. It raised the Doctor's blood pressure in a Pavlovian response.

"Come in."

Dolt opened the door and stamped in. The stamping wasn't Dolt's fault – he came from a high-gravity environment, after all – but after five years he should have been able to adjust to local conditions. Having evolved on a high-gravity planet, Dolts were short – about five feet and three inches, or one point six metres – and squashed-looking, with almost no neck. Something about them always reminded Doctor How of Humpty Dumpty, but without the associated jolliness. And, for one, he'd never bother to put Dolt back together again should he fall.

"Ah, Doctor How. Are you well?"

"As can be expected, Mr Dolt. Is this a social visit?"

"You know very well that we Dolts never make social visits, Dr How. Yet every day you ask me this, and every day I explain this to you. Your species is famed for its intellect and memory. I find it peculiar that this one fact never seems to lodge in your brain."

"Extraordinary, isn't it? Now, how may I assist you?"

Dolt thudded down into one of the two chairs in front of the Doctor's desk. He sat like a diagram of good posture. The Doctor was convinced Dolt had seen an illustration and interpreted it as prescriptive. "You have submitted forms to take on a new human assistant."

"Correct."

"I have checked my records. You have not had an assistant since the end of hostilities in the human Second World War."

"Correct."

"Why the need for an assistant now? The threat level is currently low. Human development of the first phase of digitalisation of their culture increases the risk of exposure of our operations. The choice of a human assistant at this juncture is all risk and no gain."

The Doctor stretched back in his top-of-the-range office chair and glared at Dolt, who remained expressionless and oblivious to the hostility oozing from his colleague. "As you are well aware, Mr Dolt, article eleven of the Galactic Cooperation Treaty stipulates that I am allowed an assistant."

"Yes, but the second paragraph stipulates that there must be compelling reasons to do so. Hence the reason that you and your... your colleagues, have always picked them up 'on the fly' as humans would put it."

"For your information, I did pick him up 'on the fly'."

"Incorrect, Doctor. You intervened in the life of this one some years ago."

"I intervene in many lives. That's my *job*. And it was very much on the fly – he was an unwitting proxy in an attack on my systems, and then he turned up on my doorstep."

"You were out, and he couldn't get in. You sought him out."

"To intervene positively. I saved him from a beating. And if I'd not undone the third-party hack that had set him up for it, he'd probably have lost his life."

"But I still see no emergency that would warrant an assistant, Doctor. Indeed, these last five years I have been wondering whether you and your kind are really necessary at all."

"I *do* see an emergency, you Dolt. It's my job to see these things and I sense something big."

Dolt harrumphed. "This is most irregular. The young

man is unsuitable. He has a criminal record for petty offences such as shop-lifting and handling stolen goods."

"Yes, that's what makes him such a good candidate."

"*What*?"

"He was much too good to get caught for the bigger crimes. And yet he is loyal and trustworthy."

"*Trustworthy*?"

"You will never understand humans, Dolt."

"He also has a poor education record."

"Which counts for nothing. He has a hungry mind."

"But you are in one of the great universities of the human culture, and you are a man of considerable education yourself, Doctor. How can you dismiss education in such an offhand manner?"

"He's not had the same chances as many of our students."

"I'm sorry," said Dolt, despite the fact that he clearly wasn't, "but I'll have to reject the application. There is no clear threat at the moment."

"A threat to me is a threat to the Earth."

"A minor hacking event."

"Possibly a major hack of one of my – as you would put it – 'colleagues'. Or, as I would put it, 'cousins'."

"Have you contacted him?"

"We haven't spoken in decades. As you know, we are all somewhat… estranged these days."

"It would seem somewhat lax of you not to have contacted him, Doctor. There must be a directive." Where there was a Dolt, there was a directive, a guideline, a procedure, a rule, a protocol.

"No. There isn't. And we're not in communication."

"For how long?"

"Since the Sixties."

"Some *fifty* sidereal years? That is unacceptable. Come, we must draw up a set of protocols. A weekly management meeting, perhaps. Or a monthly team-building session and an annual away-day."

Dr How held his head in his hands and spoke slowly through gritted teeth. "Given that my cousins and I have spent most of our lives travelling the length and breadth of the Pleasant universe, spanning almost its entire timeline, I hardly see the need for an annual away-day." He heard Dolt open his mouth to speak but cut him off. "Or a biennial, triennial, quadrennial – or, for that matter – once-a-decade weekend. If you've read your files you'll know very well why we've not been in touch since the Sixties. And, being a complete Dolt, I know you will have read them meticulously." Mr Dolt nodded with satisfaction. The Doctor continued. "I really don't have the time to draw up protocols. Now, please just approve my assistant and let me go back to my work."

"Not without further evidence of an emergency." Dolt got up from his seat. "Good day to you, Doctor," he added, without appreciating that it was a phrase which had a meaning.

"Good *day*," said Doctor How.

Dolt's clunking footsteps echoed down the corner. The Doctor sat and seethed for a few minutes, studying a document on the use of graphene in microprocessors for consumer products. It had been little more than a decade since he'd decided, as head of Technology Transmission, to let humans have graphene at all. They were quick on the uptake – he had to give them that. He anticipated some close questioning over the matter at the next meeting of the Galactic Council's Technology Transmission sub-committee. His argument would be that the rate of development of mankind's technology was now beyond the point of retardation; never mind control – particularly since he was apparently the only one of the six doing his job properly. Further to that, there was the ethical question as to whether it was moral that the rest of the Pleasant universe should retard or control the Earth's citizens at this stage at all.

He heard the clumping of Dolt's footsteps approaching again. It was too much to hope that he was taking a natural break and, sure enough, there was the familiar knock at his door. If he hadn't dropped his internal body temperature down to thirty degrees Celsius in preparation, his blood might have boiled.

"Come in."

"Excuse me again, Doctor How."

"Is this a social visit?"

Dolt regarded him blankly. "I understand that you might think that, given that I was with you a quarter of an hour ago. No, it is not a social visit."

"Well, what is it?"

"Protocol dictates that I tell you about an incident. Or rather, a series of incidents that have alerted the system."

"You mean we have an emergency?"

"We have an alert, Doctor."

"Because an emergency would allow me to have an assistant."

"We have an alert that needs to be assessed. You are the only person capable of assessing it under the present circumstances."

"Excellent. Show me."

They went along the corridor to Dolt's office. The Doctor still found the silence slightly disconcerting, but he had learnt thousands of years before that there was simply no point in small talk where Dolts were concerned. Conversation to them was a meaningless concept – spoken communication was strictly for the conveyance of information or orders. Dolt motioned him to join him behind his desk. He leaned over Dolt and looked at the LCD screen. All Higher systems run by the Galactic Council were, by law, ordered to interact with local systems to help mask detection. The LCD was displaying data not from Dolt's primitive laptop, but from a Higher system.

"One of our human-facing websites has reported something of merit. Our algorithms have cross-referenced it with human law-enforcement chatter and raised an alert."

"Let's have a look." The Doctor took the keyboard from Dolt and tilted the screen in his direction. "So we've got an off-duty taxi hitting an invisible object and having its fuel tank cut, then some tracks and a giant molehill. Hmm. The molehill's the weird bit, isn't it? Then just a few days later a big hole in the diesel tank of a filling station. So that's reported on an anonymous website reserved for emergency personnel. Is this ours?"

"Yes, our site. We gave the idea to a retired member of the British constabulary. Mostly it's UFO reports."

"So these are credible reports of UFOs by members of the British police service?"

"Oh, yes. You won't find a more credible source of information about such phenomena. It's perfect – it lends just the right amount of authority for human minds to dismiss it."

"I see. Very useful for keeping tabs on just how much they think they know about us."

"That was the intention. However, the Enforcement section of the Galactic Council finds it invaluable for issuing prohibition notices on malfeasants, and issuing penalties."

"Hang on a second. So we gave this retired copper the idea of setting up a website to enable serving officers to report anonymously the weird stuff they see, risking their careers and reputations in doing so?"

"Yes."

"And you use it mostly to issue traffic tickets to joy-riding aliens?"

"Yes."

"Brilliant, Dolt. Just brilliant."

"Yes, isn't it?" The Doctor's sarcasm bounced off his colleague's concrete view of the world.

The Doctor wondered how much ire he could swallow in a single morning. "And… this is cross-referenced to the destruction of five London Hackney carriages in a secure compound three days after that filling station incident. Each was turned over on its back and had its fuel tank severed."

"Exactly."

"And this is being flagged up as an emergency?"

"Well, if it isn't an emergency, Doctor, I can stand the system down with a manual override."

"I'm not inclined to think it's an emergency."

"Oh, then I shall have to de-authorise your assistant."

"What?"

"If it's an emergency, you get your assistant. Those are the rules. But, since it's not, I shall have to de-authorise that action with immediate effect. It is a binary decision."

"No, no. It's an emergency, Dolt."

"But you said it wasn't, Doctor."

"I said I wasn't *inclined* to think of it as an emergency. Of course, it is actually an emergency."

Dolt eyed the Doctor. "Why are you now inclined to say it is?"

"These are each low-probability events. The odds of three such events happening within a week are miniscule."

"But a series of low-probability events is bound to happen more often than most of us believe. I shall issue a manual override." Dolt reached for the keyboard.

Dr How snatched the keyboard away. "Wait! I see a pattern emerging. All of these happened at night, all three involve diesel fuel, and they're all in the same area of Essex."

"But surely those factors are taken into account in the

probability calculations? Let me cancel."

"No. Let me enter the data for the hacking." The Doctor tapped away furiously at the keyboard, patching the Higher system through to his home laptop, which was in turn patched through to his Spectrel's system. A split second after the data were uploaded, Dolt's system flashed a red emergency signal.

The Doctor's mood lightened. "There! We have a genuine grade one emergency, Mr Dolt." He tilted the screen towards his colleague and gloated. "That changes everything. I have my assistant. Oh, and protocols now dictate that I may now relinquish my duties on the Tech Transmission desk. All of which means…"

"You are free to go, Dr How. But I do not understand your apparent good humour at the prospect of an emergency. After all, this may involve considerable danger to your person, and the possibility of a sudden and violent death."

"Well, Mr Dolt. Please don't be offended if it appears that the prospect of such a dangerous and uncertain future is infinitely preferable to working with your good self."

Dolt pondered this for a moment. "No. I can't see how it could be."

"Which is a pretty good indication in itself. Goodbye for now." He rushed for the door.

"I shall expect regular reports, Doctor. It is stipulated in directive…"

The Doctor jogged back to his own office. The curious happenings in Essex were interesting, and worthy of investigation. But what really intrigued him was the hack. The incidents with the taxis gave him the time to investigate.

On the Tube home he felt a sense of mounting dread. The bus picked him up from Brixton and dropped him at Telford Avenue. Deep down, he disliked many aspects of the job – the hours, the stress, the danger, and the mess; particularly the mess and the dirt. He'd seen what it had done to the others, and considered himself fortunate still to be normal. He bathed in the UV light of his porch before scrubbing his hands with anti-bacterial soap for a few minutes in the downstairs bathroom whilst the house-bots cleaned his already spotless home. He felt better after those little rituals.

Chapter Six

"Great God Almighty, Kevin. I thought I told you to get some decent clothes?"

Kevin stepped out of the porch, having undergone the ritual of what he thought of as the UV shower. "This is great gear, Doc. It's the latest season from Hilfiger. D'you, like, not like it?"

"It's a hoodie, Kevin. And the letters spelling the brand name aren't even sewn on very well. They've not even bothered to trim the threads off the edges."

"That's the whole thing, man. It's what you pay for. It's the look."

"Let me correct you: it's what *I* paid for. Do you have the receipts, as I asked?"

"I'm not taking them back." Kevin handed over some crumpled pieces of paper.

The Doctor examined the receipts. "Since when were people stupid enough to pay a premium for such shoddy workmanship? The whole point of the industrial revolution was not just mass-production, but consistently higher quality. I suppose I ought to take my hat off to Mr Hilfiger for charging a premium for lowering the quality."

"Let *me* point something out to *you*, Doc. The way I figure it is that one of the reasons you hired me is because I is street. You can do, like, all this high-end stuff with physics and time travel and all that palaver, but the one thing you ain't got in your armoury is street knowledge."

"I could acquire it; like I could acquire any language or

knowledge."

"Look at you, man. You is square. In fact, you has, like, got more right angles than a cube."

"Very good, Kevin."

"Thanks. But my point is that you are an," Kevin furrowed his brow, "an anachronism. You're lucky you don't get mugged with your black suit and your white shirt."

"A time-travelling anachronism. How humorous. Do you know what a tautology is, Kevin?" He brushed the youth's answer aside, irritated that his companion might have a decent stab at the correct answer. "The gentleman's suit is one of the most versatile pieces of clothing in the Pleasant universe. Two breast pockets inside, a breast one outside and two capacious ones at the bottom, each with a shelf for change. The trousers have two pockets to the front and two to the rear, both of which button shut. In the event of a marine incident, the trousers may come off; the ends of the legs can be tied and used as a flotation device. I'm sure you must have learnt that in swimming at school using a pair of pyjamas. I will leave aside the extraordinary physical qualities of the material used in this particular suit, but the shirt is made of a lighter version of it. A shirt and suit is one of the most adaptable sartorial choices ever invented. Furthermore, it bestows authority on its wearer."

"What about a spacesuit?"

"What?"

"Neil Armstrong didn't wear a two-piece single-breasted suit to the moon. You get me?"

"Don't act the smart-ass with me, laddie. My point is that a suit will get you in anywhere."

"Yeah, like a morgue."

"I think you'll find that more people are murdered in hoodies, Kevin."

"Yeah, but more people are *seen* dead in suits. So what do you want me to do, then?"

The Doctor sighed heavily. "I suppose on the plus side your outfit doesn't smell of fried food yet. Though I'm sure you'll work on it soon enough. Look, here's another couple of hundred to get yourself another outfit for when you need to dress up a bit smarter. And for when you don't want to be subject to random stop-and-searches by the police."

"Sorry. It's just, like, this is *my* uniform. You understand me? You might think I'm more likely to get stabbed wearing this, but it's less conspicuous where I live."

"Sure. I suppose times have changed. A hundred years ago the guy sweeping the street would wear a suit. Not a great one, but nevertheless a suit. Where I go it gets me instant respect."

"That's what I'm saying, Doc. You wear a suit like that in my manor and you're the enemy, innit? Like everyone thought you was with the Feds the other night. And that landed me right in it."

"Speaking of which, how are your friends?"

Kevin smiled. "Like you said, man. They just steer clear of me at the moment. They is like scalded cats but they don't know why. Cool."

"Even so, I want you to keep clear of them. Understood?"

"Yes, boss."

"Excellent. Now, come with me."

Kevin followed the Doctor to the cellar, but hesitated at the bottom step because Trinity was sitting in the chair he'd sat in the last time. She gave a loud meowl and sat bolt upright. He walked hesitantly over and reached out to stroke her head. She pressed up into his hand, and he stroked her. "Good girl. Mind if I sit here?"

Trinity stood up and looked at him with her glowing green eyes. He understood what he had to do, and picked her up.

"Jesus, she's heavy. I've got a three-year-old cousin who

weighs less than this." He set her down on his lap. She put her front paws on his left thigh and he felt the prick of her claws through his jeans as she flexed them. He wondered how much blood they'd spilled. This was one cat that could handle herself on the streets. Spider, he reminded himself. Or *something*. She settled down and began purring.

"Oh, I forgot to mention your DNA tests the other night."

"You what? You mean the Feds have fitted me up for something?"

The Doctor looked at him for a second. "Oh, I see. You think I've checked your DNA against scenes-of-crime evidence held on the police national DNA database. No, no. That's not what I mean at all. I mean your DNA's history. And your future. Would you like to know?"

"Like, what's the downside?"

"Some people don't like to know their genetic susceptibility to cancer, Alzheimer's, heart disease and so forth."

"Can you give me a hint? Like, would I want to know how I'm going to die?"

"These are only for increased propensities, Kevin. I can only tell you what you have a greater chance of dying from if you make poor lifestyle choices. I can't tell you whether you're going to get run over by a bus next week. Though I suppose your intelligence and sensory perception might have a bearing on it."

"Like, can you just summarise?"

"As you wish. It would be a terrific idea if you were to give the fried food a rest. Your father died from heart disease, didn't he?" Kevin nodded. "Scottish," continued the Doctor. "Tie that to a loving wife who believes the way to a man's heart is through his stomach, combine it with a lethal Caledonian-Caribbean diet and… well, you know the result. Sorry. Eat more fresh fruit and veg, eh? Less KFC and more of the piri-piri. Go easy on the fries and the sodas."

"You mentioned my history?"

"So I did. Ever wondered how a Caledonian-Afro-Caribbean boy has blue eyes?"

"Yeah, I had. It's actually been remarked on. They used to bully me for being a 'coconut' at school."

"Coconut?"

"Black on the outside, white on the inside. To put it into language you can understand, Doctor, it's a common derogatory term when you don't like the behaviour or appearance of someone else of colour."

"I see. Interesting. There are none so judgemental as one's own race." The Doctor paused for thought. "True enough."

"Why is it?"

"I suppose part of it might be envy, but also a kind of racial pride. It would depend on the situation."

"No, I mean my blue eyes, man."

"Seven generations ago, one of your ancestors by the name of Ekua – from Ghana, incidentally – had the great fortune to be spared the worst. She was a comely lady, as they would have said back in those times, and caught the eye of a Mr Cruachan – a supervisor at the plantation. You are a direct descendant of the male born of their union. Your family's carried the recessive gene for blue eyes since then and your father had blue eyes. When you were conceived, those blue eyes popped out to say hello."

"Cheers, Doc. It was so worth the years of bullying. How the hell do you know all this?"

"We keep detailed records, and what we don't know we can derive or impute. Your Scottish ancestry has served you well, Kevin, and in ways you'll only come to understand in the future."

"Meaning?"

"In terms of genetics it might protect you against your

mother's family's propensity for obesity and diabetes, as well as sickle cell anaemia. You retain just enough of that gene to afford you a touch of protection against malaria. And for the rest of it, I have a feeling we'll be delving into your family history in more detail in another one of our little adventures."

"I can't wait. Really. Sorry to be rude, but can I just ask where in the space-time continuum this particular adventure we has embarked upon is going to take us?"

"Essex."

"You have *got* to be joking. What about Jupiter or Mars? Or Alpha Centauri or something?"

"Why the hell would we go there?"

"Why the hell would you go to Essex if you have the rest of the bleedin' universe to choose from? In fact, why go to Essex if you have the rest of Britain to choose from. Or *anywhere* for that matter."

"You've completely lost me, Kevin."

"Look, when the Eleventh Doctor takes on Clara Oswald as his new assistant, he asks her where she wants to go. That was in *The Rings of Akhaten*."

"Oh, dear God," said the Doctor. "That is *fiction*, Kevin. We're dealing with cold, hard reality here."

"But –"

"It's unfortunate that this particular investigation doesn't meet with your somewhat ambitious travel expectations, Kevin." The youth's eyes nearly popped out at the Doctor's understatement, but he chose to remain silent. "However, expediency suggests that Essex is our first port of call. To put it in your parlance, Dagenham is *where the action is, man*."

"It depends what kind of action you is after, Doc. If you want white racist blokes with beer-bellies then it's right up your street, innit?"

"That's a racist comment in itself – don't be such a

hypocrite."

"This *sucks*, Doc. I thought I was signing up for some kind of intergalactic adventure thing."

"It was so much easier in the past. Damn the BBC and their idiotic scriptwriters for creating these sorts of expectations. Damn them to hell." The Doctor took a deep breath. "Look, I don't know what there might be waiting for us in Essex."

"I can't wait to find out, Doc. Mind you, this is going to be my first trip in the TAR—" Kevin saw the Doctor stiffen. "In the Spectrel, innit? Man, that is just cool beyond imagining."

"What on earth makes you think we're going in the Spectrel?"

"But Time Lords always travel in the T – in their Spectrels, don't they?"

"Only if absolutely necessary."

"You *what*?"

"It's another myth put about by those scoundrels. Dramatic effect and all that. It's all *his* fault."

"What do you mean?"

"Who's fault."

"No, I asked you first."

"No, you clot. It's *Who*'s fault – Dr bloody Who. That's who!"

"Why?"

"No, not Why. I said it's *Who's fault*."

"Whose fault?"

"Yes. Who."

"What?"

"No! Listen, damn you. Don't bring Why or What into it. It's nothing to do with them. It's *Who*'s fault."

"That's what I'm trying to establish, Doctor. Whose fault is it?"

"Yes. It's Who's fault; now, can we just bloody get on

with it and stop arguing the toss and bringing the others into it?"

"Like, you *really* need talking therapy, Doc. We is uncovering some major anger-management issues here."

Trinity quaked in Kevin's lap, her head bobbing up and down.

"Sorry, this is my fault. I see that now. Let me explain a little bit more to you. There are six of us. The others are What, Why, When, Where, and Who."

"Six Time Lords? I thought there was, like, the whole planet of Gallifrey, and you've got the Master and Rana, and –" He caught a look from the Doctor. "Sorry, *Gael*frey."

"Please, Kevin. Will you just be quiet and listen to me? There are six of us. We are not Time Lords. That is a gross aggrandisement; a title which suited a certain someone. Powerful we may be, but lords we are not. We are Time *Keepers*. Referees, if you will."

"*Referees*?"

The Doctor sighed. "What was the one instruction I gave you?"

"Uh… Stick with you and do as you say?"

"Precisely, now I would like you to just shut up and listen. We are Time Keepers. We alone have free rein to make temporal journeys. Time travel is an undertaking not to be taken lightly. The consequences can be dire – cataclysmic. The sort of foul-ups that can end a universe. I'm sure you must be aware of that, even from your own culture's popular conception of it. That is not to say that we are the only ones who *can* travel in time, but we are the only ones allowed free rein to do so. Even then we are bound by an intergalactic treaty, which means we must adhere to a certain code.

"Your appointment as my assistant was a matter of some significance, not to say some controversy. I may say there were some grave reservations about your previous behaviour, but I gave a personal assurance that I understood you to be someone of the rarest good character. In some respects, rather like an ancestor of yours from the sixth century. Don't let me down. You have questions?"

"Where are the other guys? The other Time Keepers?"

"I know of their whereabouts, but not of their circumstances. We had a... disagreement. A bit of a falling-out. That was some fifty years ago. I alone chose to stay on the true path. The others have, shall we say, drifted a little. In fact, one of them first drifted about nine hundred years ago. But the serious rift was in 1963. I have a strong feeling I shall be reacquainting myself with them in the coming adventures. You will have the rare, if not privileged, opportunity to witness it."

"You said these guys are your cousins? Is that, like, for real? It's, like, not a turn of phrase?"

"What on earth do you mean?"

"Well, I refer to my bluds as cuz, sometimes. Is it like that, or is they real blood relatives?"

"Yes, four of them are cousins. One of them is my twin brother. I'm sure you can guess who."

"Who?"

"Yes."

"No, who?"

"Exactly." The Doctor's gaze was in some far-off place, his voice low and monotone. "He was always the troublesome one. He instigated the rift, cemented the separation. Blabbed to the Beeb. I can never forgive him for that. Never."

Kevin brightened. "My Mum actually knows someone who's a psychologist. Rather than wait six months on the NHS, she could see you privately. You know, for talking therapy."

The Doctor shot up from his seat. "We're going to Essex. Now."

"But I want to hear the rest of the stuff about your family. I'm actually a really big *Dr Who* fan, you know."

"Don't worry, I won't hold it against you. You – and millions of others – weren't to know. You're all innocent victims in all of this. You've been duped."

"But I want to hear –"

"All in good time, as we Gaelfreyans like to say. Some of us don't give up our secrets so easily or cheaply. Come."

One of the perks Kevin hadn't counted on was an Oyster card – the pre-paid electronic card used on London's transport network. However, the potential saving of hundreds of pounds of travel expenses was little compensation for the disappointment of not having his first trip in the Spectrel. The Doctor briefed him on the way, showing him some photographs from a website to which he was a regular visitor. Run by a retired policeman, it allowed serving officers to submit material that was too far-fetched for routine reports.

They arrived in Dagenham by rail, and the Doctor consulted his smartphone. "It's just a mile or so over to the east," he said.

"So we'll get a cab, then?"

"Heavens, no – we'll walk."

"We're going to *walk* to a taxi depot? Is this for real?"

"Yes, it's all for real, Kevin. Come on."

They arrived twenty minutes later in a semi-industrial area of tatty red brick buildings which had avoided refurbishment since their heyday in the Fifties. The compound belonging to Grove Cab Services was around fifty feet wide and a hundred long. Grey metal fencing ten feet high separated it from the road at the front and sides, and the railway embankment at the rear. The fence posts were flattened galvanised steel with a triple point at the top. A profusion of weeds grew at the bottom, and the top had been secured with razor wire. On two sides the compound was bordered by buildings – those belonging to the business were at the front, and on the other side there was the external wall of a neighbouring unit. Three cabs – their roofs scratched and windows broken – sat on the pot-holed tarmac, set at odd angles to each other as if they'd been casually put down by a giant. A white transit van that had seen better days was the only other vehicle in the yard. The crash of a piece of metal falling echoed from inside one of the buildings at the front. A passenger train rattled past on the embankment fifteen feet above as the Doctor and Kevin approached the entrance to the office.

"Let me do the talking, but follow my lead," said the Doctor. "You're my assistant. Your area of expertise is car mechanics."

"But I don't know the first thing about cars."

"Then you should be working at your local garage."

"What?"

"You'd fit in perfectly and earn a fortune on repeat business."

"I don't get you."

"That was humour, Kevin. I do it sometimes."

The Doctor pushed open the door and they found themselves in a small, basic reception area – the kind of reception area that never receives female visitors. A man looked up from a desk behind the counter. He was bald, white and in his fifties. "Can't do nothing for you, guv. Bit of an accident the other day, and the owner-drivers are all over in town. I hate to say it, but there's a private hire firm just down the road there. They usually have a couple of spare drivers."

"Mr Grove? We're from the insurance," said the Doctor.

"Eh? We had someone in yesterday doing the assessment."

"Loss adjustment," corrected the Doctor. "Who was it?

Briggs'?"

"No, Swann."

"Well, that explains everything." The Doctor lifted up a flap in the counter and moved into Grove's personal space. "We don't just underwrite them, we have to check every adjustment they make. We just need to take a quick look at the damage. Take some pictures."

"Erm. Sure. Be my guest." Mr Grove stood up, revealing a pronounced beer belly. Kevin dug the Doctor in the ribs.

"My understanding is that your business maintains its own fleet of cabs, and maintains cabs for owner-drivers," said the Doctor.

"Yeah, s'right," said Grove, leading them through to the exit at the back. He held it open for them as they stepped into the yard. Close up, they could see that the three cabs had scratches and dents on their right-hand sides. "They was all turned over on their backs when we came in. Fuel tanks severed."

"You've done a good job of cleaning up the diesel – I see no trace of it on the surface of the puddles," said the Doctor.

"There weren't none. Someone's gone to a lot of trouble to half-inch a few gallons of fuel."

"And the police didn't find any prints?"

"They dusted the side of that one." Grove drew them round to show them the side of a cab that had been covered in fine aluminium powder. "But of course you've got hundreds of members of the public all over them doors every day. Waste of time."

"And I believe the intruder or intruders got in over there?" The Doctor pointed to an area of fencing bordering the railway embankment at the back. The cross-bars at the bottom had been severed and a section several feet wide had been bent upwards to the height of a man.

"Bleedin' amazing, innit?" said Grove as they walked

over to examine it. "This is quality stuff. Cost us a fortune. You'd need an oxy-acetylene torch to get through that in a reasonable time. Then you'd want some big jacks to do the bending, wouldn't you?"

"And there's nothing to set the jacks against except the earth embankment, so the initial bending would be a problem."

"Exactly." Grove pointed towards the end of the fence. "And you'd have to haul all that kit through these brambles." He laughed. "And for what? Vandalise some black cabs? Use the jacks to turn 'em over on their backs and then cut the fuel tanks off to nick the diesel? If that makes sense to you, then you should be certified. Never 'eard of anything like it."

"Any CCTV footage?"

"Camera only covers the exit. You expect someone to try and half-inch vehicles, and – like I say – you don't expect someone to go to this bother to do this."

The Doctor pulled a camera out of his jacket pocket and took a couple of pictures from different angles. "I imagine you must feel rather hard done-by."

Grove laughed again. "Hard done-by don't even come into it, squire. Here, you'll want to see the underside of one of them cabs."

They turned and walked back to the building. Adjacent to where they'd exited the office was a metal roller-shutter, which Grove banged on. "George!" A few seconds later there was the whine of an electric motor and the shutter clattered upwards into its cover to reveal another overweight middle-aged man next to the control pad. Once it reached the height of the Doctor's head, the shutter stopped with a rattle and they walked into the workshop. There were two hydraulic platforms side by side, but only one black cab was being serviced. It was four feet off the ground. The crashing sound they'd heard earlier was evidently a damaged side panel being removed.

"Insurance," said Grove, jerking a thumb at the Doctor and Kevin. "Give her a couple more feet." He grabbed an electric light in a protective cage on the end of a cable and switched it on.

George clicked a button on the wall and the cab rose high enough for the others to get in underneath. The Doctor had to duck his head slightly.

"There you are. Clean cut. I don't know what does that. Biggest pair of pliers on God's green Earth, I should have thought." He tapped Kevin on the chest and then pointed along the fuel line. "You can see for yourself I'm going to have to replace the entire line. Yeah?"

"Goes without saying," said Kevin, trying to sound like he understood.

The Doctor took a couple more photographs and pocketed his camera. From the same pocket he brought out a glass phial with a bud sticking down into the container from the stopper at the top. "Has anyone touched this?"

"George? Did you touch the tank yet?"

"Nah. No spares for any of that. Had a side-panel in stock. Get through plenty of those. The other stuff is on order. Maybe later today."

The Doctor pulled the stopper off the top of the phial and rubbed the bud against the surfaces of the cut.

"What's that for?" asked Grove.

"Looking for traces of whatever made the cut."

"You're 'aving a giraffe, ain't you?"

"Nothing humorous about modern forensic loss-adjustment," said the Doctor. "I'd certainly be interested in what kind of tool was used."

"I'd be much happier if you could just get the readies to me. This is murder on my cash flow – not to mention damage to my reputation. Hang on… are you implying that we might have used some of our own gear to do this?"

"Not at all. What would be your motive?"

"Well, exactly. Thank you."

"If you don't mind, I'd like to examine that hole in the fence again."

"I thought you was wanting to see more of the damage to the cabs?"

"Eh? Oh, well we'd want to make sure the fence was secure to prevent a repeat. Otherwise you'd expect a jump in premiums, wouldn't you?"

"Sure. Whatever. You do what you have to do. Some of us have to work for a living." Grove went back to his office and the Doctor ushered Kevin over to the hole in the fence.

"Whatever did this was unbelievably strong," said the Doctor. He dabbed a second phial against the severed edges of the metal. "And where did it come from and go to?"

"The bushes the other side have been crushed a bit," said Kevin. "Something's been in them."

"Yes, I see that. Then further up the embankment it's all been cut back by the railway company so you can't see any traces of where whatever it was might have come from. Typical." He stepped underneath the gap and looked along the back of the fence, to where it ran into the back wall of the neighbouring business. "Bingo."

"What?"

"You should see this. The brambles have been crushed and ripped right along the back of these properties. There's a mound of fresh earth against the back wall over there. Come on, lad."

Kevin followed him along the bottom of the embankment, stumbling a couple of times when his feet snagged on bramble stems. The Doctor seemed to have little difficulty, and the youth was out of breath when they reached the edge of the pile. He flapped the bottom of his hoodie to let fresh air in.

"Smell that, Kevin?"

"Diesel, innit?"

"Exactly. See how earth has spread out against the wall? Whatever it was has burrowed into the side of the embankment, so the soil's scattered down and to the side slightly. Absolutely no sign that the police even bothered coming to look at this. Hopeless."

He climbed up the embankment to just above the disturbed soil and stamped on it. "Sounds hollow. This mound of earth wasn't dumped here; it's a burrow." He stamped hard again nearer to the edge of the earth and a clod came away underfoot, causing him to lose his balance and teeter. Once he'd recovered he kicked the clod away to reveal the top of a hole leading into the side of the embankment. He made a face and then stepped onto the earth so that he could bend down and take a look inside. He sank up to his ankles.

"Aren't you, like, scared, Doctor?"

"This was done a couple of days ago. The amount of soil displaced would indicate that this is either a small hole dug as a temporary hiding place, or that the thing that dug it is moving through the ground."

"I don't understand."

"This amount of soil," the Doctor indicated the mound he was standing on, "we can probably assume is about the size of the thing that dug it out. If it had dug a temporary hole to hide in, then it probably would have done a better job of covering up the entrance. All I can see through here is the top of more soil. So the thing is just displacing an amount of soil equal to the volume of its body as it tunnels. That's my view, anyway." He gave a rare smile. "My professional opinion, as someone who has investigated plenty of seemingly inexplicable phenomena. Whatever did this has long gone."

"Like where?"

"I have no idea. Underground. The sewers, perhaps?

Unlikely, since they are underneath the service roads for this estate, rather than to the rear. And it might be too big to fit in anything but a main sewer. You saw the size of the tailings from the first incident."

"Tailings?"

"You know: spoil. The right word for the stuff left over from mining activity. I think we can call this either tailings or spoil, since we've established that this is a burrow. Precision is key in these things, Kevin."

"Whatever."

"Oh, please don't be flippant. What else do you think we can deduce from this?"

"Are you, like, seriously asking me?"

"Of course. I want to teach you to think a little for yourself."

Kevin sucked his teeth. "We know it's incredibly strong." The Doctor nodded. "It seems to like diesel. It burrows."

"And?"

"It can cut through metal."

"Good. And what else?"

"Uh… it hates black cabs?"

"Exactly. It seems to have a little penchant for wrecking black cabs. Very good. Or it could be a 'they', rather than an 'it'. And every incident took place at night."

"Yeah. So, uh, where does that leave us?"

"Absolutely nowhere. I need to see the results of the samples I've taken. Come." The Doctor pulled his feet out of the pile of mud and shook the dirt from them. Every trace fell off, leaving behind perfectly clean black trousers and polished shoes. He started walking back through the mutilated undergrowth towards the hole in the fence.

"That's like…amazing. Can I get some clothes made of that?"

"Restricted technology," said the Doctor over his

shoulder. "Sorry." His tone brightened a little, and he added, "Though your people are getting fairly close." He chuckled to himself. "It's funny. It was way before your time, and it's not played much on the TV these days – not that I think you watch old black-and-white films anyway – but there was a film called *The Man in the White Suit*. Came out in the early Fifties. Alec Guinness played the lead. You'd know him better as –"

"Obi-Wan Kenobi in the original *Star Wars*!"

"Oh, well remembered."

"Gimme a break, Doc. Like, how could I not know that? How could I not know my man Obi-Wan?"

"If you believe the press, most inner-city children don't know that milk comes from a cow, or potatoes from the ground."

"Well, that's like, not important information, is it?"

The Doctor stopped and twisted round to look at Kevin. "You *what*?"

"Like, am I going to milk a cow in Tulse Hill, Doc? Or am I going to dig up some plant roots if I want fries? Nah, I'm just going to rock over to BK and get me some fries and a milkshake, innit? Milk comes from a bottle, or a machine if you want a shake. It's irrelevant. You get me? That information is, like, surplus to my requirements. I don't need to know that in order to survive in today's sophisticated urban environment, does I?"

"Well, I suppose you're right on one thing: those milkshakes have probably never seen a cow either. I dread to think what I'd find if I did tests on one of those."

"So get on with your story."

The Doctor ducked under the bent fence and back into the yard. "Oh, just a recollection. It was only a few years after the end of the war. Things were still fresh in the folk memory. Science had taken leaps and bounds, and a few people had seen the seemingly impossible in the previous decade – aeroplanes without propellers, for example; the jet-powered fighter. So they wrote this satire about a man who had invented a miracle material which was incredibly hard-wearing and impervious to any kind of contamination. Since it couldn't be dyed, it was white. Hence *The Man in the White Suit*."

"So what happened?"

"The factory owners and the unions realised he was a threat to the entire business, so they tried to stop him, of course. He'd have ruined them all – destroyed the industry. In the end, the material turned out to be unstable, so the suit fell apart and all was well."

"So you're afraid if you give us this cloth we'll not have a textile manufacturing industry?"

"No, not at all. You're such a vain species you'll never tire of wasteful fashions. You'd probably end up with endless landfills full of perfectly good clothes you simply didn't like."

"Thanks for yet another insult."

"Not intended. Sorry."

"Well, what's your point?"

"No point, dear boy. No point. Just an amusing anecdote about our portrayal in popular culture."

"You mean…?"

"It's difficult to keep everything a complete secret. Things leak at the sides. One of the film's writers, Alexander Mackendrick, worked for the Ministry of Information during the war."

"So what about *Doctor Who* the TV series?"

"That was a step too far. I will talk no more on this matter for now. You will find out more in our further adventures." The Doctor opened the office door in the back of the building and Kevin followed him inside.

Grove swivelled in his seat. "See all you wanted to see?"

"Yes, thank you," said the Doctor. "Just one thing. Was

the Transit van left here overnight?"

"Yeah. The van was here. So was one of the other cabs."

"*Really?*" said the Doctor.

"Well, yeah. I did mention it in the original report."

"I must have missed that. My apologies. And this other cab wasn't damaged at all?"

"Not apart from the paint and the flat battery. A couple of scratches on the roof."

"Oh?"

"Yeah, these vandals had splashed this stuff over the back of it. Took the paint off. The police said it was like that gel they use to remove graffiti. It's at the paint shop now. Corroded the rubber around the rear window too. That'll have to be replaced. It's at the paint shop now getting a respray."

"Was there anything different about this cab?"

"Jesus, you said Swann was bad. I don't think much of your outfit either. Did you actually read the report?"

"I can only apologise. They tend to send me into these things a bit blind – start from first principles and all that."

"It was an older model. FX4. Rounder lines. You know the one. Superseded by the TX1 back in, let me see, ninety-seven I think it was. Problem with the FX4 was that you can leave the lights on after taking the key out. Can't do that in the later models."

"Go on."

"Well, the driver had left the internal lights on. Oh, and the Taxi sign."

"The orange sign on the front that lights up when it's for hire?"

"Yep."

"Hmm. That's food for thought. Thank you." The Doctor raised the flap in the counter and held it open for Kevin. "I don't suppose you saw whether the police took any samples of that gunk?"

"Nah, we washed it off."

"I just need to see that. You can stay there if you like, Kevin."

"Gordon Bennett," said Grove.

The Doctor hurried out the back door and was directed to the spot where the older cab had been standing. "Where was the rear of the vehicle?"

"Just there, mate."

"About where this puddle is?"

"Yeah."

The Doctor took out another phial, dipped it into the muddy water and put the stopper back on. He held it up to the light.

"Happy now?" asked Grove.

"Oh, as I'll ever be." He walked back to the office door.

"You sure you're not with the Old Bill?"

"The police? No. As I say, we have to do these tests to try to see what caused the damage." He opened the door. "After you."

Grove walked back into his office and eyed Kevin, who was leaning against the exit, playing with his phone. "Like I say, I feel like I'm under investigation here."

"Don't worry about it."

"Can I have your card? I'd like to keep in touch. You know, in case anything else turns up."

Kevin perked up, looking ready to make a fast exit.

"My card? Certainly." The Doctor reached into his left breast pocket and took out his wallet. He took out a card and presented it.

"Michael Wallace, Loss Adjuster, Alperton Claims. Right enough then, Mr Wallace. I'll email you if I think of anything else."

"I'm much obliged to you, Mr Grove," said the Doctor, and ushered Kevin outside.

"That was impressive. I didn't realise you was a con

artist too," said Kevin, as soon as they were round the corner.

"Con artist? I didn't con Grove out of anything, and had no intention of doing so, either. I like to think of that role as being one of confidence trickster. One just needs the confidence and the props. I printed that card on an ordinary colour printer this morning. By the way, how far do you think we'd have got if we'd both been wearing hoodies?"

"Alright, I take your point. Now, it's way past my lunch and I need to eat."

"Very well, but no fried food. I need you to be fighting fit."

"If you want to eat healthy, you're in the wrong place. This is Dagenham, Doc. Get real."

Chapter Seven

Mr Grove had just settled down to eat his own lunch – two sausages and a fried egg in a white roll, heavy on the ketchup, from the catering van down the road – when the black saloon car pulled up outside, causing him to look up from his *Racing Post*. The swift and deliberate way in which its black-suited occupants exited the vehicle jolted a question into his head, namely: why had this morning's visitors arrived on foot? As the pair stepped forcefully into his office a second question offered itself: why did he never get to enjoy his lunch in peace? His hackles rose.

"Mr Grove?" asked the shorter of the two suits. He had a mean demeanour, and wore thick glasses.

"Who's asking?" growled Grove through a mouthful of food.

"MI16," said the other suit, in a distinctly female voice. A voice that could cut glass. She was about five-feet ten inches tall, and athletic-looking. Her honey-blonde hair was straight and shoulder-length, parted in the middle, and her eyes a kind blue. She smiled. "Camilla Peterson."

Her smile deflected Grove's irritation back to his two previous visitors. If it hadn't been for them and their stupid samples, he'd have had his lunch by now. He swallowed, rubbed his hands on a paper napkin, rose from his seat and offered out his right hand to her. "Brian Grove. My outfit."

Rather than finding a hand waiting to shake his, Grove found that Peterson was holding out an open leather wallet. On one side was a metal badge, and on the other an official-looking card on the kind of paper he recognised from his passport. He looked at it, confirming her name. "You're CID? Thought you might be back. The uniformed officers weren't that thorough the other day."

"No, Mr Grove. We're not CID," said the man tartly. "As Miss Peterson said, we're MI16. I'm Thickett."

"MI6?" said Grove. "Like the Secret Service?"

"No," said Thickett, clearly irritated. "M-I Six-*teen*."

"Six*teen*?" parroted Grove. "Are you sure you don't mean MI *Six*?"

"No. Six-*teen*. And we're not *like* the Secret Service. We *are* one of the secret services."

"Never 'eard of you." Grove sat down and took another bite of his roll. A splodge of ketchup squirted out onto the upper one of his three chins. He deliberately fixed his attention on his *Racing Post*. "Come back after me dinner. We're closed."

"Now look here –" began Thickett.

"So sorry to interrupt your lunch, Mr Grove," said Peterson. "Mind if we take a look out the back?"

"Look," said Grove, "I've had enough of this. The Old Bill was in two days ago. The insurance was in yesterday – useless bunch of muppets they was an' all. Then I had a couple of jokers from the loss-adjuster in this morning. Pissed me around taking samples of puddles and all sorts."

Peterson looked at Thickett. "They took samples?" she said. "Which firm were they from?"

"Here's the card," said Grove. As soon as Peterson had the card he continued eating.

Peterson looked at the card and dialled the number on it. She held her phone to her ear and then said, "What's your address? Sorry, wrong number." She turned to address her colleague. "Indian restaurant in Brixton."

Grove looked up. "You must have dialled it wrong."

"No, Mr Grove," said Peterson. "Tell me, what did these

two look like? You called them 'jokers'. Was that intentional, or just a turn of phrase?"

"Odd couple. The gaffer was in a black suit and white shirt. Looked expensive. He was maybe early forties, well-groomed. Proper gent. Well-spoken. The other guy kept his mouth shut. Mixed race, bit shorter than you, Miss, but taller than him." Grove gestured towards Thickett. "Wearing what kids that age wear. You know – hoodie, jeans, trainers. Didn't look like he knew much about motors. No oil under his fingernails for one thing. Of course, he might be a desk-jockey with the insurance, but he's a bit young to have served his time as a mechanic or panel-beater if you ask me."

Peterson gave Thickett a meaningful look. "Well, well," said Thickett, rocking up and down on his toes with glee. "Dr How. Who'd have thought it?"

"Do you really think it's him, after all these years?" asked Peterson. "Surely he'd be in his nineties by now? Or even older. Probably dead, in fact."

"The description is perfect, Miss Peterson. I told you – age doesn't matter a jot to him and his ilk." He rubbed his hands. "And he has a new assistant. He's up to something."

"Here, what's all this about?" said Grove, swallowing the last of his food.

"I want you to show us exactly what you showed the other two earlier today," said Thickett.

"I've got a business to run," said Grove, and turned his focus back to his paper.

"I don't think you understand me, Mr Grove," said Thickett, fixing the man with a stare so cold it could roll back global warming. "I think you'll find you have no choice but to cooperate with us."

"We don't wish to be heavy-handed about this, Mr Grove," said Peterson with a smile. "But we really do need you to show us what the other two were interested in. It's an issue of national security. I'll get the sampling packs from the car."

"I noticed your CCTV camera pointing towards the exit," said Thickett. "I take it that your recent visitors went in that direction?"

"Yeah, they was on foot. The monitor's over there. Captures two frames per second."

"I'm sure that's all we'll need."

Grove went over to the monitor and hard disk, which were in a secure cabinet. Peterson came back in with a black box and looked over Thickett's shoulder as Grove fiddled with the controls. "Don't ever need to do this, guv. Sorry. I reckon they arrived about half-ten. Right, here we go." Two sets of blurred legs walked into view, then the image went fuzzy for a second, before becoming clear again, showing the same view.

"Play it again. Slow-motion. One second of replay at twenty-four frames per second is twelve seconds of real time," said Thickett.

Grove did as he was told twice more in slow-motion. Each time the image went fuzzy just after the Doctor and Kevin's feet came into view, then cleared once they were out of the camera's view.

"Damn! Of all the rotten luck," said Thickett. "When did they leave? We can at least see their clothes, relative height. Maybe one might even turn to talk to the other and we'll see a profile."

"Hang on, hang on," said Grove. He spooled forward and let the video run. "Here. See? That's the edge of the door just coming into the frame there on the bottom right as it opens when they leave." The screen went fuzzy, then it cleared to reveal the empty scene again.

"What?" screamed Thickett. He put a hand on Grove's shoulder. "Did you do this? Did the Doctor tell you to do this?"

Grove pulled himself up to his full height and puffed out his chest. "I don't know nothing about no Doctor, mate. Now you come in here with your badge and your accusations but I don't know who you are. I ain't ever heard of no MI16, and if this is a wind-up you'll be eating hospital food."

"I'm sorry," said Peterson. "My colleague's a little overwrought. Our department has been trying to track down this... man, the Doctor, for quite some time."

"Yeah, but I don't know who you are, do I? For all I know, this Doctor could be the good guy and you could be the wrong 'uns."

"I assure you that we're above board, Mr Grove," said Peterson. "If you'd care to call SO15 on this number, they'll vouch for us."

"SO15? What's that?"

Thickett pushed into the conversation. "It used to be called Special Branch. If you'd prefer, we could get a warrant to search your premises, Mr Grove?"

"We would just like some answers," said Peterson. "Did you tamper with the CCTV?"

"No. But, come to think of it, the lad was alone in here for a couple of minutes whilst this Doctor fellah took a sample. But then I don't see how he could have nobbled the footage after they left."

"Right enough," said Peterson. She turned to Thickett. "I seem to recall reading something about this in the files. Some kind of intelligent disruptive device. They were notoriously difficult to photograph, and they were nondescript – an everyman." She turned to Grove. "Tell me, could you describe these two men in more detail?"

"The older chap was in a black suit, black shoes and a white shirt."

"Colour of tie?"

"I...I don't know if he was wearing a tie, Miss."

"Hair and eye colour?"

"Dark hair. Eyes were… I don't recall. Sorry. I'm normally quite good with faces. You know, when I used to pick up fares it was handy – in case they did a runner or something." Grove shook his head.

"The youth? What about the youth?" asked Thickett.

"Mixed race." He shrugged.

"The colour of the hoodie?" asked Thickett.

"It wasn't white. Grey? Or was it blue? I don't think it was red, but…I'm sorry." Grove rubbed the back of his head. "I can't really see them in my mind's eye. The more I think of them, the less I see them. Look, I'm not being funny but to be honest I don't remember too much about this morning."

"It's okay, Mr Grove," said Peterson. "Just show us where you took them. Show us the vehicles."

As they went out into the yard, Thickett touched Peterson's arm and muttered, "Do you see now? Do you see why they need to be controlled? This one, this How character – he's the most dangerous, I'm sure of that."

"My understanding was that we owe them a great debt," said Peterson. She opened the box and took a phial out to sample the same puddle that the Doctor had tested. "He hardly seems to be a threat. Quite the opposite, I'd have thought."

"Well, Miss Peterson, it is our department's remit to find and control this kind of technology. The kind of technology that your friend the Doctor uses so casually."

Peterson rolled her eyes at Thickett's provocative language. Although he was her boss in the department, it was only thanks to his long years of service. She didn't know much about his background, but was sure she'd find a wealth of disappointment and petty resentment in it. As far as she was concerned, if things didn't pick up soon she'd try her luck elsewhere. A Ph.D. in Astrophysics from Imperial

College carried no weight with a dyed-in-the-wool mid-ranking civil servant like Thickett.

She put the phial in the box and walked over to join Grove and Thickett at the bent fence. She felt a twinge of excitement coursing through her veins as she did a mental calculation of the forces that would be required to perform such a feat. She ducked down and stepped through the gap, leaving the two men in the yard. Her eyes followed the mutilated undergrowth along the back of the properties. They took in the pile of earth at the side of the embankment and she smiled. She was glad she wasn't wearing heels.

"Are you alright there, Miss Peterson?" Thickett called after her.

"Fine, thank you. Just going to take a few samples."

And there they were, in the soft earth: the Doctor's shoeprints. She placed a phial on each of them for scale, and took photographs. She could figure out his shoe-size later. If it was really him. It was trivial but here, at last, was physical proof of his existence. She touched the impressions lightly with the tips of her fingers and smiled again to herself.

Chapter Eight

The Doctor looked with disdain at the food on his plate.

"You said less of the KFC and more of the piri-piri, Doc," said Kevin.

"I meant for you, not me."

"That's proper flame-grilled chicken, that is."

The Doctor ran his Tsk Army Ultraknife over it. "It may once have seen fire, but that was around three weeks ago, in a factory. The chicken itself came from Thailand. It was merely defrosted and microwaved in the so-called kitchen."

"Straight up, your Ultraknife is a food critic too? Maybe it could start its own blog."

"No, it can't analyse food, Kevin. At least not to that extent. I was using my Ultraknife's UV function to eliminate what I'm quite certain are large colonies of bacteria. The facts behind the origin of this food are my own deduction. Those marks that are supposed to look like it's been flame-grilled on a barbecue are actually printed onto the meat."

"Is that right?" said Kevin through a mouthful of bun, chicken and spicy sauce.

"Of course. If any grill were that dirty this place would lose its licence. Although frankly, I'm surprised it got one in the first place."

"Delicious, though. And a healthy low-fat alternative to fried chicken."

The Doctor took a reluctant bite. His phone gave a quiet *ping* and he drew it out of his pocket. "Ah, preliminary results from the tests are back."

"What tests?"

"The samples we took a couple of hours ago, remember? The preliminary results are back. Now, let's see…"

"Back up a bit, Doc."

"Why?"

"You haven't taken them samples back to the lab yet."

"I didn't need to." The Doctor put his phone on the table, took another bite and continued to read the message on his phone.

"You just put them in your pocket."

"Of course. That's how they got back to the lab in the Spectrel."

"No, Doctor. Listen, listen. You are, like, telling me that you put your hand in your pocket and it reached back into the Spectrel? And you put the samples in there to be analysed?"

The Doctor thought for a moment. "Yes, I suppose that is what I am telling you. What of it?"

"Wow! Like, how does that work?"

"Do you *really* want to understand how it works?"

"Absolutely!"

"In that case, I suggest you join the Theoretical Physics department of a major university and do a Doctorate. However, I will explain it in layman's terms for you. You know computers, don't you?"

"Yeah, like some*what*, Doctor. I only hacked into the system that hacked into your system, didn't I?"

"That's a matter for some debate. My understanding was that they used you as a proxy, but we'll let that one pass. So you know what a desktop shortcut does?"

"Yeah. Put a shortcut on your desktop and you don't have to navigate all the way down through the folders to get to a file. One click and it's open."

"Exactly. And you understand how that works with a

shortened URL going to a specific page on a website too?"

"Similar sort of thing, innit."

"And you know what a zip file is?"

"Of course. Files contain a lot of repeated code. If you can crunch out all the spare code you create a much smaller file."

"Same principle."

"I still don't understand."

"That's because you don't have the doctorate. That's an analogy. Matter – all this stuff around you – is mostly empty. There's nothing really there when I tap this table." The table sounded solid enough to Kevin under the Doctor's knuckles. "It's just opposing forces meeting and not moving. The things that generate the forces are miniscule. It's mostly just empty space."

"Okay, I get that. But the shortcut?"

"Other dimensions."

"Seems simple enough."

"Excellent. I look forward to hearing you explain it to an audience of your esteemed peers when you pick up your Nobel Prize for Physics next year."

Kevin sucked his teeth. "I mean, you explained the analogy so *brilliantly*, Doctor, that even a lowly human couldn't fail to understand it. Anyway, what do the results say?"

"D'you know, they're rather interesting. Whatever the implement was that cut the steel fence and the fuel lines of the taxis wasn't made of metal. Nor, in fact, was it anything like diamond. In fact, it was biological in nature."

"Come on, Doc. That isn't possible."

The Doctor fixed his assistant with a stare. "Please don't make me go down the baboon analogy again because I couldn't face another conversation like that with your mother. *Nothing* is impossible, Kevin. Heavier-than-air flight was thought impossible. If you want to be my assistant – and especially if you want to be an assistant who survives the experience, and I hope you do, because I'd imagine the conversation with your mother would be even worse than the one about the baboon analogy – then you'd better start believing in the impossible."

"Okay, I get the message."

"Look at nature on your own planet, for heaven's sake. You have insects that can support five hundred times their own weight when they hang upside-down. They don't *need* to be able to do that, but they can do it all the same. And you've still to invent something superior to the silk produced by spiders."

"I suppose so. I've seen Trinity cut open a tin. That was out of this world, man."

"Exactly. So at least we know that we're probably dealing with something biological in nature. Or something that has a biological appendage. Though I can't see any good reason to add a biological appendage to a machine. It has been done, though. Hmm. Food for thought, and a distinct possibility."

"Yeah, it could be a machine that runs off diesel. With a jaw made of some super-hard biological material."

"Most of the things that run off petrochemicals aren't motors, Kevin."

"You what?"

"Bacteria digest petrochemicals. Diesel would be a pretty good food source for a creature that evolved in a carbon-rich environment."

"You're kidding me."

"Plenty of life-forms live off methane, often in liquid form."

"But it would have to be freezing for liquid methane."

"Nice thinking, but not if the pressure were high enough. Bees feed off sugar, which is just a crystalline hydrocarbon. Put the same molecules in a ring and you'd have an oil.

Bacteria quite happily store energy as plastic, the same way you store your excess chicken nuggets and milkshake calories as fat. Anyway, we digress. It needs diesel, for whatever reason. Almost certainly as a source of energy. That diesel tank it ruptured at the filling station must have been a bit of a shock for it. A bit like a drunk drowning in a vat of whisky. No wonder it didn't stick around."

"Wasn't there another sample? The one from the puddle."

"Hydrocarbons again – as you'd expect in a car park for taxis. But also some amino acids."

"What, amino acids as in protein?"

"Very good. Yes, amino acids of some sort. Not necessarily what you'd expect in a puddle in a car park. I did take a control sample from another puddle. The hydrocarbons in that one were human industrial in origin, and there were no amino acids."

"So you think it's like a creature, or something. Something alive, I mean."

"A pretty fair bet. A very powerful creature that feeds off diesel. I'd guess its extraordinary strength comes from its need to burrow."

"This is all well and good, Doctor," said Kevin, using the last of his bun to mop up some piri-piri sauce from his plate, "But I've no idea how we're going to track this thing down."

"And if you think I do either, you're very much mistaken."

"But that's hopeless!"

"Isn't it exciting, though? For all we know, that creature – or hundreds like it – could be tunnelling away under our feet right at this moment. Who knows when and where it – or they – might strike next?"

"So can't you work it out?"

"Eventually. But there's not enough to go on yet. I think

the answer may lie elsewhere."

"Doctor, I've had enough of Dagenham now. "I know bits of Tulse Hill is bleak, but this is just hideous. I mean all the houses are this horrible pebble-dashed grey and brown."

"These are called 'banjos' by the locals, you know. If you look at the shape of the streets from the air, they're like a giant banjo. A circular bit at one end, then a couple of parallel streets leading off back to the main road. I suppose the idea was that there wasn't any through-traffic, and you got a bit of a community feel to it. These are suburbs designed for the age of the automobile. We're in Dagenham, after all – Britain's equivalent of Detroit, I suppose."

"Yeah, Detroit without the charm. Or the glamorous architecture. Or the contribution to black music. And the problem is that if you go up one of these banjos, you have to come all the way back down before you get to the next one, innit? It's a mad idea. Especially if you is on foot. I don't know why we didn't get a cab or something. Or the Spectrel."

The Doctor had his Tsk Army Ultraknife out, and was sweeping it slowly from side to side as they walked up the street at a snail's pace. A woman pushing a pram gave them a suspicious look as she passed the other way.

"My apologies; bad management on my part. I should have explained this afternoon's objective to keep you motivated. We're trying to find where Where is. Where is here somewhere."

"Sorry?"

"I said Where is here somewhere."

"You've lost me again, Doc. Where's here?"

"Yes, exactly. Now keep your eyes peeled."

"Nah, I still don't get it. Who is where?"

"No! Where isn't Who. Nothing like him. Where is here. Somewhere. Who is elsewhere."

"Where's your cousin?"

"Well, if I knew that, I wouldn't be looking for him, would I? Pay attention, would you?"

"No, I'm saying that Where is your cousin. Your cousin is called Where."

"Of course he is. Honestly, Kevin. I thought you were pretty bright but now I'm having doubts. We're trying to find where he is."

Kevin took a couple of deep breaths and counted to five. "I take it he's not on your Christmas card list no more."

"No."

"Your family had this big falling-out, yeah? And you hasn't spoken since?"

The Doctor nodded.

"But, like, you should be able to find each other easily. You have all this hi-tech gear. It would be like trying to find an elephant in a herd of cows, surely?"

"Bad analogy. More like trying to find a tiny chameleon on a green wall covered with ordinary lizards. Actually, that's also a bad analogy because you might be able to infer the presence of the chameleon by the absence of other lizards, or the behaviour of the other lizards due to the presence of the chameleon you can't see. Maybe a tiny chameleon living on the back of a lizard on a wall covered in lizards."

"So he's like a parasite, your cousin?"

"No, no, no. Look, he's just difficult to find. Alright? He doesn't want to be found. And, to be honest, I think his powers have probably degraded somewhat – hence the fact that he got hacked. That makes him doubly hard to find because he's not giving out much in the way of signals I can pick up. Luckily, though, I'm able to pick up something from his Spectrel. It's degraded too."

"Isn't there some, like, relationship between you and your T— Spectrel?"

The Doctor stopped and faced him. "Yes, there is. That's one thing that the BBC did at least get right. There's kind of a symbiotic relationship between a Time Keeper and his Spectrel. That makes it doubly important to find Where. If he's compromised, whoever it is that tried hacking us can get at the others."

"Surely they can help you too, right?"

The Doctor snorted.

"Like I said, you should get therapy for those issues. I bet your Christmas card list is, like, really small."

"Here we go... Yes, here we go, Kevin. Up ahead – not much more than forty or fifty yards." They looked along the street, both sides of which were lined with cars in front of drab, identikit houses. "It's actually rather clever to hide somewhere so unglamorous and nondescript."

"Rather him than me."

They walked on, the Doctor waving his Ultraknife in smaller arcs. To Kevin's surprise, he began waving it more in the direction of the parked cars than the houses. Finally he was pointing it directly at a dilapidated old black cab.

"Oh, dear God," said the Doctor.

"Whassup?"

"This is it. This is his Spectrel."

"What, this piece of junk? It's filthy. And the tyres are flat too. This is ready for the scrapyard. You sure you've got it right?"

"Oh, this is Where's alright. This is bad, Kevin. This is really bad."

Kevin rubbed some of the grime off the window on the passenger's side and cupped his hands against the glass to peer inside. "Filthy inside, too. Junk and all sorts. Someone's been eating a McDonald's and just chucking it in the back." He touched the side of the vehicle and felt only cold metal. He wondered if this was how a Spectrel was supposed to feel.

"I feel faint. My poor cousin." The Doctor leaned back against a garden wall.

"Road tax is up-to-date," said Kevin, brightly. "Expires in September. If he'd not kept it taxed it would have been towed. That's encouraging, innit?"

"I suppose so." He pushed himself away from the wall again. "I wonder which house is his?"

"Um… I, like, don't think you have to look far."

The Doctor followed Kevin's gaze to the house next door to the one whose wall he'd been leaning against. The grass was completely overgrown. A buddleia had sprouted in the middle of the lawn and a blue bag trapped in its branches flapped in the breeze. The paint on the front door was peeling and the curtains were closed, both upstairs and down. All the other houses in the street had modern uPVC double-glazing fitted, but this house had retained its wooden frames. Most of the paint had peeled from them, and the wood underneath was clearly rotten.

"I feared as much," said the Doctor. "At least he has a semi-detached, I suppose. He walked up the drive between the two houses. Whilst the neighbour's garage was well-kept, his cousin's was not. The neighbours had installed a metal swing-down door, but his cousin's was the original wooden design. It was rotten at the bottom and one of the four panes of glass at the top was broken. He peered inside. "Full of junk," he called back to Kevin. He tried the gate into the back garden. It was padlocked, but when he pushed it the latch came away from its rotten surround.

"It makes the front garden look like an entry at the Chelsea Flower Show," said Kevin. The grass was knee-height, and a few sycamore saplings had taken root in the lawn. The borders were impenetrable.

"He's gone native," said the Doctor. "Look, he's even got a brick-built barbecue set on his weed-infested patio." He went over to examine it. "The coals suggest it was used just the once, then left to rust. He moved some considerable time ago. But to find this... It's just so far beneath what he was. I mean, he was always the least fastidious of us but one always assumed that whatever bottom he hit, it would be above this. Substantially above."

"It happens, Doc. You should at least be grateful he's alive. Besides, each to their own, you know? Some people are happy with less than what you've got. Like about ninety-nine percent of the population. You get me?"

"Please," said the Doctor, closing his eyes and sighing. He opened them again. "Please don't equate human affairs and human lives to ours. That's another layer of presumption and prejudice you'll have to drop if you want to succeed in your role. Just as you should judge historical figures by the time in which they lived, you should judge other species by their own culture and biology. After all, you don't judge stags for keeping harems and rutting, do you?"

"Yeah, but your cousin is intelligent, right? You should respect the fact that he had freedom of choice, no matter what his background or upbringing."

"What a very *modern* view, Kevin. The individual can do what the hell he or she likes and absolve themselves of all responsibility for their actions. Someone else can take up the slack. Just assume someone else will deal with any problems whilst you go off and live your life on a whim."

"I'm so glad you're not bitter, Doctor."

"There's a lot you don't understand, laddie. You might think I'm a bit uptight, and maybe I am. But in the coming adventures you might just begin to understand the reasons why. Right now, I have to pick up these pieces and secure us all."

"Excuse me. Are you from the council?" called a voice.

Kevin and the Doctor spun around to see a grey-haired man peering over the back fence. He was evidently standing on something.

"I filed a complaint about the state of this place eight months ago and I ain't heard nothing back. I'm glad you're finally going to do something about it. Bleeding disgrace it is. Brings the neighbourhood right down. Old Alice next door to me, when they came to sell her house and put her in a care home last year, the agent said the state of Ware's place knocked twenty grand clean off. You do the maths on that," the man pointed at the surrounding houses, "and he's knocked at least a hundred grand off all of us. Bleedin' disgrace."

"I'm not from the council," said the Doctor. "I'm a blood relative. I've not seen my cousin in decades."

"A relative? I thought he was on his Jack Jones now. Ain't seen no visitors in years."

"How long's he been here? Do you know?"

"Me and the wife moved in here in 'sixty-one and he moved in a couple of years after that. He was a decent sort at the start – a bit of a gent, actually – but he's gone and let himself go. Much more in recent years. You can't talk with him no more."

"Forgive me, but it's been such a long time since I saw my cousin. Could you tell me what he does for a living now? What are his habits?"

"Taxi driver, ain't he? Always has been. Bit of a legend actually, by all accounts. No one comes close to getting their fares where they want to be faster than he does."

"*Really*? Who told you that?"

"Me elder brother – God rest 'im – was a cabbie just about all his working life. Your Dave might have slobbed out in his personal life, but I heard he was always bang on when it comes to cabbing."

"I'm glad to hear that. I assume he works up in town. What are his habits?"

"Course he works up in town. 'Ave to don't you? All the

Knowledge is within six miles of Charing Cross. We're twice that out here."

"Yes, yes," said the Doctor. "His habits. What shifts does he work, and what bases does he use?"

"Alright, mate – keep your hair on. I can see you're just like him. Won't be told – think you know it all. I heard he preferred the City to the West End. Never much liked the tourists and the shoppers. As I said, he thinks he knows it all and you get a smarter type – all the smart-Alecs in the law firms and the banks. Not that the bankers have much common sense, if you ask me."

"Yes, but what sort of *hours* does he work?"

"Likes his nights. That's what's made it so difficult to deal with him, see? You can't ever collar him. You don't want to wake a man who's on nights. I used to do shifts at the Ford plant and –"

"I assume he uses the shelter on the Embankment. Did your brother ever mention that?"

"Look, mate. I'm just trying to be helpful. As a matter of fact, my brother would say he saw him in there more often than not. Now, when you see him, if you can tell him –"

"Don't worry, I'll tell him," said the Doctor, turning his back. "Secure it, will you?" he said to Kevin as he brushed past and walked out of the gate.

Kevin glanced around. The best he could do was to pull the gate closed and jam a twig in it. He ran to catch up with the Doctor, who was striding down the street.

"What's all that about?"

"You can't choose your family, but thank God you can choose your friends."

"You're, like, really mad at your cuz, ain't you?"

"You're dead wrong, Kevin. I'm livid. I'm absolutely *livid* with him. He's let everyone down. Badly. He's potentially put the whole project in jeopardy. I've a good mind to commandeer his Spectrel." He stopped and looked back up the street.

"Great idea! Let's use his Spectrel to get wherever it is we're going double-quick, yeah?"

"I doubt she's got it in her." He turned and began striding purposefully down the street again.

"She?"

"Yin and yang, Kevin. Time Keepers are male. Well, we're male in a simplistic sort of way for you humans to understand it."

"You mean you're not a man?"

"Of course I'm not a *man*, you stupid boy. I'm a different species. I'm no more a man than you are a giraffe, you clown."

"Look, there's no need to be like that, Doctor. I've been with you about three days and you just seem to assume I have a certain level of knowledge about the whole universe. No wonder you aren't on speaking terms with your cousins and you don't have any mates apart from a spider that thinks it's a cat. You're a stuck-up jerk, you know that? That old geezer back there was trying to help and you was just rude to him."

The Doctor stopped and turned. Kevin nearly bumped into him. The two stood face-to-face, just inches apart. "Kevin, I'm sorry. Really I am. You're right – there's no need for incivility, and I apologise unreservedly for that." He began walking again, slower, but with the same solid purpose.

"When I chose you to be my assistant it was because of certain… characteristics. Things that you can't possibly guess at right now. Characteristics and abilities you don't yet know you have. You'll come to understand that, and to grow into them. You will also come to understand just how much of a burden my cousins left on my shoulders when they chose to abdicate their responsibilities. Maybe then you'll appreciate just how much pressure I've been under the last fifty years. More than fifty years, frankly."

They strode on in silence for a minute, crossing a major road, and heading for a Tube station.

"Well, thanks for choosing me, Doc. You know, for putting some faith in me. I'll pay you back, man. I swear it. But it's frustrating, you know? I was expecting this gig to be something else – time travel, fighting evil, seeing amazing creatures and all that."

The Doctor laughed. "I'll tell Trini you're disappointed in her, shall I?"

"Jesus, no!" Kevin saw the Doctor's look, and let himself laugh from his gut.

"Be very, *very* careful what you wish for, Kevin. Even the damned BBC has occasionally let one of the assistants be killed. Death in real life is much more painful, and tends to have this awful permanence about it."

They touched their Oyster cards on the barriers and went onto the open platform to wait for a train back to town.

"You think about it, Kevin. You seriously think about it. There's something on the loose here that can cut reinforced steel like scissors through paper, and bend it like it's tinfoil. And you're not afraid of that?"

"Like, let's look at the facts, Doc. It's not physically harmed anyone yet, and it seems to live off diesel. It only comes out at night and it runs at the first sign of trouble."

The Doctor grabbed him by the shoulders and grinned. "Good man! Exactly the kind of reasoning I want to hear. Now I remember why I chose you."

"It's this yin and yang thing, innit?" said Kevin. "I'm the brainless optimist full of hope, and you're the uptight, gloomy brainbox, ain't you?"

"Something like that, except that you're not brainless. But as to whether this species of creature is dangerous or not, that's another matter. If you exclude the malaria parasite that travels in mosquitoes, the most dangerous animal in Africa isn't the lion, it's the hippopotamus. Despite the fact that hippos are vegetarians, they kill far more people. They're so powerful and aggressive they can kill crocodiles."

"Yeah, but this thing's not aggressive."

"*Yeah, but* no one's got between it and its diesel yet. Or its young, if it has them."

"Good point, Doc."

"Thanks. And I sincerely hope it *doesn't* have young. Invasive species are another constant nightmare I have to deal with."

They boarded a near-empty District line train that would take them straight to Embankment station, and sat down.

"So, do you mind if I ask you about this thing with the Spectrel, then?"

"What, exactly?"

"Like, you wanted to take his Spectrel, but you didn't. I mean, what gives with it? Why's he just left it there? I mean, left *her* there."

"Anyone – any Time Keeper, that is – can use a Spectrel. But the reality is that you grow into each other; get to know each other's strengths and weaknesses. You get energy from each other. Your Spectrel becomes an extension of your character, in a way. Unfortunately, my cousin has chosen to abuse his – or at least, not to treat her with respect. My guess is that he was using her for ordinary cabbing at some point. Can you imagine? You have the most advanced piece of kit in the entire Pleasant universe and you choose to use it as a London licensed hackney carriage? And I bet that's where his reputation came from: he was using her to transport important clients faster than humans should really be going. I could excuse it if they were important out-of-towners on serious diplomatic business, but not humans."

"Out-of-towners?"

"Oh, sorry. Out-of-towners. Extraterrestrials. Aliens, you would commonly call them."

"Aliens *exist*?"

"Of course." The Doctor used an open-palm gesture to offer himself as an example.

"No, I mean, like, little green men. Stuff like from Roswell."

"Not really listening to my point about men earlier, were you? I've met the odd alien that's a bit green around the gills, and some species are shorter than others, yes."

"That's so cool! When can we –"

The Doctor silenced him with a wave. "Anyway, I bet she got pretty sick of that quite quickly. They would have had what you'd call in human terms a bit of a falling-out."

"But, like, surely he's the boss?"

"To an extent. But a Spectrel takes its – and I mean 'its', because it's yin and yang – Time Keeper's job seriously. And if the Time Keeper goes off-mission then a Spectrel can refuse to serve anything that isn't related to that mission."

"But you said there was, like, a symbiotic relationship."

"Indeed there is, and therein lies the tragedy. In a relationship where there's no interaction, both parties suffer. His Spectrel is in such a bad way that I doubt she could function on her own. I got but the briefest greeting from her. I can understand that she was trying to conserve energy, but she remembers that I'm his cousin and we've been estranged. I'm sure she was just being a bit huffy. I hope it's nothing more serious – I have no way of knowing how bad that hack was. As I said – there are two sides to it. I know that Dave is not going to be in that good a state himself."

They were into the rush-hour now, and as the Tube train rumbled on into London the carriage became more crowded. When they reached Embankment station they had to squeeze out through the crush onto the platform.

"Yuk," said the Doctor, as they exited through the barriers onto the Embankment itself. He stopped and took out a hygienic wipe from his pocket to clean his hands. Kevin noticed that he was careful to clean between the fingers, and to rub the tips. The Doctor caught him staring. "Oh, I'm sorry. Would you like one?"

"No thanks. You're, like, meticulously clean, Doctor."

"Hygiene is key, Kevin. Public transport is filthy."

"Yeah, but you are, like, obsessive. Seriously, I think you need to talk with someone."

"What was I saying earlier about judging each by the standards of their culture?"

"Just sayin'."

It was twilight now. The London Eye rotated slowly on the other side of the river, and a commuter train rumbled loudly on its way out of Charing Cross and out over Hungerford Bridge to a town in distant Kent. "I love this view east along the river at night," said the Doctor.

"My Mum says it was pretty ugly when I was a baby."

"Ah, you should have seen it in its heyday, Kevin. Water was the fastest way to travel. Where we're standing now was in the river. Over there," he gestured towards the Strand, "was where the beach was. Strand is old English for beach, in case you didn't know. There's a gate in Embankment Gardens where Peter the Great, Tsar of Russia, disembarked. It's about fifty yards from the water's edge now."

"Sounds amazing."

"Stank to high heaven. A giant cesspit. If you fell in, you were dead. The great engineer Joseph Bazalgette built out the riverbanks to accommodate the new sewers in the Eighteen Sixties. They were able to stick the trains down there too. Also narrowed the river and speeded up the flow. It's still only about six feet deep here at low tide. Further down, the Romans were able to ford it."

"You're kidding me."

"Yes, at low tide you could ford the river nearer the City."

"Why'd they build a bridge, then?"

"Who wants to wait for low tide? Now, come on."

"Why are we going back this way?"

"I only came to see the view. You'll learn to take the time to appreciate the smaller things, like views, when you can."

Kevin followed the Doctor back along the Embankment, under Hungerford Bridge, to the bottom of Northumberland Avenue. He pointed past the steps leading down from the pedestrian bridge to an oblong panelled wooden hut. It was dark green with a tiled roof. "There it is."

"It looks like a big garden shed. Or a pixie's hut or something. What's it doing in the middle of London?"

"Scores of these were built in the Eighteen Seventies. Shelters for cab drivers. They could get warm, enjoy decent food at a low price and keep one another company. Built by a charity founded by Lord Shaftesbury. As in Shaftesbury Avenue. There are quite a few still scattered around London. Want to know why they're all that size?"

"Go on, indulge me."

"The police decreed that they should be no bigger than a horse and cart because they were built on public highways. You can get ten cabbies in there, easily."

"Not if they're as fat as most cabbies, you can't."

They heard a faint round of men's laughter from inside the building.

"Stop it. Now, they're a close-knit bunch and they're not keen on outsiders. Let me do the talking." The Doctor knocked on the door and went in. He was hit by a wave of warm, moist air laden with the smell of fatty food, toast and coffee. The conversation stopped, and the eight middle-aged men sitting on benches either side of a long table looked at him.

"We're all off duty, mate," said one, through mouthfuls of a bacon sandwich. "Taxi rank's round the corner. Opposite the Tube station. Can't miss it."

"You want to look for one with the yellow light switched on," said another, to much laughter.

"I'm not after a cab, actually."

"Well, if you want food then there's plenty of places on Villiers Street," said the cook from behind his counter at the far end. "We're closed to the public, mate. Cabbies only, I'm afraid."

"I'm looking for David – Dave – Ware. I understand this is his regular shelter."

"You Old Bill, are you?" said the one who'd joked earlier. "Takes six months to get your warrant card, four years for one of these." He waved his licence, and his mates laughed.

"I'm his cousin, actually."

"You don't look nothing like him," said another man.

"Dave's twice the man you are," said the joker. More laughter.

"So I'm right in assuming he frequents this place?"

"Oh, la-di-dah," said the joker. "David Ware *frequents* us often," he said in a mock-posh voice. "Flamin' 'eck, I always thought Dave was from good stock, but I didn't realise he was related to royalty. What's happened? Has his rich aunt died and left him a castle?"

"Yeah. Elephant and Castle," chimed another.

"*Roundabout* time someone said that," said the joker.

The Doctor waited until the laughter died down. "It's a fairly serious matter. Just… if you could please tell him his cousin is looking for him."

"Uh, Doctor," said Kevin from behind him.

"Not now, Kevin." The Doctor felt a presence behind, and noticed that all eyes were looking past him.

"You looking for me?" It was a throaty voice, but it had a familiar undertone.

"*Daibhidh*," said the Doctor.

"*How* do you pronounce that?" muttered one cabbie.

"Like I said, Dave's from royalty you know," said the joker. "All hail King David of the London Licensed Hackney Carriages."

The Doctor turned to find a large man with a shaved head, two chins and wire-framed glasses standing behind him, blocking the exit with his girth. He was a couple of inches shorter, wore a creased dress shirt, cheap workwear trousers and casual trainers. His licence didn't so much hang around his neck as rest on top of a pot belly.

"*Peadair*," he said. "You've not changed a bit."

"You've... put on a bit of weight, cousin."

"Come here, Peadair." The big man grabbed the Doctor and hugged him tightly, putting him off-balance. He put his hands lightly on his cousin's shoulders, then stepped back.

"There's tears in my eyes, Trevor," said the joker.

"We need to talk," said the Doctor. "Is there somewhere a bit more private?"

"He'll have forgotten his mates in a week," said one of the cabbies.

"I'll be back, lads. Tomorrow, most probably. Keep me seat warm, will ya?" He stepped away from the door and let the Doctor back out onto the pavement. The door closed behind him. "We can talk in my cab. It's just around the corner."

"Daibhidh, I've been worried about you. I have to say you've put on quite a bit of weight. And I can smell tobacco smoke on you." They began walking back down Northumberland Avenue, back under Hungerford Bridge. Kevin winced as the brakes of a train thundering into Charing Cross screeched from above.

"It's *Dave* now. Alright? I've built a new life for meself.

And I'm perfectly happy. If you're going to have a go at me and give me a lecture, save your breath. Right?"

"Something's afoot. I think you might need my help. I think we might all need to help each other."

David Ware stopped to cough, deep from his lungs. "Is that why you've got the lad in tow?"

"Yes."

"Bit different from the others, ain't he?"

"If you're referring to his ethnicity, then yes. I assure you he's of the highest calibre."

"I'm sure," said Ware. He reached out a large hand to Kevin, who took it. "Dave Ware. How'd you do?"

"Pleased to meet you, Dave," said Kevin. "Are you a Doctor too?"

"If you mean to ask if I'm a Time Keeper, then yes I am. There's only two proper Doctors as such, and that's him," he gestured towards How, "and his brother. They was always the academic types. Anyways, I'm retired. So don't expect no fancy tricks off of me."

"It's not something you can ever retire from," said Dr How. "Abrogate responsibility, yes; retire, no."

"Jesus, Pete, let it go."

"*Pete?*" asked Kevin.

"It's *Peadair*," said Dr How sternly. "Yes, it translates as Peter. But it is most definitely not *Pete*."

"But I thought the name of the Doctor was a question that must never be answered," said Kevin.

Dave Ware began laughing. He laughed so hard that he began coughing, a deep bronchial cough that sent him leaning against a cab to recover and catch his breath. "Oh, don't tell me you're a *Doctor Who* fan an' all, son? Peadair's got to love you for that." He coughed some more.

"My God, you must be driving him mental with your view of the – what's the word? – the *Who-niverse*." He began another laughing and coughing fit, and reached into his pockets. He leaned back against the cab in a proprietary manner and lit a cigarette. He drew deeply on it, the coal at the end glowing such a fierce yellow in the gloom that it cast light on his face. He held his breath for a couple of seconds, then blew out a thick cloud from his nostrils. He shook his head and looked at his training shoes.

"Sorry," said Ware. He slapped Kevin on the shoulder. "I shouldn't laugh. But if you didn't laugh you'd cry. Or if you didn't laugh or cry, you'd end up like my young cousin here."

He took another long draw on his cigarette and let the smoke out as he spoke, addressing Doctor How. "I can imagine it must have been quite hard on you. And I'm sorry about that. Really, I am. But I didn't want all that palaver. I just got… tired."

The Doctor's face was rigid, and he spoke between his teeth. "You're right. It hasn't been easy, Dave. Not emotionally, not physically, not mentally. My young friend here is of the same, modern, *individualistic* view as yourself. It's all very well for the individual, just so long as all the other individuals continue to pull their weight. But when it all comes down to the last individual, then it is just a mite unfair."

"The only fair I do now is fares."

"Deep down, you still have your sense of responsibility. You know who you are, and you know what you have to do. As soon as I knew you were a cabbie I guessed your regular shelter would be the Embankment. Not Maida Vale, not Temple Place, nor any of the others. It had to be Embankment."

"Excuse me, Doctor. Why Embankment?" asked Kevin, his voice small.

The Doctor gestured to the west. "Just yards from Whitehall. The centre of British power for centuries." He turned back to his cousin. "You can't deny your – our –

roots any more than I can."

Ware threw his cigarette onto the pavement and rubbed it so hard with his shoe that it disintegrated. He went round to the driver's side and opened the door. "Jump in," he said.

The Doctor and Kevin got in and sat on the back seat.

"I find it easier when I drive," said Ware, pulling on his seatbelt.

"Find what easier?" asked the Doctor.

"Everything. Just existing. Thinking and not thinking." He started the engine. "Now, where to, guv?"

"I think you know where to go, Daibhidh."

"It's *Dave*, and the surname's *Ware*. And I'm certainly not going south of the river. And especially not after dark."

Chapter Nine

It took them two hours to get back to Dagenham. To the Doctor's great irritation, Kevin and Ware insisted on stopping for fast food and eating it in the cab. Whilst his companions sat and ate, he'd gone in search of something healthier, returning with an apple, a banana and some raw nuts. This dietary choice was a source of more mirth for his cousin. Despite complaints about the chill from Kevin, the Doctor insisted on keeping the window open for the rest of the journey. He said it was to get rid of the smell of the fried food, but Kevin suspected it might be punishment.

"I shall have to have this suit dry cleaned," he said.

Ware caught Kevin's eye in the rear-view mirror. "He's got worse. You know that clobber he's wearing is all-singing, all-dancing and resistant to everything, don't you?" Kevin nodded. "Smells don't stick to it either. Tell me, does he still insist on the UV bath when you come in his house, and then make you wash your hands?"

Kevin shot an embarrassed glance at the Doctor before replying. "Yeah."

"Flippin' 'eck. It's not like he's vulnerable to any of the stuff you people carry. It's just the thought of it drives him crazy."

"You can never be too careful," muttered the Doctor.

"He's a real catastrophiser," said Ware, catching Kevin's eye in the mirror again. "A bit of a drama queen. The sky's always about to fall in."

"I'm conscientious, and always on alert. There's a

difference."

"Hyper-vigilance and paranoia. That's another symptom of mental ill-health. He was the one who could never relax. Well, him and… rhymes with Scooby-Doo."

"Who is simply deranged," spat the Doctor.

"You are."

"No, it was a statement, not a question."

"Gotcha, Pete!"

"Oh, ha-bloody-ha."

They turned the final corner into the road where Ware lived. "Home, sweet home," he said.

"Not what your neighbours think," said the Doctor.

"Leave it out. You don't really get rich just because your house goes up in value. You have to live somewhere, don't you?"

"An extra twenty-thousand pounds would have helped your elderly neighbour's relatives pay her care-home bill."

Ware shook his head. "She had ample money to pay for as much care as she needed. What her relatives were really complaining about was the fact that there was twenty grand less for them to blow on new cars or holidays."

"Be that as it may, you might at least show some consideration by spending a small sum on tidying up your own house. I certainly can't believe you're struggling for money."

Ware pulled into the driveway of his house. He unbuckled his seatbelt and turned to the Doctor. "Right, I want no nagging in me own house. You ain't me mother."

"But I do care, Dave."

"I know. I know."

The three of them got out, and Ware made for his front door. Doctor How walked the few steps back to the road, and put his right hand on the badge over the radiator grill of the old cab that was sitting there – Where's Spectrel. Ware stopped on his front step and turned to look at his cousin.

He looked down at his feet and put a hand over his glasses.

"You might at least have put her in the garage, David. For pity's sake. Even if you thought your future held nothing together, you might at least have done it for all you'd been through with her." The Doctor walked back up the path, put a hand on his cousin's upper arm and led him back to the abandoned Spectrel. When they were there, the Doctor took his cousin's right hand and placed it on the badge.

"Ow!" yelled Ware, whipping his hand away and flapping it.

Doctor How placed his hand on the badge, and in a soft voice said, "Stop it." He turned to Ware, who had his right hand under his left armpit, and was gritting his teeth. "Come." Ware shook his head. How gestured with his free left hand, and Ware reached out his right. How took it firmly again, keeping his own right hand on the badge. He addressed the Spectrel. "Now, please. I know you feel aggrieved. Daibhidh apologises, don't you Daibhidh?" Ware nodded. "I said, don't you, Daibhidh?"

"Yes. I'm sorry. Truly I am."

"Very well. Forgive him." He took Ware's hand and slowly slid his own hand away whilst replacing it with his cousin's. When Ware's hand was covering the badge fully he stepped away and walked back to where Kevin was standing, dumbfounded.

"What's that all about?" asked Kevin.

"Reconciliation. It will take some time. Let's go inside."

"It's locked."

"I have his key."

"I didn't see him give it to you."

"You have to learn many skills in my job." The Doctor unlocked the door and fumbled for a light switch. He found an old Bakelite one with a knob-and-pin mechanism. He turned it on. The dim light of the forty-Watt bulb couldn't suppress the scene it revealed.

"Oh, man," said Kevin. "I've seen homes like this on TV, innit? He's a hoarder."

"It's symptomatic of his mental state."

The carpets had gone out of fashion in the late Fifties. The wallpaper, peeling off in places, looked slightly older. To the right of the door there was a pile of papers on top of a couple of old cardboard boxes that had split open and let their contents spill out. On the stairs were more piles of paper, plus an assortment of odd objects – a spare sock, a spent light bulb, a flashlight without its end, and empty of batteries. A mouldy towel hung over the banister. The place smelled musty and damp, with a strong overtone of stale cigarette smoke.

"It's a miracle the electricity is still on," said the Doctor. "It's also rather a worry – this place is so badly in need of rewiring it's a fire hazard. And I am *not* going into the kitchen," said the Doctor.

He edged his way past a couple of piles of degraded cardboard boxes full of paper, and opened the door to the front room. He turned on the light and went in, followed by Kevin. Their feet made a curious Velcro-like sound on the carpet as they walked to the centre of the room, feeling the stickiness tugging at the soles of their feet. The smell in the hall was just a hint at the stench they now faced in the living room.

There was a twenty-year-old television and a VCR in one corner, and a filthy sofa with a low table in front of it. The table was piled with dirty dishes and mugs. The space between the sofa and the window was filled with a heap of discarded fish and chip wrappers and beer cans.

"I've been in a flat like this once," said Kevin. "Old neighbour my Mum used to drop in on. Spent all his pension on drink. The carpet was exactly like this. Like walking on flypaper, innit?"

"It's utterly revolting. We need to get him out of here. He'll never get better if he stays."

"He ain't gonna come, boss. People like that are fixed in their ways."

"How did they get your neighbour out?"

"Feet first."

"My point entirely. He needs to be in a better environment than this. I'm hoping that communing with his Spectrel will kick-start something within him."

"Pardon the mess," said Ware, stepping into the room. "My cleaning lady jacked it in a while back. I think she wanted danger money. For myself, I just can't be bothered. I just got… tired."

"How are things with your Spectrel?"

"Could be better, to be honest." Ware glanced at his watch. "I should be on shift now."

"For the love of God, Daibhidh. Do you still think your only duty is to anonymous taxi passengers in London? Is it to your bank balance? Even if you won't rejoin the battle, you might at least make more of an effort."

"She's too weak!" shouted Ware, taking a step towards Doctor How. "She's just about gone." The echo of his voice seemed to hang in the air for a couple of seconds. Then he fell forwards onto the Doctor, who staggered under his weight. Ware sobbed great heaving sobs as the Doctor manoeuvred him towards the grimy sofa, which he fell back onto. He lifted up his feet and curled into a ball, weeping and moaning softly.

"I'm a pessimist by nature," muttered the Doctor, to no one in particular, "but why is it that everything is always so much worse than I thought it would be?"

"Like, what happened?" asked Kevin.

"What *like happened*," said the Doctor, "is that he neglected his Spectrel for too long. She got as weak as he did. And then she was hacked. That's what *like happened*."

"Like, don't take it out on me."

The Doctor shut his eyes and slowly opened them again. "Sorry. I think I just have the one option." He pulled out his Tsk Army Ultraknife, concentrated on it for a second and then put it back in his pocket. He left the room.

Kevin dithered, then decided that wherever the Doctor was going had to be better than being alone in a stinking room with a man – or Time Keeper – in his fifties sobbing his heart out. The front door was open, and he slipped out into the cool night air, savouring the freshness of it, and looked around for the Doctor.

There was a red telephone box on the pavement outside. The light inside was bright – so bright that he couldn't see in – and yet the light didn't illuminate the area immediately around it. Even the black letters of the backlit TELEPHONE sign were indistinct due to the brightness of the light behind them. The obtrusiveness of the light made it difficult to see what was beyond it. As he walked slowly past Ware's black cab, he noticed that the telephone box was not reflected in its windows or polished paintwork. Thoughts of vampires crept through his imagination.

"Doctor?" he called.

"What *now*? Can't you see I'm busy?"

"Well, no."

Once he'd skirted around the phone box, Kevin could see that the Doctor was somewhat stretched. He was standing on the bonnet of the cab, with the tip of one finger on its badge and the other touching the crown symbol above the TELEPHONE sign, which was at the very limit of his reach.

"It'd be a lot easier and faster if I could put my whole hand on both of them," he said.

"What are you doing?"

"What does it *look* like I'm doing, lad?"

"Um. Is it kinda like when you have to jump-start a car

with another one?"

"Yes, it's *kinda like* that," the Doctor panted. "And before you point it out in your own wonderfully literal way, yes: I'm *kinda like* a time-travelling breakdown recovery service." He paused to catch his breath again, and winced. "And I can tell you it's not particularly pleasant being the wiring. Thankfully, Daibhidh's Spectrel should shortly recover enough to be able to take a transdimensional feed off mine."

"Right. Of course. Anything I can do to help?"

"Thanks for offering. I'm tempted to say that you could start by taking out my cousin's trash. Ouch! Excuse me. If you go back in and make sure he's not doing anything stupid, I'll join you in… Oh, about another thirty seconds, I should think. Then I'll have to jump back to this in a few minutes for a final go."

"Gotcha. It's pretty cool that you've got your Spectrel here, Doc."

"I'm so glad you got something out of this little jaunt today, Kevin."

"So will we be taking the Spectrel back home, yeah?"

"I very much doubt it. I'm afraid we'll have to get Daibhidh – sorry, *Dave* – to pull himself together enough in order to drive us home."

"I could drive us!"

"I'm sure you could, but you don't have a licence."

"Couldn't you, then? Don't you have a licence?"

"If you think I'm touching that greasy, bacteria-breeding-ground of a steering wheel, or sitting on that filthy seat, you'd better think again. Nearly done." He winced again, then let his fingers go from the two Spectrels. He jumped down from the bonnet, then shook the life back into his arms and hands. "Whoof! Hopefully the top-up should be much easier." He patted the telephone box gently and whispered "Thank you," affectionately. "Come on, let's see how David is."

Ware was sitting up on the sofa when they got back to him. His face looked bleary. "How is she?"

"Getting better. It'll be a little while, but she'll get there. Then there's going to be a period of rehabilitation and recovery."

Ware nodded. He reached out and clasped his cousin's hand. "Thanks. I mean that."

Doctor How cleared his throat. "Look, we need to get you out of this place. The sooner the better."

"I ain't got nowhere else to go."

"I meant that you could come and stay with me for a while. Get yourself together."

"But…"

"I don't see any other options. Do you?"

"Nah. I suppose not. Let me get a few things together."

"Just bring enough for tonight. We can come back tomorrow for the rest. It's getting late. Change of clothes and a toothbrush, that's all." He turned and muttered to Kevin. "God alone knows if he's got anything fresh. And I dread to think what the toothbrush will be like."

"I heard that," shouted Ware. From upstairs came the sound of heavy footsteps, and of drawers being opened and closed.

"Still got his superior senses," whispered the Doctor. "That's something. I imagine his sense of smell must be compromised, though."

"Nah, you just get used to it," called Ware. A cupboard door slammed.

"I could bring a house-bot over here tomorrow," said the Doctor. "It could clean the place up, put a lick of paint on it, and he could move back in by the end of the week. Yes. That's what we'll do."

"Are you, like, not worried about the neighbours?" Kevin nodded his head towards the open front door.

"Not especially. First, I'm sure they're glad someone's taking an interest in him. Second, I've got the light on."

"You mean the one that…?"

"Yes, the one that makes people's memories a bit fuzzy."

"But won't I –"

"No. You're fine. You're exempted. At least for now."

"What do you mean, 'at least for now'?"

The Doctor gave Kevin a look that told him he was still on probation.

"Ready," called Ware, and thudded his way down the stairs. He had changed into a clean set of identical work clothes, and was holding a blue plastic carrier bag.

"I suppose we're not going to the Riviera," said How.

"Anonymity. Isn't that what you always wanted for us?"

The Doctor's arms shot out, as if to steady himself. "Did you feel that?"

"Aren't they doing fracking somewhere?" asked Ware.

"Didn't feel as deep. Get in the cab and let's go. I'll lock up then do the last energy transfer for your Spectrel."

"Nah, she'll be alright for another night out on the street. You'll do yourself an injury giving her another jolt tonight. Let's just get back to your gaff, Peter."

Ware and Kevin left the house and got into the cab. The Doctor had a quick look around and turned the lights off. As he stood in the doorway, he heard Ware start the cab's engine. The headlights went on, catching him in the edge of their glare. He felt a distinct tremor under his feet. He paused for a couple of seconds, but there was nothing more. He glanced around the darkened hall one final time and then shut the door. He locked it, checked that it was secure and then turned to the idling cab.

Kevin lowered his window and said, "Come on, Doc. We haven't got all night."

Ware honked lightly twice, and Kevin laughed.

135

The Doctor smiled and took a couple of steps towards the cab.

There was a crash from inside the house, and the sound of splintering wood. Doctor How whipped around to see the sofa burst through the front window and tumble into the garden. It came to a stop upside down against the wall. He took a couple of steps back, pulled out his Ultraknife and held it towards the house.

"Get in the bleedin' cab and let's go!" yelled Ware.

"I want to know what it is. Kill the headlights."

"Kill the headlights? You'll kill us all. Get inside, Pete." Nevertheless, Ware turned off the headlights.

"Get in, Doctor!" shouted Kevin.

The wall beneath the living room window collapsed outward in a cloud of dust, and the radiator that sat underneath it fell with a resonating *clang* onto the rubble. Water gushed out of a piece of broken central heating pipe.

A pair of black antennae waved through the dust. They were followed by two interlocking pairs of black mandibles two feet wide that scythed back and forth in the night air.

"Oh, you absolute *beauty*," said the Doctor, lowering his Ultraknife a fraction.

"Oi, nutter! Get in the bleedin' cab, will ya?" Ware turned the headlights back on, lighting up the rest of the creature. It was six feet wide and six feet tall, with a rounded shiny black body.

"I wish you hadn't done that," said Kevin. "Get in, Doc. Let's go!"

"It's after you, David. Or your Spectrel. Or your cab. Or all three."

"Well, I don't want to stick around and find out which, do I? Get in, you bleedin' maniac!"

The Doctor opened the door and got in the front beside his cousin, who jammed the vehicle into reverse just as the creature edged forward a few feet, to where the cab had been two seconds before.

"Wait!" said the Doctor. He slammed the cab into neutral and jerked the handbrake.

"What the hell are you doing? This ain't no Spectrel – it's an ordinary bleedin' cab! We could get killed here!"

The creature jumped forward and grabbed the bumper. The cab shook violently, and Ware cracked his head on the steering wheel.

"Turn your Taxi light on!" said the Doctor.

"You *what?*" Ware tried to wrestle control of the gearstick and handbrake back from the Doctor. "You're mental!"

The creature twisted the front bumper, tipping the vehicle onto its two left wheels. The bumper gave way, and the cab slammed back down onto all four wheels. The creature held the bumper over the bonnet. It scythed its mandibles and the metal sliced neatly into two pieces, which bounced off the bonnet and rang loudly as they fell to the drive.

"Let's go, Doctor!" screamed Kevin.

"Turn the orange sign on, you oaf! It's our only hope!"

"You could kill it with your bleedin' Ultraknife!"

The creature put its front legs further up the bonnet, its mandibles twitching inches from the front windscreen.

"It's no use to us dead," said the Doctor. "Now turn the sign on!"

Ware flipped a switch and the mandibles were lit by the orange glow of the Taxi sign. The creature stopped moving.

The trio sat with bated breath, their front field of vision engulfed by the black mass of the creature. The Doctor clicked a few times with his Ultraknife.

"What are you doing?" whispered Kevin.

"Photographs."

"What do you think it's doing?" whispered Ware, mirroring his cousin's sudden calmness.

"Thinking. Thinking very primitive thoughts, I hope," said How.

The cab juddered as the creature shifted. Then it sank on its suspension as it took the full weight of the creature, and they could hear the underside of its body scraping across the roof. Its long legs scraped against the side windows, found the door pillars, and pushed against them.

"Quite gentle for something that size, actually," said Ware, with the professional tone of a seasoned wildlife commentator.

"I'll take your word for it," said Kevin, reassured by the lack of concern shown by his companions, and impressed by Ware's transformation from cowering cabbie to hardened adventurer. "But can we please get the hell out of here?"

"We'll look just a tad conspicuous with a two-ton beetle on the roof," said How. "Aside from that, this thing presents an obvious danger to the public. I have a duty to protect them."

"It's alright for you, this is going to cost me a packet." Ware paused for thought. "What's all this about, anyway? You've been preparing for this."

"You haven't heard a few odd stories in the shelters this last week?"

"Well, there's always some tall ones, but… I heard one bloke had a hit-and-run early one morning out this way. Then there's that stuff about Grove at the weekend."

"Don't tell me. You use Grove to service your vehicle."

Ware's affirmative answer was cut short by another massive jolt that caused them all to brace themselves. They turned as one to look out of the rear window, where the view was completely blocked by the underside of the creature's body. The vehicle began to rock rhythmically on its suspension as the beast thrust itself repeatedly against the rear of the cab.

"You have *got* to be kidding me," said Ware.

"What's it doing? What's happening?" asked Kevin.

"Ah. Not quite so street and savvy as you think, young man," said the Doctor. "Have you ever been in a position where an excited male dog grabs hold of your leg?"

"Oh, *man*. Talk about bump and grind," said Kevin.

"Dry-humped by a giant beetle," said Ware, shaking his head. "This is worse than kicking-out time in the West End clubs on a Saturday."

"How much longer do we have to –" began Kevin.

"I think that answers your question," said the Doctor. "I'm afraid you're going to need a paint job on the back as well."

"Let's hope it's not like Earth mammals," said Ware. "We can't hang around all night whilst it has a smoke and a kip. Besides that, we're going to have company soon." He nodded his head at neighbouring houses, where heads were poking through curtains. "You can mask the Spectrel and a few other things, but the front of the house is going to take some explaining."

"Despite what we've just witnessed, it's a shy creature," said the Doctor.

"Very Essex, though," said Kevin. "Doing its business in the street."

There was a scrabbling noise on the roof and the cab bounced violently again as the creature slid down over the bonnet, cracking the windscreen as it did so.

"Wham, bam, thank you ma'am," said Ware. "Charming."

The cab bounced up as the back of the beast slid off the bonnet. It scuttled up towards Ware's garage and bulldozed straight through the doors, reducing them to matchwood.

"Like most cabbies, I'm sure you keep an illicit drum of diesel in your garage?" said How.

"Twenty-litre job, just in case of emergencies."

"I'd say a post-coital snack for a monster like that is an

emergency."

"Quite."

In the glare of the headlights they saw the creature pierce the drum of diesel and suck greedily from it.

The Doctor grabbed Kevin's wrist as he stretched out with his smart phone. "I don't think so, Kevin."

"But –"

"I know, I know. It would make compelling viewing on YouTube, and maybe do wonders for your channel's popularity, not to mention your street cred. But there are some things people don't need to see."

The drum emptied, the creature hesitated and waved its antennae around a little. The Doctor wound down his window and held his Ultraknife at the ready. The creature scuttled back towards the cab in a series of quick moves. It stopped and waved its antennae again.

"I wonder what the recuperation time on one of those is?" said Ware.

"If it's any help, it's been four days since its last one," replied the Doctor. "As I said, quite a shy creature at heart. Oh, there we go."

The creature turned and scuttled back through the hole in the front of the house. There was the sound of more splintering wood, and large lengths of floorboard and carpet flew out into the garden. A three-foot plank, splintered at both ends, bounced off the windscreen. A few lumps of earth and clay were ejected from the hole, then an eerie silence descended.

"That settles it. Back to yours," said Ware, and took the handbrake off.

"Just a minute, just a minute," said the Doctor, and got out. He headed for the rear of the vehicle.

"Where are you off to?" asked Ware.

"He'll be wanting some fresh samples, innit?" said Kevin.

A few seconds later, a smiling Doctor How jumped back into the front passenger seat and closed the door. "Excellent. Already being analysed. Let's go."

Ware shook his head, put the cab into gear and reversed out into the road.

"You're going to need a bit more than a paint-job – it's gone through the metal in places. When it attacked Grove's place it must have been raining."

"Are you just going to leave the Spectrels here?" asked Kevin.

"Let me just correct you, Kevin. My Spectrel has decided to stay with my cousin's for the moment. I doubt she'll remain for too much longer – just enough to keep people distracted and give us a little time. Oh, here we go."

Ware pulled in to the side of the road to let a police car roar past, blue lights flashing and siren wailing. Kevin twisted in his seat to see the car drive straight past the telephone box, which looked to him like a bright beacon in the night marking out the scene of devastation.

The taxi drove for a few more yards before pulling in again as two fire engines made their way up the street. They didn't slow down as they passed Ware's house. They reached the end of the street, to the junction with the main road back to London. As they looked to their left, the police car emerged from the parallel street that made up the banjo and turned towards them. It screamed past them again, back towards the house. Ware turned the wheel and they headed towards London.

"Wasting police time is a serious criminal offence," said Ware.

"Perhaps they'll arrest themselves after a while?" said the Doctor.

"Now that we seem to be safe, can you please tell me what's going on?" asked Kevin. "Like, how did you know to turn the Taxi light on?"

"Elementary, my dear Kevin," said the Doctor. "The only cab that wasn't touched in Grove's place had its orange light left on. So it seemed that it would have some kind of protective value. As it turned out, it would appear that the female of this species displays a similar colouring in roughly the same place. It might well be the case that our sign was many times greater than needed to trigger the mating response – but that's all the better. Simple secondary school biology. You see the same thing happen in many Earth species, either with young or with mating pairs."

"But it vandalised those other taxis!"

"Competing males. Why wouldn't it? And it went straight for their major organs – or where their major organs would be. In their place it found fuel tanks filled with what it uses as food. So much the better, wouldn't you say?"

"But, like, where did they come from?"

"It, Kevin. I think there's just the one. At least for now."

"Where?"

"No idea. But I think it was sent to look for my cousin here. Just as it was difficult for me to track him down, so it was for them. They got a few more particulars by hacking his Spectrel, then the rest was following clues. As for its tunnelling ability, I'd say that in the wild it lives off crude oil. Wouldn't you, David?"

Ware nodded. "Of course it does. Hence the ability to tunnel. Digs into underground reservoirs of oil, doesn't it?"

"But wouldn't it drown?"

The two Time Keepers laughed.

"Like, I don't have your scientific background, do I?"

"Reservoirs of oil are held within rock," said the Doctor. "It's a common misconception that there are pools of the stuff. The oil itself is under pressure in porous rock strata. Drill a hole and there's so much pressure the oil oozes out of the rock. This fracking stuff that everyone's so heated about at the moment fractures the rock and lets more out into the holes. So it's easier to retrieve deposits that aren't under so much pressure. Get it?"

"Makes sense. So this thing is kinda like a worm, then? A worm burrows through the soil and digests the organic matter as it goes, doesn't it?"

"Great analogy, young man," said the Doctor. "See his qualities?" he asked Ware.

"Yeah, I get you, Peter." Ware glanced round to make eye contact with Kevin. "You handled yourself pretty well there, mate. Most humans would have wet themselves. Or gone into shock or something."

"Um, thanks."

Ware's cab crunched to a halt in Doctor How's drive just before midnight. They got out to inspect it. Apart from the missing front bumper, there were scrape marks all over the paintwork and windows, plus a few dents in the roof. The rear looked as if someone had thrown paint-stripper at it. "Well if that's what it does to its girlfriends," said Ware, "then I bet they're an endangered species."

A chink of light appeared from between the curtains of Mrs Roseby's bedroom window.

"Come on, let's get inside," said the Doctor. He let them into the porch and insisted on two UV baths back-to-back. "No offense, David," he said as he let them into the hallway.

There was a flash of black, and Ware was pinned to the porch door. He screamed.

"Doctor, stop Trini!" yelled Kevin. "She'll kill him!"

"Argh!" shouted Ware. "Get *orfm*—" His cries were muffled by Trini, who – appearing as a large black cat – had her paws on his shoulders and her jaw in his face.

"Doctor!" shouted Kevin.

The Doctor leaned back against the banisters and laughed.

Ware grasped Trini's head in both hands and pushed it away from him. "I missed you too, but I just *hate* it when you do that."

"Careful, Trini," said the Doctor, catching his breath. "You don't know what you might catch."

Trini relented and jumped down, rubbing herself against Ware's legs, purring deeply. He reached down and stroked her. "Good girl. Fifty years on and you ain't changed a bit, my darling." Ware surveyed the hallway. "And this place ain't changed none, either. I'll give you that, Peter – somehow your style is always contemporary."

"Good taste never goes out of fashion," said the Doctor, subduing a proud smile.

Ware wandered over to the paintings. "And these will be worth a ton more money now, eh?"

"Those will never have a price put on them, David. Given me by friends. The other things I've collected on the way I feel free to trade."

Ware turned to Kevin. "You want my advice, son? You stick with Peter. Brightest of the bunch. We've all done pretty well, but he's a master. Buy what he buys when he's buying, sell what he sells when he's selling."

"Still got your Hockneys?"

"Yeah, thanks for the tip. Must've been the last one you gave me."

"I hope they weren't in the house."

"Gawd, no. Vault. Always surprised you never bought his work."

The Doctor wrinkled his nose. "As I said, *good* taste never goes out of fashion. Still, I'm sure they'll appreciate even more when he passes on."

"You guys are no better than thieves," said Kevin.

"I *beg* your pardon?" said the Doctor.

"Pretty easy to speculate on the art market if you're a time traveller, isn't it? See what the prices are next year, travel back in time and buy it. Sell it in the future."

"Heaven forbid. We're strictly forbidden by intergalactic

treaty. We're trusted and licenced to travel in time, and we'd not want to lose that. No speculation allowed."

"What? Why?"

"It would distort markets. Besides, if I bought a load of gold when I thought the price was going up, then it would drive up the price at that point. When I came to sell in the future it would depress the price. Thus, I wouldn't make the killing I thought I would, would I?"

"Yeah, but futures contracts."

"Same thing, dear boy."

"Art, then."

"If I bought Constable's *Hay Wain* direct from the artist it wouldn't have the same cachet as it does today. The absence of that piece from the market might mean that all of his work was devalued."

"Yeah, but you could bring another piece back."

"Ah, then the paint and canvas wouldn't age correctly. For older *objets d'art*, the carbon dating would show it was younger than it should be. Sorry, Kevin. You're not going to get rich by temporal smuggling or speculation."

Ware laughed. "That's put a dampener on a little scheme at the back of your head, eh?" He ruffled Kevin's afro hair.

"All I'm getting is expenses!" said Kevin.

"Bleedin' 'ell!" said Ware. "You're *paying* them now, Peter?"

"Sign of the times," said the Doctor. "Decay of society. His mother even wanted some kind of apprenticeship contract."

Ware whistled. He took Kevin by the shoulders. "Wisdom is beyond price. My companions haven't done too badly in the past, either. But just a hint. When you do travel in time, you will notice the bigger trends. You can't lose money by following the bigger trades. You understand me?"

"Not really."

"Look, at the turn of the nineteenth century every smart-arse on Wall Street was buying the shares of the companies that cleaned up the horse manure in Manhattan. It was a sure bet – all the predictions were that the place would disappear under ten feet of the stuff after a year without them. Ten years later, they were all bust. Why?"

"Uh. Motor vehicles?"

"Good lad! Same thing goes with other stuff. People's houses kept blowing up because of gas lighting. Mr Edison comes along with electricity. Get it? If my cousin takes you to the future and you see driverless cars, the last thing you want to do is spend four years of your life doing the Knowledge to become a London hackney carriage licence-holder."

"Yeah. Got it. Hey, Doc – when can we go ten years in the future?"

The Doctor laughed. "We can only go where and when our missions take us."

"But we might never go ten or twenty years into the future!"

"Ah, but you can always read a history book when you get there." The Doctor switched focus, as if tapped on the shoulder. "Oh. My Spectrel has returned, David. Without yours, alas."

The other two followed him down into the basement, where his Spectrel stood in the corner, gleaming. He pressed his hand against the crown above the door. "Good news and bad, David. The good news is that mine is now in touch with yours transdimensionally – although she's still not able to take a power feed because I couldn't do that last jolt. The bad news is that she's just about to be taken into custody."

"Taken into custody?" asked Kevin.

"Half-inched?" asked Ware.

"Guess who by?" asked the Doctor.

"Don't tell me. MI16," said Ware.

"Still around after all these years," said the Doctor. "Relentless. How terribly tiresome."

Chapter Ten

Thickett was bouncing up and down on his toes again. Before that morning at Grove's, Peterson had never seen him do it in the eight years they'd been working together.

"This, Miss Peterson, is the state of the art," said Thickett, as he ran an admiring finger over the curve of the front wing of the black cab. "Something we dare only dream of." The flickering red and blue lights of the emergency vehicles made his grin look even more manic than it was. "Oh, this is a beauty alright. I've waited my whole career for this."

When they'd got to the scene, Peterson had been more interested in the glutinous liquid in the driveway. Unfortunately, the water coming out of the burst central heating system had washed all but a corner of it away, but she'd still managed to get a tiny sample, which was now safe in the car. Her colleague had shown no interest in the fact that it was four days fresher than those taken that morning, and that it hadn't been diluted with dirty rainwater. Instead, he'd taken a cursory look at the damaged house and garage, then become fixated on the black cab standing on the road outside.

"The telephone box was right next to it, do you see? One witness says she vaguely recalls a tall man in a suit touching the box and the car. Another witness says that there might have been three or four of them. That's them, you see? That's Doctor How, and his assistant. And another Doctor and his assistant. Do you understand what this means, Miss

Peterson?"

"Yes. It means that two of these Time Keepers are talking to each other. In person."

"Exactly! Exactly! That means they're up to something, doesn't it? They're on the move again. There has to be a reason for it."

"The reason seems obvious to me." said Peterson. "Something demolished this house, smashed up the adjoining garage, then disappeared back down *underneath* the house. Maybe it was looking for something, or someone. It didn't find it, so now it's on the loose again. Or maybe it was after the Doctor and the Doctor fought it off and then left? Maybe it managed to get one of them before they fought it off? Maybe what I have in my sample is the blood of the thing that attacked them? And according to eye-witnesses this thing was rather big and scary. Unfortunately, their memories are fading as fast as the fluids that it left behind." Despite the coolness of the night air, the rest of the glutinous liquid had evaporated. "And it looks like it managed to attack the vehicle the Doctor was travelling in. And, correct me if I'm wrong, the vehicle was a black cab – what's left of the bumper matches this one."

"Yes, yes," said Thickett. He tried the driver's door for the twentieth time but it wouldn't budge. "But this is the other Doctor's. The house belongs to one David Ware, a licenced cab driver. David *Ware*. *Where*, you see? Doctor Where. This is his –" he lowered his voice so that the police and fire crews couldn't hear – "time-machine. His *Spectrel*." He hissed that last word in an awed whisper.

"So you think he drove off in his other taxi and left it behind?"

"Yes."

"So it must be broken. I mean, look at it – it's got flat tyres. That's not state-of-the-art, is it? Surely he might have taken his Spectrel."

"He has his reasons. *They* have their reasons. Maybe they're spying on us?"

"Then it could be a trap. Or a piece of misdirection?"

"Ah, maybe that's what the Doctor – the *Doctors* – want us to believe."

"The Doctor isn't a threat, Mr Thickett. However, whatever demolished this house presents a clear and obvious threat to the British public. Our remit is to protect them."

"Yes, yes," snapped Thickett. "But it's also to protect them by advancing and incorporating scientific knowledge. This beauty is *mine*. Imagine what we're going to learn from it. Ah, here we are."

A parking enforcement truck pulled up. It was the kind which had a small crane with a sling, capable of lifting a vehicle onto its back. Thickett went over to the driver, shouted some orders over the noise of the engine and gesticulated at the black cab.

Peterson shook her head and looked back at the house. Thickett would be shocked if he knew what she thought she knew about the Doctors and their Spectrels. The fire crew had turned off the water at the mains, as well as the electricity and gas. Two of them were tightening a piece of scaffolding in the centre of the smashed front of the house to shore it up. Their watch supervisor came over to her.

"It's safe now, Miss. Want to take a look inside?"

"Sure."

They walked over the detritus on the lawn – pieces of splintered floorboard and ripped carpet – and stepped through the hole into the remains of the living room. The ceiling had been caked in mud as the creature had burrowed into the layer of heavy clay that lay beneath the fertile topsoil of Essex.

"Don't know how you explain that one on the household insurance," said the fireman.

"I don't know how you explain all the soil in this room. How would you? Ever seen anything like it?"

"Nope. If you asked me, I'd say you might mistake it for a low-velocity gas explosion. You know – one that didn't quite go supersonic and create enough of a shockwave to blow everything to bits. Just enough of the right methane-air mix to create a mess, blow the window out, churn up the soil."

"Except that…?" prompted Peterson.

"Except that there was no gas leak, no evidence of fire, and if the explosion was strong enough to blow the front of the house out then why's the back and everything else still alright?"

"Nor would that explain the damage to the garage. So how *do* you explain it?"

"No idea, but I'm open to suggestions. I understand you're the expert."

"Not necessarily an expert *per se*, but I'm a scientific officer who is charged with explaining the otherwise inexplicable."

"Oh, very *X-Files*. MI16, your boss said. You've seen something like it before?"

"Somewhat like it. Been a bit of a spate of them. I'm sure it has a perfectly rational explanation."

"Well, let me know when you do." The fireman picked up a piece of newspaper from the detritus and scribbled his number on it. "I'd love to hear more about your glamorous line of work over a drink sometime."

"Thank you, I'm flattered," said Peterson, putting the paper in her wallet. She emptied it of such scraps on a monthly basis. In her head she kept a bar chart which displayed the number of solicitations per month, and she carried out multivariate analyses of the various factors she felt affected it – clothing, makeup, weather – to see how they affected the number of hits. She tried her best to minimise the attention because it was a distraction to her work. Of course, the running analysis was itself a distraction, so she recognised she was in a zero-sum game with her subjects. She wished she could dump the research, but her brain never seemed to be short of memory or processing capacity so it just kept accumulating the data and analysing it without her consciously doing so.

"It's no more glamorous than your line of work," she said, then realised what an insult it probably felt like to a man who was used to veneration by members of her sex. She took a few photos of the mess, doubtful they'd be of any use. Whilst she knew blood-spatter patterns could reveal a great deal about a murder scene, she doubted mud-spatter would cast much light on the incident.

"Going to board it up now, boss," said one of the fire crew at the front of the house, so they picked their way back to the hole and stepped into the front garden.

"Were your team first on the scene?" she asked.

"Yeah, we were as it happens. I thought I knew the area, but I have to admit we were a bit confused. All these roads – they call them banjos round here – are a bit alike. I reckon we must have passed it at least twice before we found it."

"Oh, that happens."

"Well, we get measured on response times, so I'm for the high-jump."

"So do you actually remember driving past it the first couple of times?"

"Between you and me, the whole thing's a bit hazy. I could have sworn we passed a telephone box. But there isn't one on this road. I mean, there would never be one in the middle of a banjo, would there? Why do you ask?"

"Just curious. Here's my card. Give me a call if you recall anything else – no matter how trivial you think it might be." She gave him a smile that she'd mathematically proven would make most men remember her instructions.

The pitch of the parking enforcement truck's engine changed, and she looked round to see it straining to lift the dilapidated cab. Thickett watched impatiently from the kerb as the driver worked the controls at the side. "Too heavy!" he shouted above the din.

"It can't be too heavy. Try again," insisted Thickett.

The driver went back to his controls. This time the cab lifted immediately, causing the truck to rock dangerously as the cab swung back and forth.

"Careful!" yelled Thickett.

"I am being careful!" shouted back the driver. "It's too light now."

"You must be mistaken," said Thickett.

"Must have been stuck," said the driver. "I didn't see nothing. You sure the engine's not dropped out or something?" He left the controls and studied the underside of the cab, and the area where it had been parked. "Inertia," he said.

Thickett made eye contact with Peterson and made excited gestures which she took to be about the apparent variation in weight and its impossibility.

The driver swung the cab slowly into position, two feet above the back of the truck, and lined it up. There was an ominous creaking noise from the neck of the crane, and the truck groaned uncomfortably as it settled down onto its suspension. Its wheels flattened against the road. There was a loud retort as the bolts that fastened the neck of the crane to the hydraulic pistons shattered and the driver jumped for his life. The cab slammed down onto the back of the truck with a massive crash. The truck's windows shattered and the crane neck bounced off the roof of the cab then fell onto the roof of a car parked on the other side of the road, crushing it and spraying shattered glass everywhere. The car's alarm activated, and wailed to the neighbourhood.

"Be careful!" said Thickett.

"You be careful!" said the driver. "What the hell is this thing?"

"If it's damaged I'll hold you responsible," said Thickett, climbing up onto the truck to inspect the miraculously undamaged cab.

"You never told me anything about this," said the driver. "I'm off the job, mate."

"Oh, yeah?" said Thicket, jumping back down and pulling himself up to his full height, which fell short of the driver's by several inches. "Well, I don't think you've got much choice, have you? You're not getting it off in a hurry. Your equipment's clearly sub-standard, and I'll hold you personally responsible if this specimen isn't delivered to our depot by nine tomorrow morning. Do you understand?"

"*Specimen?*" said the driver. "Jesus. I'm not going anywhere with this. No way."

"You have to," snapped Thickett. "Remember who you're under contract to." He pulled out his wallet and stuck his badge in the man's face. "Now get moving."

"Well, I'm not going without my crane."

A couple of police officers had taken an interest, and stepped between the two men. One of them explained that the crane would have to stay where it was, pending an investigation by the Health and Safety Inspectorate the following morning. It was explained to Thickett that driving a truck with a shattered windscreen would be a serious traffic violation. Either the truck and the cab would have to be towed, or the windscreen would have to be repaired *in situ*.

"If you don't mind, Mr Thickett," said Peterson, "I think I'll call it a night here. I think we've reached a logical impasse. Don't you?"

Thickett glared up at her. "You saw it, didn't you? You saw that it could vary its weight. How do you explain that within your current understanding of the physical universe,

Doctor Peterson?"

"As I said, Mr Thickett, I was much more interested in the danger presented by whatever demolished the house. Quite why you remained so interested in an apparently unrelated object is something that defies rational explanation in itself."

"I'm looking to the future, Miss Peterson," said Thickett, between clenched teeth.

"So am I. I'm looking to the future and hoping to prevent whatever this thing is from destroying any more property. It's my job. God forbid there's more than one of them. I can't imagine the trouble we'll be in if an invasive species like this starts breeding. I'll drop these samples back at the lab and see you in the morning. Goodnight, Mr Thickett."

"She's not a happy Spectrel, is she?" said Dr How. They had been looking at a projection of the scene in Dagenham from the point of view of the Spectrel's badge. The three-dimensional image hovered in the air in front of Dr How's Spectrel.

"She's a bit grumpy, that's all," said Ware. "I don't know where she gets it from," he said to Kevin, with a grin. "Still, she's done herself proud, resisting arrest."

"Unfortunately, she's used up quite a bit of energy by throwing a tantrum. She's also drawn a little more attention to herself than she perhaps should have done. She could have gone along quietly, then just waited for us to rescue her."

"Well, you gotta understand what she's been through, Peter. I ain't proud of the neglect, am I? Then there's this cyber-attack you were talking about. She's got a right to defend herself."

"Yes, yes. We could just do without the attention of these people."

"Who are they?" asked Kevin.

"Mmm? Oh, MI16," said Dr How. "Directorate of Military Intelligence, Section Sixteen. Formed in 1945 to deal with scientific intelligence."

"The Nazis had funded all this scientific research, you see," said Ware. "The V-1 Guided missile, the V-2 ballistic missile – and a host of other stuff. They needed a whole new department to gather the documents, the artefacts, and interrogate the actual scientists."

"But I thought there was just MI5 and MI6?" said Kevin.

"Nah," said Ware. "There was MI sections right up to Nineteen. I must say, I thought Sixteen was disbanded and shoved into Six after a while."

"Section One became GCHQ," said Dr How. "The big base of eavesdroppers based in Cheltenham. The ones who crack codes, hack emails and listen to telephone conversations."

"Anyway, they were more than a little interested in us Time Keepers," chipped in Ware. "But we didn't want to talk to them."

"We'd done our bit for Britain during the War," said Dr How. "As always. But we digress." He turned to his Spectrel. "Thank you," he said, and the projection stopped. "She'll be okay, but we have to get her back soon. She's going to need extensive repairs."

"Again, my apologies for the complications," said Ware.

"It happens, cousin. Just so long as you're back with the cause now."

"I'm back."

"So, like, who do you think is attacking you?" asked Kevin.

"Could be anyone," said Ware.

"Or, indeed, any*thing*," said Dr How.

"Yeah, but like, do you really think it's this beetle thing?"

"If you're asking me whether the beetle is attacking us – or, more specifically, my cousin – of its own volition, then the answer is almost certainly no."

"Like, how do you know?"

"Come on, Kevin, look at the facts. It's a fairly dumb critter, as they go. Give it something that looks even just a little like a member of the opposite sex and it's happy. Give it some food and it's pretty passive. No, something's controlling it. And it's no coincidence that it attacked so soon after we arrived on the scene."

"Well it might be obvious to you, but I'm new to all this. Like, do you have any enemies?"

Both of the Time Keepers laughed.

"Come on, guys," protested Kevin. "You can't expect me to know all of this stuff."

"Sorry," said Ware. "It's just that – even if you were going off your BBC knowledge – you should realise that there are plenty of people who'd rather we weren't around."

"Yes, but *who*?" said Kevin.

"Oh, don't mention that word in Peter's house," said Ware, and slapped the youth on the shoulder.

"I just want to understand what the situation is," protested Kevin. "I mean, Dr How's told me that there are aliens all over the place, but he hasn't told me who they are, what they want, why they're here – none of that. I think I've got a right to know. I mean, why are you two here anyway?"

Dr How gave him a serious look again. "As I think I've told you, Kevin, we Time Keepers operate under an intergalactic treaty. We are, if you will, peace keepers, of sorts. We're entrusted to do certain things. That's why we're called Time Keepers. As for the other aliens, there are delegations from many different cultures. They're here to observe and to represent their civilisations." Kevin opened his mouth to speak. "And, no, they're not here to kidnap people on lonely country roads; nor do they carve up cattle in the Mid-Western United States."

"Not for the most part, anyway," said Ware.

"There are miscreants, yes. But most civilisations mean well."

"And there are ones that don't?" asked Kevin.

"There's always a small percentage of otherwise intelligent beings who want to destabilise, or control."

"Or just trash the status quo," added Ware. "Who knows what they want?" He flashed a look at his cousin. "Who hasn't a bleedin' clue, actually."

"Enough, David."

"What about the other Doctors? I mean, the other Time Keepers?" asked Kevin.

"As we like to say on Gaelfrey, Kevin, 'All in good time'. Now, we must all rest. We have much to do tomorrow. Trinity will show you to your rooms." The other two glanced at the stairs, surprised to see the big black cat swishing her tail silently.

"I'd better call my Mum and let her know I'm staying out."

"I took the liberty of having my Spectrel leave an explanatory message in your voice earlier," said the Doctor. "She'd not be grateful for a call at this hour in the morning. I bid you goodnight. Oh, and just one thing."

"What's that?" asked Ware.

"Both of you – please shower thoroughly before you go to bed. You know I… Look, it's just this cleanliness thing. Okay?"

"Where are you sleeping, Doctor?"

"A good Time Keeper sleeps in his Spectrel," said Ware, putting a hand in the middle of Kevin's back, and guiding him in the direction of the stairs. Trinity was already climbing them.

Kevin glanced back over his shoulder. The chair at the desk was empty and the red telephone box glowed in the corner.

The Doctor was gone.

Chapter Eleven

Dr How had known who it was the instant the doorbell had rung.

"Mrs Roseby, good morning," he said. "And to what do I owe this great pleasure at this early hour?"

"Don't you try sweet-talking me, Doctor How. You know very well why I'm here."

"No, really, I don't."

"You arrived back at God-alone-knows what hour last night in a scruffy-looking cab with a couple of very dodgy-looking people and woke my Albert up. And I'm concerned that this wreck of a vehicle," she gesticulated at Ware's cab, "is bringing down the neighbourhood."

Inside his pocket, Dr How's fingers curled around his Ultraknife. He made a conscious effort to let it go and bring his hand out empty. "Mrs Roseby, I have every right to arrive at my own home in whatever means of transport I choose at any time of the day or night, with whomever I choose to do so. Domestic cats are semi-nocturnal so it's only natural that Albert was awake. As for my guest's cab, it has every right to park on my property. However, if you feel it's affecting the value of your house, I'd be delighted to move it before you put it up for sale. I have to say I'm glad to hear you're considering moving into a nursing home; your niece has often expressed concern about your safety."

Doctor How had chosen to press several buttons at once. It put him in mind of pulling the lever on a one-armed bandit, and he could almost hear the words lining up in his neighbour's head as the wheels stopped spinning.

"Oh! Don't tell me that… that *boy* is staying with you?"

A jackpot line, bar one wheel.

"You mean my new assistant?"

Nudge.

"*Assistant?*"

Jackpot.

"Yes. Kevin's my new assistant."

"…"

"He's from the Tulse Hill estate."

Bonus.

"Don't tell me he's one of them illegal immigrants. I shall have the police round to arrest him if anything goes missing from my house."

"He's as British as you are, Mrs Roseby. Born and bred. Believe me, I do share your concerns about illegal aliens. More than you might care to imagine. Now that I've covered Kevin, how else may I help?"

She recovered her composure. "Well, I won't stand for having a cab service operating from these premises, Doctor How. It's quite against planning restrictions, and I shall bring down the full weight of the residents' association; not to say the council planning officers."

"You have no need for concern there, Mrs Roseby. That's my cousin's cab. His house is undergoing an unexpected refurbishment after a small accident yesterday."

"Well, I think it's in a disgraceful state and I shall be reporting it at the next meeting. And he can't be operating it from domestic premises."

"If there's nothing else I can help you with, Mrs Roseby, then I'll bid you good morning." He didn't quite slam the door in her face, and went back into the house.

"That woman was a cantankerous old bag when she was a blushing bride," said Ware from the bottom of the stairs. He was only wearing his underwear, and his unsightly potbelly made the Doctor shudder.

"Age has not mellowed her, nor will it ever. How did you sleep?"

"Not bad. My Spectrel was in my dreams. She's insisting we get her back. Today."

"Yes, yes. It's on my ever-burgeoning to-do list. If you get Kevin up and breakfasted we can crack on. And if you can make sure you both have a shower before joining me in the basement."

"Anything else?"

"If you could remember to tell the house-bot to clean up after you, that would be much appreciated."

"And you wonder why you don't have visitors."

"No, I don't wonder. I don't have visitors because they make everything so untidy. And unclean."

Chapter Twelve

"Good morning, Miss Peterson," said Thickett drily. "I'm so glad you could join me."

She had no idea where Thickett got his energy from. He could only have had three or four hours' sleep the previous night by her estimate. In her opinion, the man was borderline psychotic. "Good morning, Mr Thickett. I see you got it back in one piece," she said with a forced smile.

"More than can be said for the pick-up truck," he chortled. "Oh, the *power* of this thing."

They were in an observation gallery overlooking a concrete vault fifty feet square and thirty high. Ware's Spectrel was in the middle of the chamber, brightly lit by strip-lights from above and the sides. Peterson had not been in this particular area before. Judging by her route through the labyrinth of tunnels under Holborn, she thought they must be somewhere under Kingsway – probably at a depth of well over two hundred feet – deeper than the Central Line station which lay to the north. On the side opposite the gallery were armoured steel doors painted a drab military green. There was a three-colour traffic light next to the door to control the traffic going in and out of what would be a long single-lane tunnel to the surface. She knew enough to work out that this would have been built in the Fifties, along with other Cold war bunkers. She guessed that its purpose would have been to quarantine vehicles or supplies whilst they were decontaminated from nuclear or biological material. Below the gallery would be another armoured door, allowing access to the rest of the complex.

"And what's your plan?" she asked.

"Slowly drain it of power, then we'll be able to get in."

"Great plan. You could be here quite a while."

"Oh really? What makes you so certain? We're not detecting anything from it at the moment." He nodded towards a bank of monitors.

"Well… It's just that you'd expect something like this to have plenty of reserves on hand." She looked away a little too quickly.

"At the very least, they'll have to come and get it sooner or later. They can't just leave it in this state."

A slam echoed around the chamber, and the floor shuddered, distracting Thickett. Two technicians dressed in black rubber nuclear, biological and chemical suits – NBC suits; often called Noddy suits in the military – came into view and made their way towards the cab. Each was carrying a heavy toolkit. When they reached the vehicle, one of them turned and waved up at the observation gallery. Thickett waved back, and turned a button next to a speaker.

"Testing," said a man's muffled voice. "Jackson here."

"Roger, Jackson," said Thickett. "Test all the doors."

The men did as they were told, testing all four doors, which didn't open. They looked back up at the gallery and shook their heads. "No luck," came Jackson's voice.

"Try the boot and the bonnet," said Thickett.

The other man went round to the back of the vehicle. They saw it bounce slightly on its suspension as he grappled with the boot handle. Once his colleague at the rear was clear, Jackson felt under the lip of the bonnet. "I feel the catch," he said. He tugged and shook his head. He put his hand on the cab's badge to steady himself as he tugged hard, and a scream came from the speaker. "That hurt! It felt like an electric shock. But I'm totally insulated in my Noddy suit, so it can't be."

"Gotcha!" said Thickett. "There it is, Miss Peterson. A deliberate assault on a member of the security services by the Time Keepers."

"Oh, hardly," said Peterson. "This is a waste of time. None of these monitors even flickered. The lab should have the results back by now. Let me know if anything interesting happens."

There was a sound like a distant explosion. Peterson felt a tremor in the floor beneath her feet, and the monitors on the wall rattled on their mountings. The men in the Noddy suits looked around at the door then, puzzled, looked up expectantly at Thickett and Peterson.

"On second thoughts, I'll stay," she said.

Chapter Thirteen

"Like, for real, we're going to travel in the Spectrel this morning?" said Kevin.

"Yes, Kevin. This is 'for real', not some parallel universe. As you can see, David's Spectrel is in a Cold War bunker under Kingsway."

They were in the Doctor's basement looking at two projections, which occupied the middle of the room. One showed a three-dimensional representation of the secret complex, including the buildings immediately above it. Kevin was captivated by it: the detail was extraordinary. The other projection was a live three-dimensional feed from Ware's Spectrel.

"It's like that bit in *Star Wars*, innit?" said Kevin. "Like where R2D2 is showing Luke the recording by Princess Leia, when she's asking for help from Obi-Wan Kenobi."

"Nah," said Ware. "Surely it's more like the bit where they see the 3D model of the Death Star? Or the bit in *Return of the Jedi* when they see the Death Star coming into firing position round the forest moon of Endor."

"Yeah, or there's this bit in –"

"Can I just remind you that the reason we're able to mount this rescue mission at all is because I was doing my job, rather than gorging myself on contemporary human cinema?" snapped the Doctor.

Ware turned to Kevin and muttered, "To be fair, he did get a bit less sleep than the pair of us."

"So our Spectrels estimate that they'll have to be in

close proximity for ten sidereal minutes to get the power transfer completed. Unfortunately, it looks like she's under some scrutiny. Now, that needn't necessarily be a problem just so long as I can get the connection back." The Doctor nodded towards his Spectrel and the projections vanished.

"Excuse me, Doctor. Do you mind if I ask a stupid question?"

"There's no such thing as a stupid question. Fire away, but make it quick."

"Like, if you're using this transdimensional feed, why can't you use it from a distance?"

"Good question. There are four forces. Gravity is the weakest, but it makes its presence felt at almost infinitely greater distances than the others. The ones that apply on a subatomic level are unimaginably stronger than gravity, but make their presence felt over almost infinitesimally small distances. They bind subatomic particles together, but as soon as those particles are a short distance away – even just a couple of radii of those particles – then they are much weaker. This is a bit like that. Got it?"

"Um. I think so."

"Well it's a bit like the way I can reach the lab in the Spectrel through my pocket. Does that make sense now?"

"Not really."

"That's because you've not done the Ph.D. in Astrophysics yet. I take it you're postponing your Nobel acceptance speech by another decade."

"Is he always this sarcastic?" Kevin asked Ware.

"Nah, he's going easy on you. His full sarcasm has been banned by intergalactic treaty."

"So," said the Doctor. "First rule of time: the sooner we start, the sooner we're back."

"Uh, another stupid question if I may," said Kevin.

"Go on."

"Like, can't we just go back in time and stop them from

taking David's Spectrel?"

"No, not really."

"But why not?"

"Misuse of time travel."

"But I don't understand."

"That's because, not only have you failed to complete your Ph.D. in Astrophysics, you have neglected to read the Laws of Time Travel, to which David and I are both signatories and of which we are both enforcers. We can do this another way, and so we must. Or, if you want to put it another way, because I say so, Kevin. Now hop in."

Doctor How opened the door of the red telephone box and held it. Kevin looked at Ware and How. He looked at the inside. There was a telephone and a shelf, just as he would have expected to see in any other box on any British high street.

"Okay, me first," said David. "Been a while, ain't it?" he squeezed into the telephone box and glanced around. He took a firm step forwards and disappeared. He didn't disappear into the back of the box as if stepping behind a curtain – he just ceased to be there.

"But where is he?"

"My cousin Where is now elsewhere, if you'll indulge my humour."

"Yeah, but where?"

"Quite literally, he's nowhere. Nowhere so far as you're capable of experiencing at the moment. He doesn't exist anywhere you could experience him."

"Yeah, but isn't that dangerous? I mean, what if –"

"I haven't got time to talk hypotheticals and probabilities right now. Just do as he did and I'll follow."

Kevin stepped into the phone box and looked back at the Doctor, who waved him on impatiently. He took a step forward, and ceased to be.

He was at the side of a control room. He felt a sudden

force in his back and was thrown forwards. A hand grabbed his hoodie from behind and stopped him from falling to the floor.

"Hell's bells, Kevin," said the Doctor. "What did you stop in the doorway for? You're like those bloody tourists who stop outside Tube stations and block the exit for everyone else. Stop rubbernecking and take a seat, lad."

Kevin glanced behind him. There was no door behind the Doctor that he could see.

"Leave it, Peter," said David. "It's his first time. No one's that confident their first time, are they?"

"Oh, I suppose," said the Doctor. "Sorry."

Kevin looked around the circular room. It was a brilliant white – so bright that it overwhelmed his eyes. He felt it should have been painful, but it was calming. In the centre of the room was a semi-circular control panel with a single seat. He moved towards it.

"No, not there," said the Doctor. "Passenger seat." He indicated one of several comfortable-looking black seats in rows around the side of the room.

"Come and sit beside me," said Ware. "And I'll answer any questions you might have."

"Why are there no seatbelts?"

"Not needed. Forget your preconceptions about travel. You're not travelling at all."

"Oh, but if we're not travelling…"

"Then how do we get there? Easy. I don't know how much Peter's explained to you."

"He told me it's all a bit like zip files and things."

"Hmm. This bit isn't. There are all these other dimensions that you don't – and, indeed, most of the Pleasant universe – doesn't experience on a day-to-day basis. That's mainly because most of them don't harbour life."

"Most?"

"Well, some do, by implication. Obviously."

"It might be obvious to you."

"If I say 'most don't', then some obviously do. Keep up, sunshine. So when we stepped into the Spectrel we stepped into a space elsewhere. If you were looking at it from any angle, it would always be going away from you to get there because it's always perpendicular to your own dimensions. Does that make sense?"

"Not really."

"Good. Nor should it, if you were being totally honest. Now, let me give you an analogy as to how this works, if you're interested." Kevin nodded. "So the Spectrel provides us with a door into that other space. We just close the door behind us in the Pleasant universe and then open it somewhere else. We've not really moved in this particular dimension, but we've changed the Cartesian coordinates of the door in the Pleasant universe."

"Uh. I think I get the analogy."

"Oh. Have you read Philip Pullman's *His Dark Materials* trilogy?" asked Ware.

"As a matter of fact, I read it when I was off school with 'flu. This Amazon parcel arrived when my Mum was out. Wrong address, but I kept it. Like, I delivered it to the right address when I was better. I just borrowed it, you know?"

Across at the console, the Doctor stifled a smile.

"*The Subtle Knife* is about the best explanation of the physics I've read in your culture," said Ware. "Will is able to cut a hole into other universes. It's a bit like that. Except without the other universes. Oh, and we always close the doors behind us. Bit dangerous if you don't."

"So, like, where's the Spectrel? Are we tumbling through the Time Vortex?"

"For God's sake, don't let him catch you talking mumbo-jumbo like that. This Spectrel doesn't exist. None of them do."

"What? But we're in it."

"Sure, but it doesn't exist in your world. It's just a projection of forces. Did Peter at least explain to you that nothing is actually there where we think it is?"

"Um. Yes. Like a table isn't really composed of anything at all. It's just forces, with a tiny bit of matter."

"So it's not there. In the same way as nothing else is there."

"Yes, but how come we're able to exist in another dimension?"

Ware tapped the side of his nose. "Very good, Kevin. That's the secret the Time Keepers have which makes us the Time Keepers. The rest of the Pleasant universe would love to know."

"Well, why don't you tell them?"

"Mayhem. For all our many faults, we do see fit to abide by a strict set of Laws. We're respected for our adherence to them, and for our all-round goodness."

"Sorry to sound cynical, but that's, like, subjective, innit? One man's goody is another man's baddy."

Ware grinned. "Oh, no. No, Kevin. Believe me; you'll know the baddies when you meet them. You think some of the lads on your estate are bad 'uns? You don't wanna meet some of the nasty entities hanging around out there." Ware swept his hand in an arc.

"And what's this Pleasant universe you and the Doctor are always talking about?"

"If I say something like 'most of' and what's left over is therefore 'some of, but not all', then if I say Pleasant universe, then…?"

"Then there's an Unpleasant universe. And… and the Unpleasant universe is what doesn't make up the Pleasant universe?"

"Got it in one."

"But that still doesn't explain –"

"I think David has explained quite enough for now," said Doctor How.

"Are we there yet?" joked Ware.

The Doctor rolled his eyes and then addressed Kevin. "We've always been there. Unfortunately, time has moved whilst you've been yakking. You may have noticed that it has a tendency to do that. That movement of time has allowed events to unfold, as you can see." Above the control panel was a projection of the bunker in which the Spectrel was being held. Thickett and Peterson were visible in the gallery.

"As I said, he does sarcasm by the bucket," said Ware. "He could move into wholesale."

"But if we're already there, and if we've been there all along, why couldn't we charge David's Spectrel?" said Kevin, exasperated.

"Because we're still nowhere. We're all around this place, but we're at right-angles to it," said Ware.

"Then how will we get there?"

"Just open the door and we'll be there. You'll see."

"I'm sorry, this is making exactly no sense at all," said Kevin.

"I said leave it for now," said the Doctor. "David, I'll hold you personally responsible if the poor lad suffers a brain aneurysm. I should warn you that his mother is fearsome. Now, look at this."

"That's the MI16 agents," said Kevin. "She's well cute."

"And there was me thinking that it was just our giant beetle's sex-drive that would be a problem on this mission. She was at Imperial. Saw her there as a doctoral student. Peterson. Camilla. Good reputation. The other man is Thickett. Career civil servant. Exactly in the mould of others we've seen before in Sixteen. She'll be the one with the scientific mind and he'll be the odious pen-pusher."

They watched as the two men in NBC suits emerged

from the armoured door under the viewing gallery.

"So what's the plan?" asked Ware. "This is your op."

"After we enter the chamber I need to reconnect the Spectrels. We'll jam all the security services' systems, of course – doors and alarms. You two just need to keep those goons in the Noddy suits busy whilst I work my magic as a jump-start lead."

"Gotcha," said Kevin. "Like, how long do you need?"

"Maybe thirty seconds."

"That's actually quite a long time, Doc," said Kevin. "For example, to smash and grab from a car you've got five, max. A good shoplifting move is, like, two."

"Kids these days, eh?" said Ware. "Still, I'm glad you're an equal-opportunities employer and looking to fill that critical thieving skills gap so prevalent in the time-travelling community." He winked at Kevin. "It's alright Kevin. You know, his brother –"

"Leave my brother out of this, David. Please, be serious. I'm relying on you both to keep them busy for thirty seconds. That's all."

"What do you suggest we do?" asked Kevin.

"Oh, I don't know. Perform a comedy sketch, ask them what brand of shampoo they use, run around a bit or something. They won't be expecting us, so you'll take them completely by surprise. Now, come on, let's go to the door."

Doctor How walked to where he and Kevin had entered. A crack of darkness opened in the dazzling white of the wall and formed the shape of a doorway. Kevin stood directly behind him and Ware right behind Kevin. From the projection above the console they could hear Jackson cry out with pain as he touched the badge on the cab. Ware laughed. "That's my girl," he said.

"Okay," said Doctor How. "Double-quick. Go!"

The Doctor leapt forward and disappeared. Kevin took two quick steps and found himself in the concrete chamber, next to Ware's Spectrel. The two men in Noddy suits were just a few feet away and were looking up at the viewing gallery. He gawped for a second at the extraordinary transition he had made from nowhere to this place. Ware slammed into his back and he sprawled to the floor, which seemed to be shaking under his body.

"Don't you learn? Never stop in a doorway," said Ware, grabbing his hoodie and pulling him to his feet.

Kevin glanced around. Doctor How's red telephone box was glowing brightly right in front of the black cab. The Doctor had climbed up onto the bonnet and was stretching out to connect its badge with the crown on his own Spectrel using his hands as the contacts.

"That's them!" echoed Thickett's voice from a loudspeaker. It echoed around the chamber. The men in the Noddy suits turned and took a step back as they took in the sudden appearance of a glowing telephone box and three intruders in such a secure installation. "Get them! Arrest those three men!" yelled Thickett.

"*Argh!*" croaked Doctor How, as his hands connected the two Spectrels. His body shook and his hair stood on end.

The two men stepped towards Kevin, who began running. "It's not me you want – it's him!" said Kevin, gesticulating up at Thickett. "He's a paedo!"

"Metropolitan Police, Child Sexual Crimes Section," said Ware, standing his ground. "Mr Thickett is wanted for perverting the course of justice. And being a pervert."

"*Urgh,*" gargled Doctor How.

The concrete floor shook again, enough to make the Doctor slip on the cab's bonnet and lose touch with the crown of his Spectrel. One of the men in Noddy suits fell over. Ware steadied himself against his Spectrel. Kevin tripped over a slab of concrete, which had been pushed up as cracks appeared in the floor. As he lay on the shaking concrete, the floor in front of him erupted in a spray of concrete and mud. He twisted his body just fast enough to dodge a chunk slamming down where he'd been lying. As he tried to get up he felt himself being lifted as the floor rose next to his head and left him at a forty-five degree angle. A pair of black mandibles sliced through the steel reinforcement embedded in the concrete, the slab jerked up to ninety degrees and he pushed back onto his feet. The stench of oil made his head swim.

A three-foot black antenna swished through the air and knocked him on the left side of his head, crushing the top of his ear against his skull. He felt blood on his hand, and ran back as the front end of a huge black creature emerged from the hole. The slab that Kevin had been lifted on slammed backwards onto the floor with a deafening bang which reverberated around the chamber. One of the creature's legs caught on a metal toolbox and its contents went flying, the tools ringing and clattering to the floor.

Doctor How took his position on the bonnet of the cab again. The two men in Noddy suits ran for the exit under the viewing gallery and hammered on the massive steel door.

"*Yurgh!* David. For God's sake, stun it with your Ultraknife," shouted the Doctor. "It's our only hope."

"I can't. It's in the glove compartment."

"Well, open your Spectrel and get it. *Argh*!" The Doctor's body jerked under the strain of the power coursing through his body between the Spectrels.

"No, it's in me cab what's back at your place."

"You left your…? *EEE*!"

The rest of the beast crashed through into the chamber, scattering more mud and pieces of concrete across the floor. The panicked men in Noddy suits stopped hammering at the exit, turned and stared in awe and terror, their backs pressed against the door.

"It was useful on the job. You know, tricky customers, starting the cab on a cold morning, that sort of thing."

"You idiot. *Argh*! You know you should never... *Ugh*! Misuse of...*Oonf*!"

"Give him your Ultraknife, Doctor!" screamed Kevin, as the beast turned and began to focus its attention on the humans and Time Keepers.

"I. *Urgh*! I can't. Security. It's in my pocket. Can't reach. *Yerrgh*!"

"You're bleedin' useless, the pair of you!"

"Get in the Spectrel," yelled the Doctor. "Turn the Taxi light on."

"She still won't let me in."

Jackson and the other man resumed their futile banging at the security door. "Get them!" Thickett screamed. "They control the creature. Do something!"

Jackson picked up a hammer which had fallen near his feet. He took aim and threw it at the creature's mouth. The hammer hit a set of inner mandibles and the creature hissed, turning its attention fully on the men in Noddy suits.

"Noooo!" screamed the Doctor.

It was too late – the creature lunged for the men, punching and ripping a hole in the steel door with a mandible. The Doctor jumped down from the bonnet and reached into his pocket. The creature jerked around and caught Jackson's leg with a mandible, slicing it off below the knee. The severed leg and foot arced up in the air and bounced off the window of the viewing gallery, smearing it with blood.

"Kill it, Doctor!" shouted Thickett.

"I can't!" shouted the Doctor. "It's petrochemical. We have no idea what happens when it dies – it could blow us all to smithereens!"

"The Taxi light just came on!" shouted Kevin. "I'll get its attention."

The creature was waving its antennae over Jackson, who lay paralysed, blood from his severed leg pouring out onto the floor.

Kevin ran from the cab and kicked the creature in the area where he thought its reproductive organs would be, then jumped back as it turned to face him. He vaulted the bonnet of the cab. The creature took in the information and hissed. The Doctor ran for Jackson. The creature hesitated, then nature took its course as it saw the amber light on top of the cab. It scuttled around the back of the Spectrel and began to mount it.

"You're going to be alright," said the Doctor to Jackson, who was losing consciousness. He took out a bandage from his pocket and tied a tourniquet above the man's knee. Jackson's colleague approached him, carrying a heavy spanner. "Drop it," said the Doctor. The man raised the spanner and the Doctor whipped out his Ultraknife and stunned him. The man fell to the floor. The clang of the spanner caused the creature to turn its attention back to Jackson and the Doctor.

"He's attacking our men!" shouted Thickett over the intercom.

"He's defending himself," protested Peterson.

"Well, why didn't he stun the creature?"

"It could blow up – don't you listen?"

All this time, Ware had been leaning back against the driver's door of his Spectrel, his palms spread on its flanks, strangely calm and passive. Now that the creature was mounting the rear of the cab, he edged away and turned his back to the Doctor, who was moving his Ultraknife back and forth across Jackson's bloody stump.

"Kevin, bring me that man's leg," said the Doctor.

Kevin looked at the creature, looked at Ware, then ran to get the severed leg from the corner of the chamber. The limb was still in its one-piece rubber trouser and boot. The ragged end of the rubber Noddy suit was smeared with blood. It was heavier than he'd thought it would be, and jiggled around in the boot in a sickening way as he jogged over to where the Doctor was kneeling beside the groaning Jackson and his unconscious colleague.

"Can you…?" asked Kevin.

"Maybe," said the Doctor. "It's a clean cut, but if I can just…" He peeled back the rubber from above the knee, and took the lower leg from its boot. "If I can just connect the major veins and arteries… bit tricky, even in the best of circumstances."

Kevin glanced around. The creature was absorbed in its act of passion. Ware had climbed onto the bonnet of the cab, just three feet from the creature's head. "Dave," he said under his breath, amazed at Ware's bravery.

The Doctor looked up and followed Kevin's gaze to see his cousin place the palm of his hand on the crown of the telephone box. "David! No! You're not fit enough."

"Cobblers. I feel like me old self, Peter. Just you watch this, me old China." Ware reached his palm down to the badge on the nose of the cab.

"No!" shouted the Doctor. "Get away from there!"

"I cannot deny my timeline," said Ware. "I am Where once more!"

Where's palm made contact and closed the connection between the two Spectrels. His scream sent a shock down Kevin's spine. In that instant Where's Spectrel vanished from beneath him. He fell, his head hit the floor with a *thwack* and his body went limp. The creature's impact with the concrete was louder. It paused for a couple of seconds then let out a loud hiss, its mouth just a couple of feet from Where's unconscious body.

"Where's his Spectrel gone?" asked Kevin.

"I haven't got time to explain." The Doctor glanced at his patient, then at the creature, which was turning its attention towards them again. "We have to get out of here, all of us. Now. Grab these and hold them tight."

Kevin took hold of Jackson's upper and lower leg and pushed them together.

"David, you bloody idiot," muttered the Doctor. He began creeping towards his fallen cousin.

"Doctor, how can we help?" asked Peterson over the intercom.

"Not stealing things you don't understand, for a start," he shouted back.

"What can we do now?"

The Doctor glanced around him. "If you can turn that amber traffic light on." He pointed to the set of lights by the exit to the surface.

"It's a trick," said Thickett. "He wants you to open the exit so that he can escape with his monster."

"It's not a trick," said Peterson.

"How do you know?"

"That thing is distracted by amber lights. Didn't you see? Now, get out of my way."

"Miss Peterson –"

"It's *Doctor* Peterson, Mr Thickett. In scientific matters you have to give way to my superior training. *This*, Mr Thickett, is just such a time."

"We will be talking about your conduct in this situation at your next performance review," seethed Thickett.

The Doctor continued creeping towards Where. The creature jerked to the right to bring its full attention on him. "Good boy," he said. "You don't like eating things."

Peterson began flicking switches up in the viewing gallery.

"No luck?" called the Doctor.

"I'm trying, I'm trying," said Peterson. "Keep it distracted."

"Easy for you to say."

The creature took a step towards the Doctor. He inched back, then began skirting around behind his Spectrel, away from Kevin and Jackson.

"Don't leave me, Doctor!" shouted Kevin.

"No one's abandoning you, Kevin," said the Doctor, continuing to circle round to the creature's right. "You're the least of my worries right now because you're doing very well."

He came back into the creature's view from behind his Spectrel. The creature shifted position once more to keep him in view. "Oh, drat, double-drat, drat squared, and drat to the power of drat. You're not at all mesmerised by my Spectrel's light are you, my coleopteran cretin? Oh, who gave you a big body but kept your brain the size of pinhead? I would love to know. You're so brainless you could be a human politician." He kept on moving round and the creature shifted again to keep him in view.

"Can't you, like, shine an amber light from your Ultraknife?" said Kevin.

"Oh, thank you Kevin. I really hadn't thought of that."

"It's just that it can –"

"Well, it just can't flaming well do that. Alright?"

"Sorry, just trying to help."

The creature lunged at the Doctor, who leapt sideways as it slammed into the wall, sending a shower of concrete fragments rattling to the floor.

"It's not happy, Doctor Peterson."

"I can see that, Doctor," said Peterson. The sound of her desperately flicking switches was audible over the intercom.

The Doctor moved towards the main exit, which was as far away from his own Spectrel as he could be in the chamber without backing into a corner. He raised his Ultraknife as the creature began moving towards him again.

"Kevin, start dragging that chap over to the Spectrel, will you? Put your hands under his shoulders and drag him."

"He's going to take a hostage," said Thickett. "I'll make sure he gets fifteen years for that."

Kevin pulled Jackson towards the telephone box. The severed lower leg was now hanging on to the upper part of the limb by a couple of shreds of tissue.

"Got it!" said Peterson.

The Doctor heard a click above him and glanced up at the traffic light. "You're colour-blind, Doctor Peterson – that's green."

"I'm nearly there."

The beast hunkered down on its feet, ready to leap forwards again at the Doctor. He held up his Ultraknife and braced himself. "I don't want to do this, beastie," he said softly. "It might hurt all of us as much as it'll hurt you."

Click.

The beast jumped, the Doctor dived, rolled to the side and scrabbled to his feet, his Ultraknife still pointing at the beast. The creature had leapt onto the wall and was caressing the amber light with its antennae.

"Okay, Kevin, let's go!" shouted the Doctor. He ran to help Kevin pull Jackson the last couple of yards to the door of the telephone box. "We need to get David. Hurry."

They each put their hands under one of Where's armpits and pulled with all their might to drag him next to Jackson. "If he recovers, he's going on a diet immediately," gasped the Doctor. "Now, get that man into the Spectrel."

On the other side of the chamber, Jackson's colleague staggered to his feet, taking in the situation. He bent down to pick up his heavy spanner again.

The Spectrel's door swung open. Kevin got behind Jackson's head and pulled him the last couple of feet into the Spectrel. They disappeared and the door closed.

"See that?" gasped Thickett. "Kidnapping."

"Right, come on, you big lump," said the Doctor, grabbing his cousin under the armpits. The Spectrel's door opened again.

Jackson's colleague lumbered towards the Doctor and

raised the spanner.

The Doctor fumbled for his Ultraknife and jabbed at it. The man collapsed and the spanner clanged to the floor. "Sorry!" said the Doctor. With a loud grunt he pulled his cousin into the Spectrel and disappeared. The door closed.

Peterson and Thickett looked at each other, then back down at the chamber. The creature was halfway up the wall next to the main exit, grinding its lower body against the surface. The other member of their team was lying unconscious in his Noddy suit on the floor. The chamber itself was a wreck – a gaping hole towards one corner, and damage to the wall in a couple of places.

"I don't know what you propose to do now, Miss Peterson," said Thickett.

"What *I* intend to do, Mr Thickett? You chose to take Where's Spectrel."

"How am I going to explain this to the minister?" wailed Thickett. "And what do we do with the creature? Our communications are still jammed. We're helpless."

"He's still here," said Peterson.

The red telephone box continued to glow in the chamber below.

"He's still got our internal communications jammed," said Thickett.

"I doubt there's much anyone could do to help us."

The door of the Spectrel opened again, and the Doctor stepped out and glanced around. "Look, sorry about the mess. Technically it's not my fault. This thing – or maybe these *things* plural, are after either my cousin or me. We don't know why. They seem to home in on the signal from a weakened Spectrel. Bit of an own goal, bringing one here after my cousin's Spectrel had been pinpointed by whoever it is. I do hope you're insured."

"What are we going to do about that creature?" asked Peterson.

"I've not seen it go quite that long. Oh, there we go." Fluid splashed onto the wall beneath the creature. A few drops hit the armoured steel door to its left, and the metal hissed. "Quick, turn the light off!"

Peterson turned off the amber light. The creature lay motionless on the wall.

"I think we can save your man Jackson's leg," said the Doctor. "He'll probably have a hell of a limp."

"That's kidnapping. I'm going to have you for that, Doctor How. I know what you're up to – you're going to interrogate him under duress and steal our secrets."

"Oh, please, Mr Thicko –"

"It's *Thickett*, and I'm proud of it."

"I can't imagine what you might possibly think you have that's worth knowing that I don't know already, or couldn't find out if I could be bothered to spend a nanosecond hacking your systems, Mr Thicky."

"*Thickett!*"

"Whatever. Look, we'll pop Jackson somewhere safe. Probably a bit later today, if that's alright."

"Where?" asked Thickett.

"Tsh. Can't have you knowing my movements in advance, Mr Twit."

The creature began to stir.

"For the last time, it's *Thickett*. That… that *thing* could break into the control room. We have to stop it. You have to get rid of it, Doctor. I'll hold you personally responsible for this."

"Really, it'll get bored in a minute. Needs a post-coital snackette. It'd be great if you had some volatile petroleum products," said the Doctor. "Look, if it's okay with you I'll be off for now. But I'd be grateful if you could go back to defending the Realm from those who would do harm to Her Brittanic Majesty's citizens, or whatever it is you're supposed to be doing, rather than hassling harmless helpers."

The creature dropped to the floor. The Doctor stepped into the Spectrel and raised his hand to wave.

"It's going to get Smith!" said Thickett. "Turn that light back on!"

"No!" shouted Peterson and the Doctor simultaneously.

Thickett pushed Peterson out of the way and flicked the switch.

Click.

The Spectrel's door slammed shut and it winked out of existence. Peterson jumped on top of Thickett, slamming him onto the floor of the control room, pinning him to it with her body.

The departure of the Spectrel took the jamming from the control room's systems, which began to reboot. An old-fashioned steady alarm-bell rang, and a modern siren warbled into life.

Nothing happened for a couple of seconds. Peterson raised her head a fraction, and Thickett opened his mouth to reprimand her. If they had been able to see out of the control room, they would have seen that something *had* happened. If they'd turned their heads to the monitors, they would have seen them wink into life just in time to show the last two seconds of images that they would ever display.

The creature's acid ejaculate had melted through the wiring of the traffic light. There had been a spark as the light had been turned on, and a small flame had been ignited. It flashed down the wall and licked around the posterior of the creature, where fluid still dripped from its failed congress. The creature breathed out through the spiracles in its abdomen, and a yellow flame lit off the breath that came out of two on its right side, like a couple of miniature flares from an oil refinery. The twinge of pain made it breathe in sharply with shock. Deep inside the tubes of the creature's respiratory system the flame found the perfect mix of oxygen and combustible vapour.

The explosion blew out the bullet-proof windows of the control room from their surrounds and a couple of pieces of burning black body casing and a mandible bounced off the far wall and hit the floor. Oily black smoke poured off the body parts as yellow-orange flames crackled furiously from them.

"Stay on the ground!" shouted Peterson. She crawled beneath the thickening layer of smoke to where she knew there was a fire extinguisher. She grabbed it and sprayed the fragments with inert powder.

The door burst open, and four Ministry of Defence firemen in breathing apparatus ran into the room. They pulled Thickett and Peterson out into the corridor, where a pair of medics clapped oxygen masks on their faces.

"Smith! Get Smith! He's in the chamber," shouted Peterson.

"How and Where!" said Thickett.

"This one's not making much sense," said one of the medics to a doctor, who had just arrived, out of breath.

"The Doctors! It was the Doctors!"

"Who?" asked the doctor.

"No! Not Who. How and Where!" said Thickett.

"Shock," said the doctor to the medics. "Just relax, sir," he said to Thickett. He took out a syringe and tapped it for bubbles as he squeezed the plunger. "Going to feel nice and sleepy now."

"No! Get Who, you nincompoop! Get the Doctors!"

"That's it," said the doctor. "I'm a doctor and I'm here now. Breathing deeply now, and going to sleep. Relaaaax. That's it."

A man arrived in a military Noddy suit. "Smith and Jackson," he panted. Where are they, Peterson?"

"Jackson's being looked after by the Doctor," said Peterson. "Smith… Oh, God. Smith's down there, in the chamber."

"So this is Jackson?" said the doctor.

"No, that's Thickett," said Peterson. "Jackson had an accident, the Doctor... Oh, never mind." She turned to the man in the Noddy suit. "Smith was down there when the explosion happened."

"He's not there now," said the man in the Noddy suit. "No bodies. No human bodies."

"The Doctor must have come back for him. Thank God for that."

"Shock," said the doctor to the man in the Noddy suit. "She'll be fine. The other one was hysterical. Had to sedate him. Come on, Miss. Don't try to stand yet – we don't know what sort of damage you might have."

"It's Doctor," she said. "I'm a doctor. Well, not that kind of doctor. Not your kind of doctor – my kind of doctor."

"Oh, dear," said the doctor. He took out another syringe and tapped it for bubbles.

"No, that's really not necessary, doctor. I'm perfectly alright."

"Of course you are. How about a drink or dinner sometime?"

"Thank you, but I think I'm going to be extremely busy for the immediate future."

Chapter Fourteen

"Give me a hand, will you?" said the Doctor, collapsing back into the Spectrel, with Smith's head landing on his stomach. The soles of the man's boots had melted at the edges, and gave off an acrid smell of burnt rubber.

"I saw the explosion on the projection," said Kevin, taking Smith's weight off the Doctor. The two of them dragged the unconscious man to a clear piece of floor. "It was awesome! Wait 'til you see the replay."

"Great – I nearly lost my neck and you want to put it on *You've Been Framed*. I do hope that little incident made up for your earlier disappointment about the lack of monsters in your life. How are the other two?"

A couple of med-bots were tending to Where and Jackson. Kevin hadn't been that impressed when the two white boxes had each hovered in from under their respective passenger seats and taken up position over a patient. Then he'd watched in wonder as tiny hatches opened up all over the one assigned to Jackson, and intricate sensors and slender robot arms had reached out to tend to his leg. Two ancillary med-bots had arrived seconds later. One cut away the head and neck of the Noddy suit and planted an oxygen mask over the man's face. The other carried a plastic pouch of fluid, and used three arms to cut open the Noddy suit on Jackson's left arm. After peeling away the suit and the clothing from underneath, a fourth arm inserted the intravenous drip. Kevin had gone in closer for a look as microscopic stitches were made in veins and arteries, and tiny squirts of various fluids applied to the flesh. He'd had to look away when a drill began cutting into a bone.

"Like, these med-bots are the coolest thing ever. I so want to take one back to show my Mum. The guy with the amputated leg seems alright. I don't know about Dave, though."

The med-bot above Where was hovering in position above his chest.

"I don't think I know about David either," said the Doctor. "He has the family traits of compulsion and bravado – that's mostly what did for him."

"Can you explain, in really simple terms, what happened?"

"What happened was fifty years of neglect – both of himself and his duty."

"Like, I think I've heard that bit."

The Doctor sighed and sat at the Spectrel's controls. "There's a kind of symbiosis between a Time Keeper and his Spectrel. A bit like a married couple in many respects. As the relationship grows, you grow into each other. For whatever reason, David chose to opt out. It was the Sixties, I suppose. We were all tired and jaded after the War. But in my view we were entering a new and much more dangerous age. Humans had finally learnt to unleash the power of the nucleus and the atom – though you've still a long way to go in controlling them. So far as David was concerned, the genie was out of the bottle and it was up to others to perform different duties. You know, sometimes a routine life can seem like an adventure. He was obviously abusing the relationship with his Spectrel. Using her to ferry passengers around London is just the pits, frankly. You saw his lifestyle – drinking, smoking... not to mention a terrible diet."

"Yeah, but what about what happened back there?"

"Hmm? Oh, heart attack. You see, just as his Spectrel

was weakened by his lack of care for it, so he was weakened. That little incident we had with the beast at his place reawakened something in him. As I'd hoped, the old David was still in there. You saw how much better he was. He got a decent night's sleep and then overdid it. *Simple as*, as your generation would say. Luckily, he does have a second heart. But it's not like the second one is in any fit state either."

"And his Spectrel?"

"She clearly decided she was better off elsewhere."

"But, like, where?"

The Doctor swept his open hand in a broad arc.

"So… when will she be coming back?"

The Doctor shrugged.

"Well, at least David's alive and the monster's dead, innit? And that Thicko guy didn't get anything. So, like, round one to us. Right?"

The Doctor snorted. "Let us compare ourselves to where we were just a short while ago. We had two Time Keepers and two Spectrels. We now have one of each. We now also have a couple of unwanted passengers and have further piqued the interest of Sixteen. Oh, and so far as they're concerned, it looks like we were party to an attack which resulted in a massive explosion at one of their most secret locations. With the destruction of the monster, we've lost another piece of evidence that might have told me who the hell is doing this to us. Another day like this and they will have won." The Doctor glanced at his watch. "In fact, given that it's not even noon, we could be utterly defeated by tea-time."

"Do we still have that map of the underground thing in Essex?"

"Yes."

"Can't we, like, do something with that?"

"There it is. The unrelenting optimist – the reason I hired

you. Thank you, Kevin, for your can-do attitude. Yes, we could take a visit. But a number of different treaties to which I am a signatory – and in a couple of instances an enforcer of last resort – as well as common decency and sense, dictate that we have to look after Tweedledum and Tweedledee over there first. Furthermore, what you would call in your lexicon *the baddies* are just a tad cheesed off at the moment."

"Alright, alright – don't go wholesale with it. Like, we do have the advantage of surprise, innit?"

"Ah, you're looking at a *Battle of Midway* option, eh?"

"Um…"

"He with the best reconnaissance, and who refuels and reloads first, wins."

"Right you are. That was it: the *Battle of Midway* option. You got me."

The Doctor got up and wandered over to Smith's unconscious body. The med-bot tending to him had cut away the Noddy suit's head to let him breathe more easily. It had the end of a clear plastic tube clipped to his nostrils. It turned a sensor to the Doctor, who nodded in response. "Well, he's fine. Just needs to stay sedated. Won't remember much."

He turned to Jackson's med-bot, which popped out a similar sensor to communicate with the Doctor. "Remarkable, even by our standards. Helped that it was such a clean cut. And, of course, that we acted so quickly. Surgery will be finished in the next few seconds – all veins and major nerves reattached. Ah, here we go."

The med-bot withdrew its instruments and another two bots appeared. They unrolled a thin metallic tray and manoeuvred Jackson's limp body onto it. With a bot at each end, the tray was lifted a foot into the air and Jackson and the med-bot seemed to Kevin to disappear through a wall.

"Where have they taken him?" asked Kevin.

"Let's call it accelerated healing therapy, shall we? The prognosis is that we should be able to dump him into a reasonably competent hospital within the hour. We'd have to leave a note, of course. Something a bit more detailed than 'Please look after this bear'."

"You could show a bit more sympathy, Doctor."

"You're right; I could. However, things weren't going too badly for him until he threw a hammer."

"True. What about David?"

The med-bot looking after the Doctor's cousin pointed its communicator at him. "Days? A week? More? It's not just his heart." He seemed to nod to the med-bot.

Two bots came into the cabin and unrolled a silver foil tray next to Where. He wasn't sure whether they were the same two bots that had moved Jackson, because they all looked alike to him. He watched the two bots, the med-bot and Where disappear through the same section of wall as Jackson.

"Man, I really miss him. No offence to you, Doc, but I think I shared quite a bit of wavelength with David. You get me?"

"I get you, Kevin."

The youth's face brightened again. "Like, is this his *regeneration*? Is he going to come out of this totally changed? And as good as new?"

"That, my friend, is part of the problem. You can only regenerate in conjunction with your Spectrel. It's that whole relationship and growth thing I was telling you about. Come on, let's look at the map of this place under Essex."

"Um…"

"What?"

"I need to know where the facilities are. And, like, do you have any food?"

"I'm sorry. Not much of a host. Not used to it. Not recently, at least. Sorry. Through there." The Doctor pointed to part of the wall between two rows of passenger seats, where the bots and the bodies had disappeared.

Kevin saw that there was the slight hint of a black line in the shape of a door.

"Do I…?"

"Just walk through, yes."

The Doctor flipped on a projection of the underground facility in Essex.

Kevin returned a few minutes later. "This is a well-cool place, man. I hope you don't mind, but I took a bit of a tour. It's huge."

"The two great things about real estate which doesn't actually exist are that it's terribly cheap and you don't need planning permission. And, since it doesn't even exist, remodelling is a breeze."

"You mean this is all just complex force projections? There's no matter there at all?"

"Yes. Well put."

"Like, that makes me feel *really* uncomfortable. Knowing that there's nothing out there beyond these walls that don't exist is kinda spooky."

"Kevin, nothing in your world exists either. It's *all* just forces."

"Yeah, but I'm totally comfortable with the way the world doesn't exist. It doesn't exist in a totally natural and not in-your-face kinda way. You get me?"

"Not really. You should be more scared in an aeroplane flying at 35,000 feet. Same sort of thing in terms of forces keeping you alive there, but you've just got some human at the controls and you could slam into a mountain."

"Maybe, but it's matter."

"No, it isn't. It's unimaginably small bits of matter that aren't really matter at all, with forces around them. Pay attention. All we've done is remove the unnecessary bits."

"Yeah, like the matter."

"Well, I'm sure you've eaten a fish fillet."

"What's that got to do with anything?"

"You enjoyed eating the fish, but you just ate the flesh – you didn't have to waste your time on all the bits that made the fish a fish, did you? Like the head, the tail and fins. And when you've eaten it, you've got a clean plate – no waste. See?"

"No, that's a totally mental comparison. And it kinda makes my point about my fear about there being nothing left and it all going horribly wrong."

"As you wish. Now, speaking of food, did you get anything to eat?"

"Yeah, I ordered something from some machine that asked me what I wanted. It'll be delivered shortly, I expect."

"Good. We couldn't have you going more than three hours without food."

Kevin rolled his eyes. He nodded towards the projection of the Essex installation. "So you got it figured out, Doc? And why's it not so detailed?"

"This is just the upload of what was intercepted during the hack. We're being jammed from getting a decent read, which at least proves it's not human. At one level it's blindingly obvious, really. These beetles are GM and –"

"Sorry, GM?"

"Genetically modified. You know, like the crops that people protest about. Not naturally bred.

"You mean not organic bread?" Kevin grinned.

"Very droll. Where they come from there's not much oxygen. And you can see why that would be an advantage, given their diet and their physiology. They've evolved to live off crude oil, so distillates like diesel are like refined sugar or starch are to your physiology. With me so far?"

"Yup. My Mum's always nattering about this stuff."

"Good. So here they can take advantage of the comparatively high oxygen content in the air and grow much larger and more powerful. But there's the obvious risk of combustion, as you saw." Kevin nodded. "The clever bit is that southern England has a massive deposit of oil-bearing shale underneath it. In between video games you may have seen this on the news." Kevin nodded again. "So they can burrow through that, feeding on the way. Any vibration they produce is explained away by shale gas drilling, or fracking, as it's more commonly called."

"Totally makes sense. Weird and kinda unbelievable, but it hangs together."

"I think it hangs together better than most episodes of... Well, the least said, the better about your favourite sci-fi programme."

A shiny metal tray with a polished metal dome slid through the air from the door and drifted to a stop at waist height next to Kevin. "Oh, wow. Great service, and I'm guessing I don't have to tip." He removed the polished metal dome from the tray to reveal two golden Jamaican patties. The spicy smell filled the cabin. "Oh, I'm lovin' that smell, man. Jus' like at home!" Kevin picked one up and bit into it. "Man, that's *outrageously* good. It's the real thing! Go on, be my guest, Doc."

"I can't tell you how grateful I am that I have such excellent deodorising air filters. Well, I suppose I can at least be sure of the provenance of these." He took a small bite and nodded his approval.

After they had finished their patties, the Doctor said, "Nothing left of the constituents, you see?"

"You what?"

"The patties. Nothing left of them, or the ingredients they were made from – the chickens, the plants that grew the vegetables that were part of the recipe. And yet they were real, weren't they? Do you follow?"

"I don't know whether you had any plans to become one of those guys on TV who explains things like physics and astronomy but, well… I guess you're a pretty good Time Keeper. Although maybe the competition isn't exactly hot on that front, eh?"

"I think I'll have to take whatever compliments come my way. Oh. Your ear."

Kevin touched his ear, which was still throbbing. His hand came away with coagulated blood. "It's alright. Bleeding's stopped."

"It needs to be seen to." The Doctor nodded to the med-bot holding the bag of fluid for Jackson. It handed the bag to another med-bot. "Take a seat," he told Kevin.

Kevin took a seat and the med-bot hovered near his head. He heard the faint whine of tiny electric motors and felt the touch of tiny robotic appendages on his ear. It went numb, and he heard more noises.

"So now we've refuelled, what's the plan, Doc?"

"Drop off our guests at hospital in fifty minutes from now and then the Doctor will make a house call that somebody won't forget in a hurry."

Chapter Fifteen

Thickett ripped the oxygen mask from his face. "Police," he said. "I want police at every emergency clinic in London."

"He's come out rather suddenly," said the doctor. "Nurse, get ready with another shot."

"Don't you dare put anything else into my body, or I'll have you disciplined," said Thickett, getting up off the gurney. "I'll have your guts for garters unless you get me to a secure phone in the next thirty seconds."

"You might find you're a bit –"

Thickett took a couple of steps and fell over, splitting his head open on an unfortunately-placed table.

"–unsteady on your feet at first."

Thicket held a hand to his head and sobbed with pain.

"Oh dear. Let me help you up."

"You… you idiot," moaned Thickett.

"Now, I've got to warn you that abusing medical personnel is an actionable disciplinary matter," said the doctor. "But given the crack you've had I can let it pass this time. The nurse will show you the way to a secure line. Quite happily. And when you're done with your phone call you can come back for a couple of stitches if you're in a better mood."

Thickett was already out of the door and stumbling down the corridor after the nurse. Without a word of thanks to her, he snatched the receiver from the cradle and stabbed at the keypad. He was a vindicated man whose triumphant hour had come. He spoke with the thundering voice of authority – the voice of a righteous man whose truth has been denied for decades, but who finally holds in his hands the evidence he needs to prove his unlikely belief. This was his Churchill moment. "Thickett here, Sixteen. This is a Code One. I need armed police at all London emergency clinics." He paused for dramatic effect before saying, "The Time Keepers are here."

The gloating smile faded from his face.

"*Catering*? When did the number change? Why wasn't I told? Well what is the Met liaison number? Do you not have a bloody directory there? I said *Thickett*. How dare –"

"There's an internal telephone directory here, Mr Thicky," said the nurse. "Would you like me to dial a number for you?"

Thickett snatched the directory from the nurse. "No. Thank you." He flipped the pages, muttering madly, found what he wanted and then jabbed at the telephone deliberately whilst glowering at the nurse. "It's Thickett," he said. "Remember that name, because you'll be hearing a lot more of it. Oh, yes." He puffed himself back up to his full height again and cleared his throat.

"Is that Metropolitan Police liaison? Good. My name is Thickett. No, *Thickett*. T-H-I-C-K-E-T-T. Yes. Head of Sixteen. What do you…? Military Intelligence, Section Six*teen*. Yes there *is*, and I'm head of it. No, it *wasn't* disbanded. Peterson? Yes, she's one of mine. Yes, the only one as it happens. Very memorable face, so I'm told, but I can't say I've noticed myself. I'm sure she'll be glad to hear that, and I'll be sure to tell her. Look, this is an *emergency*." Thickett snapped and screamed down the phone: "This is a Code One. Officers down at MI6. Yes, *Six*. I know I said Sixteen, but they were helping us. As previously stated, there are only bloody two of us, you fool! Officers down and kidnapped. I want Met Police officers at every emergency clinic in the Greater London area. Expect casualties. No. No, no they're not going to be attacked. Expect casualties to be *delivered*. No, by the *kidnappers*. Do it. *Now*. Thank you." He slammed down the phone, exhausted.

"Oh, is that Doctor Peterson you were talking about?" said the nurse. "Such a lovely person. I didn't realise Sixteen still existed."

"No," said Thickett. "Apparently you're not the only one."

Chapter Sixteen

Jackson's body appeared, hovering on the silver tray between the two bots, with the med-bot at his side holding a drip. His Noddy suit had gone, and he was dressed in the civilian clothes he'd been wearing underneath, all of which were freshly laundered. Except that he wasn't wearing any trousers or shoes – from the waist down he was in underpants and socks only, showing the fresh red amputation scar on his left leg.

His trousers were neatly folded on his chest, with a drip resting on top. The left leg happened to be uppermost, and a fine layer of stitching was visible just below the knee. The bots laid the body on the floor and withdrew. The med-bot directed its communicator at the Doctor.

More conspicuous to Kevin than the man's state of partial undress was that the face had a week's worth of stubble on it. "Like, what happened?" said Kevin. "Does this accelerated healing therapy cause rapid ageing, or something?"

The Doctor coughed awkwardly. "Well, I *said* 'accelerated healing therapy' but what I really did was to have him go round the houses a bit."

"What do you mean, 'go round the houses'?"

"So here we all are at this point in space and time, right?"

"Yeah."

"So I sent him on a rather circuitous journey."

"I'm not sure I follow, Doc."

"This sort of thing will be second nature once you get your Ph.D. Basically, I sent him on a long journey. Time-wise long, rather than length-wise. He's had a week of just lying there recuperating, which is why he's not in his NBC suit. You can't leave a man for a week in one of those things. I shudder at the thought of the hygiene problems."

"What about this other geezer?" Kevin pointed at Smith's body.

"Didn't need it. Nothing much wrong with him. Hopalong's been given a subcutaneous slow-release healing agent capsule to last him the next couple of days. A bit naughty to leave something that advanced in there without supervision, but if they pick it up on an MRI they won't want to take it out until the rest of the leg's fully healed, by which time it'll have dissolved. The doctors should be left wondering if it was just a blip."

"Man, the NHS needs some of this kit."

"Looks like we're all done," said the Doctor, as the med-bot attending to Jackson withdrew the last of its probes and hovered expectantly above the body. "Print care instructions. Homo sapiens, early 21st century, United Kingdom. Oh, pre-collapse."

"Pre-*what*?" asked Kevin.

"Pre-collapse."

"What are you talking about?"

"Just giving the med-bot a context for the care of our friend here. It'll look at the care regime available at that particular time and then advise medical personnel on how best to care for the patient within the parameters of the drugs and treatment regimens available at that time. I mean, if we'd just helped a knight from the mediaeval period there'd be no use us giving care instructions that involved penicillin or paracetamol, would there? The best anti-septic for the wound would be honey, and the best painkiller and blood-thinner would be bark from the willow tree, which contains aspirin. With me?"

"You said early 21st century, pre-collapse."

"Yes."

"But what about –"

"Don't worry about it."

"But –"

"Smile, it might never happen. I thought you were an optimist? Let's just get on with the job in hand and not worry about the future, shall we?"

"But your whole job is to look after the future, isn't it?"

"Yes, and I'm telling you to *please* not worry about it right now. Forgive me – I didn't realise you were so sensitive about it."

"Well, when you tell me there's a collapse coming, what am I supposed to think?"

The Doctor looked away from Kevin's earnest eyes and went over to the control panel to make a few adjustments. "First, I didn't tell you there's a collapse coming. I just said pre-collapse." Kevin opened his mouth but the Doctor cut him off. "Just a turn of phrase. If I tell you there's nothing to worry about, then trust me on it. Now, please, time is of the essence." The med-bot held out two printed sheets of paper for the Doctor. He glanced over them, nodded, and handed them back to the bot, which pinned one to each of the two unconscious men.

"Okay," said the Doctor, "let's get ready by the door. You take out the uninjured one first and I'll follow with Hopalong."

"Like, can't we get the bots to lift them out, or something?"

"We *could*, Kevin. However, this little mission is already becoming a little *too* overt for my liking. We'll have the cloaking on of course, but it's far easier to bamboozle people with the ordinariness of two men with a body each."

"I'll have to take your word for that, Doc."

"Come on, then."

A three-dimensional projection of a busy emergency department appeared, with the planned position of the Spectrel's appearance. Kevin eyed it. Something nagged at his brain.

Kevin and the Doctor put their hands under the armpits of their respective patients. "One, two, three –" said the Doctor.

"But Doctor, that's –"

"Go!" yelled the Doctor.

Kevin lifted Smith and dragged him backwards. In a second he was dragging Smith out of the Spectrel and into the waiting area of the emergency department. Learning from his previous mistakes, he continued to drag the body away from the Spectrel. He saw the Doctor appear out of the red telephone box with Jackson, bumped into someone behind him and fell over. The back of Smith's head banged loudly on the blue linoleum floor.

"What the hell do you think you're doing, young man?" said a deep, stern woman's voice behind him. Kevin felt a strong, irresistible force pulling him to his feet, and a primeval dread in his heart.

"Mum! I can explain everything!"

The Doctor looked back and lowered Jackson's head gently to the floor. The intravenous drip was taped to the man's chest. Now that he looked at Smith and Jackson, he realised what a bizarre sight they made. Smith was in a black Noddy suit with its head cut off, his face was bruised, and he had a drip into a cut-away area of the Noddy suit. Jackson was half-naked with a drip sitting on a pair of trousers.

"I can take full responsibility," said the Doctor, standing.

Mrs Thomson's nurse's training took over. "Doctor!" she yelled. "My God, what have you done to this man?"

"He saved his leg, Mum. It was, like, amputated."

"You're filling his head full of nonsense again, Doctor. I said *doctor!*"

"Yes, alright, alright, Mrs Thomson, I'm here."

"No, I'm calling for a *hospital* doctor, you silly man. Doctor! Charge nurse!"

"Look, I've left care instructions pinned to their chests. This one's just had a bit of a bad tumble. The other's had his leg reattached."

"*Reattached?*" Mrs Thomson's attention snapped from the Doctor's face to a point a few feet behind him. "And what the hell do *you* people want?"

The Doctor turned to see three Metropolitan Police officers jogging across the room towards them. They impacted with a doctor and two nurses running out of the treatment area.

"Well, lovely to see you, Mrs Thomson," said the Doctor, backing towards the Spectrel. "Kevin and I must be going. I've got an urgent house call to make. Kevin's doing very well, by the way. Come on, lad!" The Doctor disappeared into the Spectrel.

The police and medical staff disentangled themselves. The charge nurse shouted some comments at the officers whilst the doctor examined Jackson's leg and the other nurse made sure Smith's airways were clear.

"Like, I gotta go, Mum," said Kevin, and took a determined step towards the Spectrel, which the Doctor was entering.

"Don't you *dare* walk away from your mother whilst she's speaking," said his mother. Referring to herself in the third person touched Kevin's fear nerve on a deeper level than it had been when the giant beetle had broken through concrete inches from his head.

"Mum, it's urgent. I've got responsibilities."

"You've got responsibilities? Are you responsible for what happened to these men?"

The largest of the police officers grabbed Kevin and turned him to face the wall. A second was calling in backup and a policewoman closed in on Mrs Thomson, separating her from her son.

"Is he the Doctor?" asked the policewoman.

"No, the doctor's down there helping the patient," said Mrs Thomson. "I'm a nurse, I have to help too."

"We're looking for two men. One of them fits this man's description. I take it he's your son. Is he the Doctor's assistant?"

Kevin was still facing the wall. The large officer had put on blue latex gloves and was searching his pockets. His familiarity with the routine allowed him to relax – at least he was safe from his mother's questioning.

"Yes, yes, he's been assisting the Doctor. Now, let him go. He did a very good thing by bringing in two injured men."

"Madam, we were at the entrance to the building and we didn't see them come in. We don't know how he got these men in on his own. He must have several accomplices. Right now, I'd say that you look like you're under suspicion."

"What the hell is wrong with a man bringing injured people into an accident and emergency department? Are you out of your mind?"

"We were told to be on alert for two men delivering injured men who had been kidnapped. My colleague's just had confirmation that they were wearing nuclear, biological and chemical suits."

"They're here and they're alive, officer."

"Yes, but they were kidnapped."

"Well, they don't seem to be kidnapped right now, do they?"

The doctor had finished her initial examination of both men, and each was being lifted onto a gurney. "Excuse me, officer," she said. "I need nurse Thomson to attend to some patients, if you don't mind."

"How are they, doctor?" asked Mrs Thomson.

"Astonishingly well, if what's on the notes is correct. If this was April the first I'm not sure what I'd be thinking. The one with the leg injury's just heading up to MRI. We'll know more after that. But it looks like someone's quick intervention saved that man's leg. Do you have a problem with that, officer?"

"We just need some questions answered," said the officer. "Like how they got here. And where the other man is who helped this one. We're looking for a white male in his forties. Slim, smartly dressed."

"So am I," said the doctor. "Heck, if he's got money and a good sense of humour, I'll even pay you a commission. Now, why don't you just leave my staff and their relations out of this. Kevin's a good lad, and I can vouch for him. He was just in here to see his mother."

"We had a description of two men. One just as I've described and the other a black male matching his description," the officer nodded over at Kevin, who now had his back to the wall. He smiled over at the doctor.

"And you couldn't find the matching white male so you just grab the nearest black guy next to the two patients. Marvellous."

"But he matches the description."

"As do a significant number of other males in this room," said the doctor, gesturing towards the silent sea of waiting patients, whose eyes were glued to the conversation. "You chose the one guy who'd stepped up to help the casualties. And his reward is that he's humiliated publicly in front of his peers. I can't say I'm that impressed." She stared coldly at the officer.

"We've got his details if we need to question him further," said the policewoman to her large colleague, who let him go. Kevin picked up the contents of his pockets from a nearby table.

"Thanks again, Kevin," said the doctor, and glanced back pointedly at the policewoman before putting a hand on Mrs Thomson's shoulder and leading her into the treatment area.

"Thanks, doctor. Laters, Mum. Alright?" He gave a half-wave to his mother. "Look, I'll just be making my way back home, alright?" he said to the large officer. The man didn't move out of the way, and Kevin had to step around him. The officers followed him through the crowded rows of silent, seated people waiting for treatment. The doors slid open in front of him and he exited into the cool air of Denmark Hill. The officers followed him out and stopped at the top of the stone steps. Kevin skipped lightly down them and turned.

"So, like, I'll see you round, yeah?" he said. "Good luck with… whatever. You know?" He glanced around. He'd not normally be able to afford the train, but the Oyster card the Doctor had given him meant he could upgrade from the 45 bus. The train was almost risk-free because gangs from other postcodes couldn't monitor the passengers the way they could with buses. The adventure with the Doctor was clearly over – at least for now. He felt conflicting pangs of relief and regret that he'd not be joining the Time Keeper in the trip to the lair under Essex.

There was the sound of police sirens closing in from two directions and he saw a carrier touch its brakes as it ran the lights at the crossroads near the station before roaring in through the gates to the emergency ward. Kevin stood rooted to the spot. Two police cars raced up the hill from Camberwell and parked on the double yellow lines outside. Officers from the carrier jumped out. He flinched as they ran past him. Five other officers, two armed, got out of the cars and moved more cautiously towards the other police.

Kevin felt eyes boring into his back, but as he turned to go towards the train station he glanced back one last time to make sure the officers weren't following him. Sure enough, thirteen pairs of eyes were staring at him.

Next to the entrance to the A&E department was a red telephone box. He couldn't recall there having been one there before. Even in the daylight it seemed to glow from within. He stopped and turned around fully. The police continued to stare at him.

Sorry," he said. "I need to phone a friend." They continued to stare at him as he closed the fifteen yards towards the box. Two of the original officers pointed and made comments that he couldn't hear. He smiled back sheepishly. "Just going to… Mobile's out of juice, you see?"

His heart was pounding as he opened the door and stepped in. He took a deep breath and took a confident step towards the back of the box.

He found himself inside the cool white space of the Spectrel.

"Ah, there you are, Kevin. Glad you could make it." The Doctor fiddled with some dials.

A wave of relief washed over Kevin, followed immediately by one of anger. "You just left me out there to dry, man! Like, thanks a *lot!*"

"I did the best I could, dear fellow."

"No you didn't!"

"Shush. Let me explain. I couldn't just start messing with people's memories inside a hospital, could I? There are sick people being treated. If I'd done that, I'd have had to take over their treatment myself or they'd have suffered the consequences. As it is, the cops will barely recall a thing. Your mum and that doctor aren't going to create a stink."

"But you –"

"If you're a bit more invisible to a trio of Her Majesty's

Constabulary in the future, is that going to be a handicap?"

"Um…"

"No. Didn't think so. Now, I've just got to get Trini."

"What, we're at home now?"

"I didn't realise you'd moved in."

The Doctor brushed past him and left the Spectrel for a couple of seconds. When he stepped back in he was followed by Trinity in her cat form. She made a beeline for Kevin's legs, and rubbed up against them, purring. He bent down and stroked her head.

"Trinity, darling," said the Doctor. "I think you might want to go and change."

The cat broke away from Kevin and disappeared through the door into the Spectrel beyond the cabin.

"Does she, like, not change in public?"

"Have you ever known a classy female who would?"

"No, but I assumed…"

"You really don't want to see her change, Kevin. Really." The Doctor sat at the control panel and made some adjustments.

Trinity popped back silently into the room in her spider format. Her two main glowing green eyes were the same as they had been in her cat form, but the six surrounding them – and her spider form – still spooked Kevin. He tensed as she crawled soundlessly towards him. She put her two front feet up onto his stomach, and two on the legs of his trousers. He could feel the weight of her as she stared up at him, her mandibles about level with his groin. He reached down and put a hand on her head. The fur felt the same as it did in her cat form, but the surface underneath was not skin – it was a hard shell, rather like the cuticle of the oversized beetle. He stroked Trini's head, and found it helped overcome his discomfort.

"Trini, I don't suppose you've seen any giant beetles in your travels?" said Kevin.

"She's never mentioned any," said the Doctor. "Mind you, doesn't mean to say she hasn't. Unlikely, though. Trini comes from a jungle environment."

"Jungle? Really? I'd have thought rocks. Or maybe desert or something."

"No, you need jungle to support something like her. Hugely productive, jungle, in terms of edible biomass. Sort of the terrestrial equivalent of a coral reef."

"I imagine her jaws must have come in useful for chopping off the occasional branch, eh?"

"Unlikely. More like cutting through the hard outer casing of some prey."

"So do you think –"

"She'd be any use against the beetles? Don't know. Aside from that, they're oil-based. How do you like the taste of petroleum products?"

"I don't."

"Same for Trini. Eats the same sort of things as you, finds the same sorts of things distasteful. Haven't tried her on Jamaican patties, though. Besides, she much prefers her food raw."

A 3D projection popped into being in front of the control panel. "Right, both of you, eyes front. All eight please, Trinity."

"Not very good, is it?"

"I'm so sorry that it's not to your apparently sudden very high standards, Kevin. Spectacularly high, given that you come from a society which believes a three-in-one dishwasher tablet that leaves glass clean is a technological breakthrough. What next for your scientists? Paint that dries? As previously explained, we can only go on the data from the hack. There's also interference."

Kevin rolled his eyes. "So, like, we have no data at all?"

"Nope."

"We're just going in blind? We could be ambushed, or

anything!"

"Absolutely right. Well spotted. You're in exactly the same position as your forebears who died fighting for your country."

"Like, could you not emphasise the *died* bit? Maybe if you said *fought*."

"Sorry, not selling this very well, am I? Perhaps if I told you it came with an added revolutionary teeth-whitening agent?"

"Can you just be straight with me, Doc? Like, what's the plan?"

"Well…"

"You mean you don't even have a plan? Jeez-Louise! Even those numbskulls in the Tulse Hill Crew always have a plan, man!"

"Aha, but they always end up in prison. Eventually."

"Oh. Right. I think the consequences of an epic fail here are a bit worse, Doc. Like, what's your objective?"

"Thank you for asking, Kevin," sighed the Doctor. "First, it's intelligence. I want to know who they are and their intentions. Second, I want to destroy or disrupt if I deem it necessary."

"Good. Now tell me how you intend to do that."

"Since I can't hack into their systems from here – and frankly I don't want to run the risk of a cyber-attack on my Spectrel either – I need to get in there with the old Tsk Army Ultraknife and see what they're up to."

Kevin nodded his head slowly. "Riiight. And I'm guessing me and Trini are going to keep these guys occupied whilst you do that?"

The Doctor brightened. "Excellent," he said. "So much better when people volunteer, rather than me having to bark orders at them."

"Trini, is he always this bad at delegating?"

The spider dipped her head twice.

"So you've got your Ultraknife and Trini's got her natural fighting ability. What do I get?"

"You've already got it, Kevin: your very own wit and guile. You did tremendously well in this morning's little scrape. You'll be fine. Really. And Trini will look after your back. Won't you Trini?"

Trini hesitated, then her head bobbed up and down as she hissed.

"If it's okay with you, I'd prefer, like, a blaster or something."

"A *blaster*?"

"Well, yeah. You know, a laser, or maybe a plasma weapon of some sort. Failing that, I'd settle for a Glock like the Met use."

"The thing is, Kevin, is that these beetles do have a tendency to explode, as demonstrated earlier."

"I don't want to shoot at the beetles. I want to shoot at the bad guys."

"Look, shooting at people is generally a really, really bad idea."

"Yeah? Why?"

"They tend to shoot back." Kevin opened his mouth but the Doctor was losing his patience and cut him off with a wave. "You will be wearing some protective gear, though." A bot came out of the door that led into the rest of the Spectrel. Hanging underneath were a helmet, goggles, a balaclava, boots, a two-piece suit and some gloves.

"Oh, cool, man!" Kevin had no qualms about changing in front of his companions. The top garment slipped over his head and had a roll-neck that went to his chin. He'd been expecting something thick and cushioned, but remembered what the Doctor had said about the properties of his own ordinary-looking suit and shirt, and realised that technology would have moved on. Although it clung tightly to him, it didn't restrict his movements. Indeed, it seemed to enhance them in a way he couldn't quite understand. The trousers were of the same material. The boots weighed much less than he'd thought, and their fit and grip were unlike anything he'd experienced. When he put the balaclava on he'd expected to find his breath restricted and to feel the moisture of his own breath, but the restriction was minimal. The helmet adjusted its internal dimensions to fit his head perfectly, and when he put on the goggles it didn't seem like he was wearing them at all. The bot picked up his discarded clothes and hovered out of the room.

"You'll still be able to smell things through the face-mask, but it won't let anything through in toxic quantities. Just don't get over-confident in that kit. It'll protect you against a multitude of things, including poisoned gas, vacuum and fire – but stupidity isn't one of them. And, before you ask, the answer is no – you're not allowed to keep it. Restricted technology. Only for use on missions authorised by me."

"Well, I might just tiptoe out wearing it."

"And you wonder why I didn't issue you with it this morning?"

"My God, you never did. I could've been killed!"

"This morning wasn't supposed to be dangerous. Besides, you handled yourself perfectly well."

"I tell you, you're not going to get me out of this clobber in a hurry. I'm wearing this when I go back to the Hill, man, and you ain't stopping me."

The Doctor chuckled. "I think you'll find the 'clobber' has a will of its own."

"You what?" He felt a sudden restriction in his groin area. "Nuff said. I get the message."

The bot returned with a thick black rod dangling under it and hovered to a stop next to Kevin. "What's this? Looks like a slimmed down baseball bat."

"Grab it by the handle and swing it around a bit."

Kevin took the rod in his gloved hand and swung it. "Oh, *wow*. I can't tell you what this feels like. I feel like I could knock a home run on every ball!"

"That's not strictly true, because the ball would disintegrate with the force you're able to exert."

"Oh, *baby*," said Kevin, and swung the bat around some more. "It's like that scene in *Star Wars* when they're in the *Millennium Falcon* and Luke Skywalker's using the force to block the shots from the training globe."

"No it's not, and kindly don't swing that thing in here. It does have friend-or-foe recognition, but you're making the Spectrel nervous. And me."

"What is it?"

"A Tsk Army Con-Bat."

"Combat?"

"No, Con-Bat. Con, as in against. Bat, as in bat. *For those situations requiring a special kind of force*, was how the advertising went."

"These Tsk people are *fierce*."

"I'll say. Now throwing spears at each other back on their home planet."

"You *what*?" Kevin stopped swinging the Con-Bat.

"Quite literally bombed themselves back to the stone age."

"But –"

"Civilisations rise and fall. Some more easily and frequently than others."

"How did you get it?"

The Doctor shrugged. "Visited them at the end of their second civilisation, of course."

"It feels like my body is like, *superpowered*, or something, Doc." Kevin was moving around the cabin of the Spectrel.

"That's the suit. It's power-assist, rather than just passive. I did warn you not to get too confident in it because you might –"

Kevin jumped, hit the ceiling and fell back to the floor.

"– do something stupid."

"It's actually pretty good at cushioning impacts, isn't it?"

"Don't push it too far, lad. Now, we've been delayed long enough. This whole installation is about twelve thousand feet below the surface. We're going to enter here," the Doctor put a finger into the projection, "which I think is the main computer network room. It's separated from a much larger room by a wall on one side. I don't know what the larger room is."

"Umm, that looks like a dead-end, Doc."

"That's right. Just the one exit – or entrance – so far as I can see. Easier to guard."

"I don't much fancy the idea of being caught in a dead end. You hear what I'm saying?"

"I share your concern, Kevin."

"But at least we'll be able to get out in the Spectrel."

"The Spectrel will disengage immediately and await further instructions."

"You've got to be kidding me!"

"They've already hacked into David's Spectrel. We can't risk mine."

"You're out of your mind, Doc."

"Not at all. She'll be waiting for us."

"And the signal is?"

"There's no signal. She'll just know."

"Man, this *sucks*."

"Well, if you want out, Kevin…?"

"No chance. It might suck, but reality sucks even more. Let's do this thing!"

Chapter Seventeen

"I'll go left two yards," said the Doctor. "Kevin, you go right two yards." He took the Ultraknife from his pocket. Kevin gripped his Tsk Army Con-Bat.

"On my count," said the Doctor. "Three, two, one. Go!"

The Doctor ran at the exit, followed by Trinity. Kevin launched himself at the door and jumped to the right. He found himself in a dimly lit grey room about twenty feet wide and ten deep. Out of the corner of his eye, he saw the Spectrel wink out of existence. As his eyes adjusted, he realised that the only light was coming from the rows of panels that covered the opposite wall. Little chinks of light escaped into the room from the gaps between the panels. The Doctor was twelve feet away to his left. He couldn't see Trinity.

"Doc," he whispered. "Where's Trini?"

The Doctor pointed upwards. Kevin followed his finger. Trinity was upside down on the ceiling, crouched like a spring. He waved at her and one of her green eyes winked. He'd not seen her do that before and couldn't remember having seen eyelids on her. The thought was a distracting one and he glanced back up. Trini had disappeared. A green eye blinked open and shut – *or was it on and off?* he wondered – from a point a foot below the ceiling, and he was able just to discern the outline of her features. As with the winking, he'd been unaware of her ability to blend in like a chameleon. Then he noticed that he couldn't see his own arms and hands – or the Tsk Army Con-Bat which he could still feel in his right hand. He waved it and it became partly visible again. He waved it around some more.

He heard a *psst* to his left and became aware of the Doctor waving at him furiously from behind a counter. He tiptoed over to join him.

"What the hell are you doing, you clown?" hissed the Doctor.

"Just following your instructions," he whispered back.

"I didn't tell you to stand around like an idiot waving your bat."

"Chill, man. No harm done." A hard stare told Kevin he might be wrong. "Sorry, Doc."

"This looks like the processing centre," said the Doctor, holding his Ultraknife out towards the wall of panels. "Superfast quantum computing. And lots of it. The really big room is on the other side of those processors."

"Why's it here?"

"Because they need it, of course."

"What for?"

"Hack into Spectrels for one thing. I don't like the look of this one bit. And this sort of thing really isn't allowed on Earth."

"What do you mean?"

"What the hell do you think I mean? It's not allowed. Same thing as you're only allowed to wear that kit on my say-so. A long way ahead of where your people are now. Restricted technology."

"Gotcha. So how did it get here?"

"Behind my back. And I'm not happy. This has to be removed or destroyed, that's for sure."

"Just give me the order and I'll get stuck in, Boss."

"Not so hasty. First I want to raid it for data. This thing we're hiding behind seems to be the interface."

"Where are the bad guys?"

The Doctor shrugged and rose slowly to his feet. Kevin

did the same. They looked around the room again. "Keep an eye on that door," said the Doctor, indicating the single door into the rest of the complex. "I'm going to figure out a way in."

"Gotcha."

"Where are you off to?"

"I'm off to guard the door, innit? Not much use if I'm over here. Basic, man. Didn't you ever play *Black Ops*?"

"Some of us are too busy dealing with harsh realities to engage in fantasy."

Kevin rolled his eyes and walked towards the door. He glanced upwards but could see no sign of Trini.

The door itself was a disappointment to him. He'd wanted one of the sphincter variety that closed towards the centre, like he'd seen in sci-fi movies. What he was faced with was a solid metal sliding door with a mundane-looking control panel on the right side at his chest height. The door was about the same width as a domestic door but slightly taller. He imagined that might be to accommodate a species taller than humans, and made a mental note to ask the Doctor whether he was allowed to see any documentaries on alien species. Above all, he was curious to know whether the descriptions of aliens on obscure websites bore any relation to reality. He stood with his back to the wall on the opposite side of the door to the control panel. That way, he'd get a good forearm swing at whoever – or whatever – came in.

He looked over at the Doctor, who was busying himself in the gloom with his Ultraknife. A green glow suddenly lit his face from the top of the counter, giving his face a ghoulish, shadowy appearance. He looked pleased as he concentrated on whatever it was in front of him. The light on his face flickered slightly as the data changed. After a couple of minutes he looked satisfied. He left his Ultraknife on the counter and walked over to Kevin.

"What's the deal?" whispered Kevin. "Who is it?"

"No idea," whispered the Doctor. "But I've set up a transdimensional data link back through the Ultraknife to the Spectrel. That avoids the jamming that a normal data feed would suffer. Sucking up a huge amount of data. The Spectrel will analyse it and we'll see what we have."

"There's another way to find out, you know."

"Such as?"

"Open this door and take a look."

"Let me ask you a hypothetical question."

"Shoot, Doc."

"Suppose you were in a bank vault. No, let's make it easier for you to relate to. Let's say you were burgling your local computer shop and you'd got right to the most valuable stuff. You were just about to go back the way you came and get away with it."

"Right."

"Would you want to go and open a door that would set an alarm off?"

"Um, right. I get your point."

"Good. Well, if you just stay there and leave this in my hands, we'll be out before you know it." The Doctor walked over to the wall of panels and took in the expanse of it. He put his hand on the back of one of the half-metre square blocks and leaned in to look at one of the chinks of light. Keeping his focus on the chink of light, he reached into his pocket, took out a thin screwdriver and inserted it into the crack.

Kevin felt his grip tense on his Con-Bat and looked nervously around the room. He still couldn't see Trini.

The Doctor drew the screwdriver along the crack and seemed to connect with something. He fiddled with the screwdriver and then shook his head. He fiddled again and then stopped. There was a tiny rattling noise, like the proverbial pin dropping, over and over again. *Rrrat-tat.*

Rrrat-tat. Rrrat-tat.

Kevin stopped breathing, feeling his heart thumping in his chest. Whatever it was – a dislodged screw, Kevin imagined – rattled its way slowly down the column of panels before ending its journey with a final *tat*.

The Doctor looked back at the green glow around the counter. It continued to shimmer as data surged through the connection to the Spectrel. He glanced round at Kevin and shrugged.

Kevin breathed again and stood easy, shaking some life back into his tense legs.

The Doctor continued his exploration of the panels with the screwdriver, this time higher, and towards Kevin's end of the room. He reached another point of interest and fiddled again, then stopped, attentive. He fiddled again and there was another faint rattle. *Rrrat-tat. Rrrat-tat. Rrrat-tat. Rrrat-tat.*

Kevin followed the Doctor's gaze back to the counter, where the data continued to stream. He felt a pang of nerves and wished the Doctor would stop his explorations. He jiggled his knees and shifted his stance.

The Doctor felt his way over to the end of a row of panels, so that he was now just a few feet from Kevin, in the corner of the room. He took out another screwdriver of the same size and explored around a panel with both of them, ears pressed against the back of it. There was a *ping* and then a *Rrrat-tat. Rrrat-tat. Rrrat-tat.* There hadn't been a *ping* before, and the Doctor glanced over his shoulder to make eye contact with Kevin, who adopted a more alert stance.

There was another *ping* further to the Doctor's left, followed by a *Rrrat-tat. Rrrat-tat.* Then came another *ping*, and another, and another, each followed by its own *Rrrat-tat. Rrrat-tat. Rrrat-tat.* Within five seconds the air was filled with the sound of little *ping* noises and their cascades of *Rrrat-tat. Rrrat-tat. Rrrat-tat. Rrrat-tat.*

Kevin knew the noise was faint, but to his heightened senses it sounded like dried peas raining on a snare drum. The Doctor tiptoed back towards him.

"What the hell are you doing?" hissed Kevin.

"I just wanted to see if I could get a couple of sample components out and identify the manufacturer."

"Jesus, Doc. You're scaring me witless, man. Like, what components?"

"No idea. Couldn't really see."

"Lost without your bleedin' Ultraknife, ain't ya?"

"Relax. Listen."

The components stopped raining down inside the processing bank and silence returned to the room. The Doctor smiled.

Kevin loosened his stance again. "Man, you'll be the death of me. How much longer's left on the download, d'you reckon?"

"A couple more minutes and we should be done. Then we can get back in the Spectrel, analyse the data and then clear this mess up. We'll be back in time for tea."

Crash!

A panel shattered against the floor, sending pieces skittering everywhere. The echo reverberated and died down.

Bright light shone through a gap at the top of the wall where the panel had been. Kevin and the Doctor froze as the neighbouring panels moved perceptibly out of position, then back.

The Doctor relaxed again. "It's okay," he said.

A split second later, the entire edifice of panels cascaded to the floor; an endless, deafening crashing and shattering – like a truckload of beer bottles overturning.

Kevin instinctively flinched and covered his eyes as pieces flew towards him. He felt them hit his protective gear ineffectually and reminded himself he was safe. He crouched, grasping the Con-Bat in both hands and looked up. The wall had gone. It had been entirely made of the panels, which he now realised had formed the back of a gigantic display system for what was clearly the real control room, which was several times the size of the room they'd entered in the Spectrel. He could see movement.

"Oh, *drat*," said the Doctor.

Kevin shot him a toxic look. "*I'm* the clown?"

The Doctor ran back to the counter, slipped on a piece of debris, slammed into the opposite wall and cried out in pain as he fell to the floor.

There was confusion in the larger room, Kevin could tell that much. Several tall beings – two arms and two legs – in white suits with opaque spheres where the head of a human would be. Several small metal boxes – bots of some kind, he guessed – rushed towards the area where the display had been. Four looked like they were converging on the Doctor and one towards him. Fighting his fear, he stood stock-still as the metal box bore down on him, trusting that he'd be difficult to see or sense if he didn't move.

A rasping, guttural sound boomed around the room, which seemed to command the beings to head towards the rear of the room, where a door slid open.

"They're evacuating!" said the Doctor.

The box slowed down as it made its final approach at head-height, and two cable-like arms emerged from the side. When it was just four feet away Kevin stepped forward and swung the Con-Bat. He felt his suit speed his body through the range of motion and refine his aim. The Con-Bat itself seemed to accelerate of its own accord. As the ends of the cables reached out to grasp Kevin, his Con-Bat slammed down onto the top of the bot, bashing the centre of it to half the height and sending it smashing to the floor. It was the most strangely satisfying physical movement Kevin had ever made, and he felt elated and pumped full of confidence. The rearmost of the bots broke off its approach to the Doctor and veered towards him instead.

The Doctor had got up onto his knees and was reaching for his Ultraknife. A bot looped a metal cable around his wrist and pulled it away from the Ultraknife. A second cable grabbed the Doctor's other wrist, and a third looped around his neck.

The bot bounced in the air and the cables were severed in quick succession. The Doctor shook them off and they fell limply to the floor. The bot spun in confusion, showering sparks. "Thanks, Trini!" he said. The bot behind it paused for a second in mid-air. It had two cables reaching forward, which hesitated for a second, then went limp as the bot was crushed by an unseen force. It fell to the floor.

Kevin jumped several feet through the air and met the rearmost bot with a blow that nearly cut it in half. It flew as gracefully as the piece of scrap metal that it had become and hit a counter similar to the one the Doctor had been using. Kevin saw a few sparks fly from the counter as he landed back on his feet and moved towards the remaining bot, which backed off and seemed to consider its options.

"Ah, download finished!" said the Doctor. He grabbed his Ultraknife and pointed it at the last bot. It remained hovering in the air. "There," said the Doctor, and put the Ultraknife back in the inside breast pocket of his jacket. Trinity reappeared as her usual black-furred self, next to the bot that she'd crushed.

"Let me take care of it," said Kevin.

"Leave it, Kevin."

"But you haven't finished it off."

"Good enough," said the Doctor. The bot floated uselessly in the air. "Components. Wouldn't mind taking a look."

"Yeah, suppose."

"They wanted us alive, that's for sure. A Time Keeper or a Spectrel is still their ultimate prize."

"Well, if you've got what you want, there's no sense in us staying here any longer. Call your Spectrel and let's get the hell out of here."

"Not so hasty. I want to have a look around and try to figure some of this out for myself."

"So you've, like, still no idea who this might be?"

"Could be anyone."

"They looked pretty distinctive to me."

"Oh really, Kevin? Describe them."

"Well, uh. Tall and slim. Two arms, two legs. Heads, obviously. Difficult to say much else coz they was wearing spacesuits."

"Okay."

"But you must know who that is, surely?"

The Doctor shrugged. "Could be anyone. For all I know it might have been a team of basketball players from your description. Do you think I should go and arrest the Harlem Globetrotters on suspicion?"

"No."

"Oh really? And why not?"

"There wasn't a funny short one."

"Very droll, Kevin."

"I mean, come on, Doc. That must narrow it down."

"I'm afraid not. It's a big place, the universe," said the Doctor. "You might suppose from that description that they're from a low-gravity home planet. But then they might have spent aeons living in a low-G environment after leaving their home planet. Or they might have decided to engineer themselves those kinds of bodies."

"What about the language? Did you understand that?"

"Of course, but it was a lingua franca."

"A what?"

"A language that everyone understands. Like Latin used

to be for science."

"What about the accent?"

The Doctor laughed and put an arm around his companion's shoulder. "A while from now you're going to be savvy to all this, and you'll laugh at your naivety. Anyway, great fight Kevin – you're taking to this like a pro."

"Like, the suit and the Con-Bat, man. They're just *wild*."

"So long as you realise that it's them and not you who have the superpowers, you'll be alright. Don't go trying to be a hero without them or you'll get yourself killed. Someone very close to me began to believe it was himself who was the super-being. He lost his sense of perspective and his ego ran out of control. Then…" The Doctor shook his head.

"Are you talking about, you-know-who?"

"Some other time." The Doctor took his arm from around Kevin's shoulder and walked off down the rows of counters. "Now, let's wrap this mission up. Something doesn't seem quite right here, but I can't figure out what it is."

"To be honest, Doc, that seemed a little bit too easy."

"Yes, I'd figured that bit out, but what I don't know is *why*." The Doctor tapped the top of one of the counters with his Ultraknife, and a 3D display flicked into life. It was showing fuzzy static.

"In all the *Bond* movies and things like that, the baddies always destroy the evidence behind them, innit? To be honest, it wasn't much of a fight, and they've left all this kit lying around. I can bash it with the Con-Bat, if you like. I need the practice."

"Oh, don't worry about that," said the Doctor. "The whole place is going to blow up in about T-minus four minutes."

"You freakin' *what*?"

"There's a counter over there on the wall." The Doctor kept his attention on the counter in front of him and motioned disinterestedly at the far right corner of the room, where a blue display showed a rapidly-changing sequence of characters.

"Christ! This is like the last scene in *Predator*, where Arnie's gonna get blown up by the alien!"

"Sorry," said the Doctor, concentrating on the counter. "Didn't see it."

"I can't bleedin' read it, Doc! That's what I'm saying!"

"Of course you can't, it's in Squill. That's the lingua franca I was talking about."

"If it's going to blow, then let's get outta here!"

"Relax, lad. As I said, we've got about four minutes. Plenty of time for the Spectrel to pick us up."

"You said 'about four minutes' ten seconds ago!"

"Oh, they're not using sidereal time so I'm just judging an approximation. Let me see…" He glanced up at the blue display. "I'd say we have exactly three minutes and forty-five seconds…*Now*. Happy?"

His fingers trembling, Kevin flipped through the functions on his watch and then clicked on the stopwatch function. "Right, I have to take away about three seconds from whatever's on this. Look, can't we just vacate the area immediately?"

"Do you know, if they didn't manage to capture a Spectrel I think it would serve their purposes quite well to neutralise me. To take me out – by which I mean kill, rather than treat me on a date to a fancy restaurant."

"Doc, will you just *do* something?"

"I *am*, Kevin. I'm trying to work this whole thing out. Frankly, I'm a bit annoyed that the Spectrel's not already been in touch with the answer."

Trinity let out a high-pitched sound.

"What's that, Trini? Oh. That makes sense."

"What? *What?*" screamed Kevin.

"Those big bugs are back. If you were wanting to leave no trace of your activity, you'd want to get rid of them too, wouldn't you?"

"You mean those things are heading here?"

"Now you can understand why they were wearing suits and didn't want their security bots using kinetic or explosive weapons."

"Great. I have to admit I was going to have trouble sleeping tonight if you'd not told me that. Now can we *please* just *leave?* We've got, like, three minutes now."

"You're right, we should go. Never any sense in cutting these things fine. Come on." He motioned Kevin and Trinity back towards the area where they'd entered the complex.

The three of them stood for a couple of seconds. Trinity and Kevin looked expectantly at the Doctor.

"We seem to have a slight difficulty," he said.

"You - freakin' - *what*? Where's the Spectrel?"

"Not entirely sure. Sorry about this, chaps. We might be better advised to use the emergency exit at the other end of the room. That might just lead us out of here."

"Might?!"

There was a massive crunching noise as the wall at the far end caved in. The room shook and fragments of shale rock flew into the rows of counters, causing a few to blow up. Two beetles appeared out of the debris, and Kevin could smell a whiff of something petrochemical through his balaclava.

"Oh dear," said the Doctor. "Looks like the emergency exit's permanently out of action."

The walls on either side split, and the room juddered again. A beetle broke through on each side, their massive antennae waving as they oriented themselves. Then the middle of the ceiling gave way and a fifth beetle crashed through onto the counters, one of which fizzed and crackled as it short-circuited. The beetle began to flail and let out a screech as a flame took hold of one of its legs.

"Drat!" yelled the Doctor. He pulled a blue canister off the wall and rushed at the beetle. He pulled a lever on the canister and a cloud of gas blew out of the other end, dousing the fire on the beetle's leg.

"What are you doing, man?" shouted Kevin, swinging his Con-Bat in preparation.

"Oh, don't thank me, Kevin," said the Doctor, running back to join his companions. "If one of those blows then we're done for."

"But we're done for in two minutes anyway!"

"I just added two minutes to your life and you're *complaining?* We'll think of something."

"Well you'd better hurry!"

The beetles that had come through the walls were closing in on them, their metre-long mandibles swishing through the air like black swords.

"What's up with Trini, Doc? She's frozen!"

"Nonsense. She's examining their physiology. I told you all that stuff when you first met her."

Trinity turned grey to match the décor and leapt through the air, landing on the back of the one to their right. She cut through one of its antennae. The creature arched its head back and hissed, but couldn't get to its attacker. She removed the other antenna with a twitch of her mandibles and jumped onto the ceiling as the creature reared up on its four hind legs.

Kevin bounded forwards and swung the Con-Bat at the beast's mouth. It connected with a crunch. He had to leap to the side as the creature dropped back onto six legs and jerked towards him. He jumped six feet into the air as it bore down on him, and dealt it a massive blow to the top of its head. The shiny black cuticle crumpled and a thick black liquid welled out. Kevin landed with one foot on a counter, lost his balance and fell back to the floor. The creature took another couple of steps towards him, mandibles flailing, cutting through consoles. A spark ignited the black liquid on the creature's head-wound and it writhed in agony as oily yellow flames took hold. Kevin scrabbled away on his back. A gob of burning black fluid spattered onto the floor where he'd been lying. The beetle collapsed, dead.

"Are you alright?" yelled the Doctor, who jumped out of the way of an attack by the creature on the left.

"Less than ninety seconds!" shouted Kevin. "Got a plan yet, Doc?"

The Doctor pulled the lever on the blue canister and rushed at the burning beetle, dousing the flames with the inert gas. The jet sputtered and went out, so he threw the empty canister at the mouth of the other beetle. There was an explosion as the canister was pierced, and a fragment bounced off Kevin's goggles. The creature was stunned, but only for a couple of seconds.

"It's no use," said Kevin. "Too many of them for us."

The Doctor pointed his Ultraknife at the beetle which had come through the roof and it arched its head up, its front pair of legs grasping in agony at the air. A second later its head exploded without flames, sending thick black liquid spraying onto the walls and ceiling. The creature slumped, but some of the patches of liquid ignited and burnt with a thick oily flame.

"Double-drat," muttered the Doctor.

"One minute!" said Kevin, and readied himself to take on the creature on the left. The two beetles which had broken through the rear wall were now almost upon them. Trinity jumped onto the head of the beetle on the left but had to jump straight back to the ceiling because one of the creatures behind lunged at her. It was no use; they were penned in.

A black cab appeared ten feet from the ground, to their

228

right. Its amber Taxi light was on. It honked its horn at the beetles.

"Wow! It's –"

"Shh. Stand still," whispered the Doctor. "Let nature take its course."

"But we've only got about forty-five seconds," hissed Kevin, swinging his bat.

The beetles' attention switched to the cab. It glided away from the three companions, keeping its amber sign directed at the creatures, which turned first their heads, then their bodies, to face it. All three lunged lustily for the cab, then fell in a heap as it dodged out of the way.

"Thirty seconds."

"Patience."

"*Patience?*"

The beetles began fighting amongst themselves – a hissing mound of writhing legs and mandibles. A severed leg flew out of the pile and landed on a pool of burning black liquid.

"Triple-drat."

"Fifteen seconds!"

The Spectrel disappeared from in front of the heap of fighting beetles.

"Aw, Doc! *Now* what? Ten seconds!"

The dismembered leg exploded, sending flaming fragments around the room, streaming oily black smoke behind them. One landed on the crushed head of the beetle Kevin had slain and it burst into flames again.

"Drat squared."

The Spectrel appeared beside them, and the rear left passenger door opened.

"Five seconds!"

"Shut up and jump in!"

Something spider-shaped flashed past Kevin and he felt a dab on his chest as it passed him. He looked down and saw a thin thread. Just as it clicked what it was, he felt himself heaved forwards towards the open door. At the same time he felt the Doctor slam into him from behind and his hands grab him around the waist. He landed with a thud on the floor of the cab. The Doctor landed on top of him. There was a massive flash and then it went quiet.

Chapter Eighteen

"How's your head?" asked Peterson, walking into the sick bay, where Thickett had been ordered to stay, under light sedation, for a few hours. She was holding something long and thin, wrapped in a black plastic bag.

"My head is the least of my worries, Miss Peterson," said Thickett. "Where's the Doctor?"

"I'm right here," said the doctor.

"No! Not you!" shouted Thickett.

"He keeps talking about me in a very abstract sense," said the doctor.

"I can see why that might have been a problem," said Peterson. "Too many doctors. It may not sound like it, but he *is* actually making sense."

"Well," said the doctor, "if that makes sense to you, then maybe you need a bit of R and R. Do give me a call when your field work calms down. I know a fabulous Kashmiri restaurant just around the corner. You can have ten minutes with him, then he'll need some more rest."

"Thank you, doctor." The doctor left the room.

"What happened?" asked Thickett. "Did they get the Doctor? What about Smith and Jackson?"

"I think we owe the Doctor a bit of a favour. Smith and Jackson were… dropped off at King's A&E this afternoon. Both of them are fine. Smith's being discharged in an hour. Neither he nor Jackson remember anything after Doctor How's Spectrel arrived. They're keeping Jackson in – for how long I don't know. The Doctor did an amazing job on his leg, and they reckon he should make a full recovery. Something else they can't quite explain is that he was out of his Noddy suit, there was no trace of blood on his clothes and he had a week's worth of stubble on his face."

"*Time travel,*" gasped Thickett. "That's how he healed him so quickly. Don't you see?"

"Forget that," chuckled Peterson. "Everyone wants to know what brand of detergent got those bloodstains out."

Thickett spluttered. "Did they nab them?"

"The attending police were a bit hazy, apparently. They did a stop-and-search on one suspect but they aren't clear how our guys got into A&E. Shall I let Jackson know you were asking after him?"

"Stuff Jackson. I wanted the Doctor. He's responsible for all of this. How am I going to explain the damage to Whitehall? How are we going to cover it up? There'll be an enquiry. I'll be crucified!"

"Nothing's going to happen, Mr Thickett. The cover-up is in action. The British Geological Survey is stating that it's related to fracking. And the radar traces from air traffic control were too indistinct. They're being explained by freak echoes from the London Array; you know, the big wind turbines in the Thames Estuary – reflecting off cirrus clouds in the upper atmosphere."

"What? What radar traces?"

"Over Essex. This afternoon. Impossibly fast-moving objects travelling at high speed straight up and out of the atmosphere. Probably a couple of escape pods."

"*What?*"

"Fractional radar traces. No sonic booms, either. Very impressive."

"Well, where did they come from?"

"Rural Essex. Oh, sorry. You don't know. It's not just the tremor under central London we had to explain. There was a much larger one somewhere under Essex late this afternoon. About half an hour after Smith and Jackson were left at King's."

"What the hell happened?"

"The BGS put the depth at about twelve thousand feet. A bit large for a fracking-related tremor, but that's how we're explaining it."

"We need to get a drill down there!"

"Calm down, Mr Thickett. It would take months to get a drill to that depth, and the chances of us hitting anything significant are miniscule. And it would cost millions. I think some things are better left as they are, don't you?"

"Miss Peterson."

"*Doctor* Peterson."

"Our department was formed to capture and make the best use of exactly this kind of advanced technology. We need answers, and we need them *now*."

"Some things are just beyond immediate explanation."

"This isn't going to look good at your performance review, Miss Peterson."

"I did warn you not to bring that Spectrel into the complex, Mr Thickett."

"Damn that Doctor How. I'll nail him and his ilk one day."

"You'll never get him, Mr Thickett. We can never match his technology, and we shouldn't question his motives. Just be grateful he saved the day today."

"He ruined my career! I've got nothing to show for this other than two injured men and millions of pounds worth of damage. *Nothing*."

Dr Peterson smiled. "Not at all." She unwrapped the black polythene bag. There was a whiff of petrol as she produced a section of mandible eighteen inches long. "We've got a souvenir. Something for the trophy cabinet."

Thickett glowered. "A jaw. You've got a bit of the beetle's jaw, Miss Peterson? That's not going to cut it with

Whitehall."

"Oh, really?" said Peterson. She swung the mandible at the metal arm of the bedside chair and it cut through the half-inch chrome piping.

"Lord above," said Thickett.

"Exactly the sort of technology MI16 is supposed to capture."

"Thank God for that. Oh, thank God for that," said Thickett. "You've saved my career. Thank you, Dr Peterson."

"I have a few contacts at my alma mater who will be very interested in this. It would be a massive leap forward if we can analyse the molecular structure and harness the technology."

"Where was your alma mater again?"

"Imperial. They've got an excellent Technology Transfer unit."

"Excellent. I can't wait to see what they make of it. This will be as big in Tech Transfer as graphene."

Dr Peterson smiled and put the mandible back in the bag. She wished him a swift recovery, but hoped he had a longer one.

She thought she understood why her memory of the Doctor and his Spectrel hadn't faded like those of the other witnesses, but didn't know why Thickett's hadn't either. She hoped he wasn't as curious about her lack of memory loss as she was about his.

Chapter Nineteen

Kevin found himself face-down on a grey ribbed floor that smelled like rubber and stale cigarettes. Somebody was lying on top of him.

"Sorry about that," said the Doctor, climbing off him. He took out his handkerchief and brushed a fast-food wrapper off his lapel. "*Yuk*! You have to learn to be a bit quicker, Kevin. Another second and we'd have been roasted like your piri-piri chicken. Although I still say it's supplied frozen and microwaved at the point of sale."

"Jesus, Doc. We nearly got fried like McNuggets and you lecture me about that?" Kevin took off his helmet and goggles, then pulled the balaclava off.

"Humour. Always the best cure for a bit of post-traumatic stress disorder. Best administered immediately afterwards."

"You had, like, no plan, man. We were goners in there."

"I did have a plan, Kevin. The best laid schemes o' mice an' men gang aft agley," said the Doctor in a Scottish accent. "Same goes for Time Keepers occasionally."

"And I ain't in the mood for no Scottish poetry, neither."

"Ah, one day our adventures will teach you a little more about your heritage."

"Hey – this is David's Spectrel. Like, what happened to yours?"

"I'd love to know. But at least David's is on-side, and we should all be grateful to her for that."

Kevin looked around at the Spectrel's interior. "It's,

uh… different to yours."

"As I've explained before, every Spectrel reflects its Time Keeper's character – whether she likes it or not."

"I can't see anyone being happy with this." Kevin surveyed the room. The ribbed rubber floor was strewn with food wrappers and empty drinks cartons. There were sticky dark patches which he took to be dried spillages from carbonated drinks. The walls and ceiling were of grey industrial carpet. The room was square and cramped, with black vinyl seating arranged in three rows of three facing towards the back of a single large seat, which was placed in front of a control panel.

"Depressing and functional," said the Doctor. "He was always low on aesthetics."

"I'm off to explore the rest of the… ship," said Kevin.

The Doctor put a hand on his shoulder. "It's really best that you don't."

"But I'm, like, hungry."

"You wouldn't go exploring a friend's house uninvited if you'd never been in before."

"I just want a bite to eat, man."

The Doctor firmed his grip. "No. She doesn't want you in there."

"She?"

"The Spectrel," hissed the Doctor. "She has feelings too, you know."

"Uh. Oh. Like, I'm sorry, Spectrel," said Kevin, looking around the ceiling. "So, Doc. Where are we going now?"

"We'll be at home momentarily. I know it doesn't seem like a long distance to you. Physically it's not, in your world, but she's not done this in a while. And she's still weak."

"So what's happened with…?" He now knew the Doctor's look that meant he should stop asking. He sat back in a vinyl seat with a farting noise. He put his goggles and balaclava into the helmet and placed it on a seat next to him. The Doctor paced up and down.

"Right," said the Doctor, and he exited the Spectrel. Trinity followed him. Kevin picked up his helmet and Con-Bat and took a last look around the interior. "Thanks, Spectrel. You saved my ass," he said, then left, finding himself climbing out of the rear left door of a black cab parked on the road outside the Doctor's house in Streatham Hill. Trinity wasn't anywhere in sight.

It was early evening, and Mrs Roseby was hovering with her watering can. "Argh!" she screamed. She dropped the can. There was a *clang* and a tortured *miaow*. She clutched her hand to her chest. "You nearly gave me and my Albert an 'eart attack!" she shouted. "I knew I should have told the residents' association about that first cab." She eyed Kevin suspiciously. "Is he the licensed driver? I shall have his Hackney Carriage Number for this." A grey, fat old tabby cat leapt up onto the wall between Mrs Roseby's and the Doctor's. It hissed. "What's he doing dressed like that and carrying a baseball bat? I shall have the police onto him."

"Please, Mrs Roseby. We're just returning by cab after rather a hectic day's work." The Doctor put a hand on Kevin's back and guided him towards the front door.

Kevin saw a pair of bright green eyes underneath David's real black cab. One eye winked at him. He put a hand on the front door of the house and it opened. A bolt of black shot past Kevin's legs and into the porch. Mrs Roseby's cat shrieked an un-cat-like shriek and leapt two feet into the air, landing on the old woman, claws digging into her shoulder. The old woman shrieked her own shriek and grabbed the cat.

"Doctor How!" she shouted. "I don't know what you're up to but I'm complaining to the association this evening. And I'm minded to call the police to have that cab towed. The tax had better be up-to-date on it."

"I look forward to being copied on your letter of complaint, Mrs Roseby. Good evening to you. And your cat."

The Doctor closed the porch door behind him, held up his arms and spread his legs. Kevin adopted the same pose. The UV light came on and bathed them. The door to the house opened and they went in. Kevin placed his Con-Bat in the umbrella stand by the door.

"Like, why won't David's Spectrel come in?"

"Kevin, I just don't know the answer to some questions. Still a little distrustful I think, and mad at David. At least she's proximate now. I wish I could say the same for mine."

"Do you know…?"

The Doctor turned to face him. "Hacked, I think. In the hands of these enemies? I don't know. She was able to send for help. And thank God that help was available. Can I get her back? Hopefully. How? I'm not sure." The Doctor let out a deep sigh. "This is a fine pickle, Kevin. I've lost my Spectrel, and my cousin with it. I could kick myself for not offloading him here with a med-bot. We only have his Spectrel, and she's not up to much. I've got no idea who these people are who are attacking us. What a fix. I was joking earlier when I said we could be defeated by tea-time. This whole thing has been an elaborate set-up. A trap. And I fell for it. I didn't even get so much as a screw from that array of display processors. What a waste."

Kevin put a hand on the Doctor's shoulder. "Sorry, boss. Look, there's one thing about us south London boys."

"Really?" said the Doctor, flatly.

"You can take the boy out of south London, but you can't take south London out of the boy." He reached into his pocket, brought out a piece of metal with writing engraved on it and handed it to the Doctor. "I nicked this. I know I shouldn't have, but… you know, a souvenir, innit?"

"You're right; you absolutely shouldn't have taken it.

Worse than taking pictures, in a way. But I knew there was a reason I needed you. Thank you. This is a start."

The doorbell rang.

"Damn that woman," said the Doctor. "As if I haven't got enough on my plate. Answer that for me, will you Kevin?" He turned to go into the downstairs washroom.

Trinity stood alert at the base of stairs as Kevin went into the porch. Through the mottled glass of the external door he could see the head of a figure wearing a black peaked cap with a gold badge at its centre. His heart sank.

He opened the door. A postman was standing on the step, wearing a grey uniform that looked like something he'd seen in old photographs. He was shorter than Kevin, and in his mid-forties. His short hair was a light red. His sharp grey eyes reminded Kevin of someone, except that they were behind a pair of black plastic-framed spectacles of the type that would once have been called NHS specs.

"Oh," said the postman. "I was quite sure Doctor How lived here. Is he in?"

Something caught Kevin's eye. To the side of the Doctor's drive, just visible over the wall, was a red post box of the traditional solid pillar design. He couldn't remember there being a post box on the Doctor's road at all.

"Who wants to see him?" asked Kevin, wishing he'd thought to have the Con-Bat with him.

"D-d-does he?" asked the postman, surprised. He nudged his specs up the bridge of his nose.

Kevin squinted.

"Sorry," said the postman. "I thought you meant something else. Tell him it's…" The postman looked over Kevin's shoulder.

"Well, well," said the Doctor from just behind Kevin. "It's cousin When."

End of book one

Thanks for reading – I hope you enjoyed it!

The Doctor needs your support in the forthcoming battle.
Please do one (or more!) of these:
- Like him on Facebook: facebook.com/DoctorHow.tv
- Follow him on Twitter: @DoctorHow_tv

More author info: markspeed.co.uk

Acknowledgements

Thanks to Lynda Thornhill for proofing. Thanks to ace beta-readers Ian Sturgeon and Suzanne C. Cope CBT for early feedback and encouragement.

6974614R00134

Printed in Great Britain
by Amazon.co.uk, Ltd.,
Marston Gate.